I0586773

PLACE

LISA J HOBMAN

First Edition, 2017
License Notes

This book is licensed for your personal enjoyment only.
This book may not be re-sold or given away to other
people. If you would like to share this book with another
person, please purchase an additional copy for each
recipient. If you're reading this book and did not purchase
it, or it was not purchased for your use only, then please
return to the book store and purchase your own copy.
Thank you for respecting the hard work of the author.

Copyright © 2017 Lisa J Hobman
All rights reserved

No part of this book may be reproduced in any form of by
any electronic or mechanical means, including
information and retrieval systems, without permission in
writing from the publisher except by a reviewer who may
quote brief passages in a review.

This is a work of fiction, names, characters, places and
incidents either are products of the author's imagination or
are used fictitiously.

Any resemblance to actual events, locales or persons, living
or dead, is entirely coincidental.

ISBN: 978-0-9956658-3-5

For the man I fell in love with in 1992
and still love with all my heart.

CHAPTER 1

Si

Drummers always get stick. Okay, there's a pun in there somewhere. But it's true. Whenever you hear musician jokes, it's always about the skin hitter. The 'how many drummers to change a light bulb' jokes, and my personal favourite, 'how do you get a drummer off your doorstep? Pay him ten quid for the pizza.'

Drummers are allegedly the talentless, sofa surfing, women repelling, drooling idiots of the band. In Sonic Idols, that's me. Si. Known by my mother for the past twenty-four and a half years as Simeon Delaney. I started drumming with the band when they first broke out into the 'big time'. Although, it was a bittersweet pill to swallow.

Aged nineteen, I was thrust into the limelight after the death of my big brother and best friend, Joe—the band's original drummer. I don't think I ever recovered from the situation. Some say I withdrew into myself. Some say I completely changed. My mother thought I used the drums to express the pent-up anger I felt deep inside at his loss.

It would appear everyone is an amateur psychologist these days.

I looked up to Joe. He was my hero. Almost four years my senior, he was the epitome of everything I wanted to be. He started to learn the drums aged ten, and I'm sure I used to drive him crazy when he was practising on his kit. I'd sit with a pair of my mum's knitting needles, banging on whatever happened to be lying around in the garage where his gear was set up.

But instead of telling me to piss off, he'd come over and sit beside me. "Here, like this, kiddo." He'd put his hands over mine and tap out a beat on the upturned bucket with the makeshift sticks while I sat there with a huge grin on my face, gazing up adoringly at him. My fantastic big brother.

"I want to be you when I grow up, Joey," I'd tell him.

I had no clue how ironic that sentence would become later in my life.

♫♫♫

Sonic Idols were doing a rock club tour down in London just after they'd signed with Blue Demon Records. I had just started uni in Sheffield and I missed Joe like mad. He hadn't gone to university, choosing to follow his dream instead. Although Joe had taught me everything he knew and insisted I could be in a band, I never felt able to go for it. *He* was the talented one. I was the bookish one. And I didn't mind being in his shadow. In fact, I willingly put myself there. That's how much I idolised him.

I'd been out with some of the guys from my course on the Friday night, and to say I was hungover was an understatement. I was feeling guilty for not being with Joe. He'd asked me to go on the tour with the band and I had chosen to stay at my digs instead. Worst decision of my life.

I awoke on Saturday to a ringing sound that seemed to vibrate around my tender skull, and when I realised it was my phone, I grabbed for it, dropping it twice in my hurry. I'd decided I was going to travel down and join Sonic Idols for a week. Sod my coursework. That could wait. I was so excited to tell Joe the news.

"Hello? How's it going, mate?" I asked, without even checking it was Joe's number.

"Simeon? Simeon, it's… it's Dad."

I yawned and stretched. "Hi, Dad. I thought you were Joe." A sob travelled over the airwaves causing a shiver to travel down my back. I sat bolt upright. "Dad? Are you okay?" I knew something terrible was wrong. And not just from the sobbing I could hear. A deep-seated fear gripped my insides and knotted them tight.

My dad spoke again. "It's… it's Joe, son. He's… he's d-dead."

There was a loud swooshing in my head and I dropped the phone.

♫♫♫

Joe had never been into drugs. He'd never even smoked. He took good care of his body and ate healthily in between stints of training at the gym. What the hell had possessed him to try drugs on that fateful night is beyond comprehension.

If I'd *been* there. If I'd gone on tour like he asked me to, he wouldn't have done it. He was always determined to be the good example a kid brother needed. Someone I could look up to—and I did. If I had been there, he would've been too busy looking out for me to even contemplate something so stupid.

As soon as I'd heard the news, I came home from university on the next train I could get. The familiar scenery outside the window was dull and grey; mirroring the intense sadness that had taken up residence inside of me. Buildings blurred past me and I'm not sure if it was because of the speed of the train or the tears that continually threatened but I refused to allow free. Usually, going home was an exciting time—regardless of where I returning from. My family meant the world to me and I was always eager to hug them. But on that particular day I was gripped with dread. How do you face your parents knowing that you are now their only remaining child? How do you comfort them after such a catastrophic loss? I had no clue.

I took a cab from the train station and tried to rehearse what I could say to Mum and Dad once I arrived home. But nothing seemed sufficient. Nothing seemed to express the immense loss I was feeling let alone what they must've been experiencing. He was their first born. A model son. A credit to his upbringing. Even though Joe had moved out months before, walking into the house we grew up in felt strange. None of the preparation I had tried to make had prepared me for the pain I would feel at seeing both my parents so bereft. When you're growing up your parents are the strong ones. They're the ones to kiss your *poorlies* and chase away the monsters under the bed. I think you forget that they're only human until you see them break. They hugged me tight and we sobbed. We stood in the middle of the living room, just holding each other up, holding on tight as if we were scared to let go in case one of us collapsed under the weight of the grief.

After I'd been there around half an hour, Joe's poor fiancée, Allie, arrived. God, she was devastated. Her auburn hair was scraped back from her make-up free face and her skin was pale. I couldn't speak to her. My folks held her as she cried, and the pain she was going through made my own heart break all over again. But I couldn't face her after what had happened. I knew she'd be angry with me and I couldn't bear to look her in the eye. If *I* had been there, she wouldn't have lost the man she was going to marry.

Joe adored Allie from the minute he laid eyes on her. They had been together since they met aged seventeen on our family holiday to Northumberland. She had travelled down from the Scottish Borders and we had travelled up from Leeds, and we were all camping on the same site near Bamburgh Castle. They met at the campsite playpark when Joe was watching over me as I drove my remote-control car around the sandpit whilst my folks prepared a barbecue. It had been love at first sight for both of them. She had long auburn hair with natural waves, and there were freckles dotted over her nose. She was incredibly pretty and had this really sweet Scottish accent. I'd never seen Joe look that way at a girl before. As much as I wanted to poke fun at him for being all doe-eyed, I just couldn't. It was clear from the start they were meant to be. Allie spent most of her family holiday with us, and her parents even joined us for dinner a couple of times. There were lots of jokes about future wedding bells, but I guess none of them thought that's where the two teens were actually headed. Things change over time, after all. People move on. Not Joe and Allie though. The day we were all leaving for home and travelling in opposite directions was hard for everyone, I think. It had been the best holiday ever. There had been a teary goodbye with lots of hugs and hand holding. They were so reluctant to part. Even I cried a little bit, but then again, *I* was a kid. Almost as soon as we got home, Joe was on the phone with Allie, telling her how much he missed her. After that, they kept in touch by letters and more phone calls. They were just so right together.

Allie had eventually moved to London to be with him when the band relocated there, and she went to every single gig that followed. Except his last. She had been ill with the flu on the night he died and hadn't been able to go. Other than one gig before the band was signed, it was the only occasion she didn't go see him play.

And I wasn't there to save him.

She must have hated me so fucking much.

I left her downstairs with my mum and dad and went to take my bag up to the room me and Joe had shared. I opened the door and walked inside but the immediate onslaught of memories hurt so much physically that I crumpled to the floor and broke down.

He would *never* be here with me again. We'd never again stay up until the early hours sneakily watching films.

I'd never hear his voice again.

Through a fog of tears, I glanced around our room. Posters of Joe's favourite rock bands—his idols—adorned the walls, and above his old desk was a pin board covered in old photos—most of which were of me and him. Me on Joe's shoulders. Joe with his arm proudly around me. Joe teaching me the drum solo from my favourite Bon Jovi song. Such happy memories that were now all I had left of my best friend in the whole world. He was gone and I didn't know how to deal with that. How could I just carry on? I honestly had no clue.

For the couple of days prior to the funeral, Allie stayed with her folks in a bed and breakfast up the road from our house, but she visited regularly. Every time she walked in, I walked out. We made eye contact a couple of times but the expression of sadness in her eyes was too much to bear. There were simply no words to justify my own actions and decisions, and trying to speak to her would have been too painful. The guilt weighing me down was draining the life from me.

On the day of the funeral, I walked into the kitchen to see Allie staring out of the window over the huge garden where we had all spent many a happy hour eating barbecue and laughing. She glanced at me as my feet hit the tile floor and I stopped dead in my tracks.

"Oh, hello, Si. How are you?" Her sweet Scottish accent lilted through the still air and tugged at my heart.

I scrunched my face as I searched for what to say. "Erm… pretty shit really, all things considered." I swallowed hard as I assessed her pain-filled gaze. I wanted to ask her the same question but I was so very afraid of the answer that I couldn't form the words. "Sorry, erm… I seem to have forgotten my…" I turned and rushed from the room as quick as my legs would take me, and once in the privacy of my own room, I slid down the door and rested my head in my hands.

CHAPTER 2

Allie

I watched Si retreat from the room like he couldn't bear to be near me and my lip quivered as more tears formed in my eyes. He hated me and I couldn't blame him. Thanks to me, his brother was dead, and nothing I could say would help. Nothing I could say would take away the agony of knowing his brother was never coming home. Why hadn't I just taken some medicine, put on my big girl panties, and gone to the gig? It was flu but it wasn't so bad that I couldn't have made the effort. Hindsight is a wonderful thing, and how I wish time machines had been invented. But all I could do now was beat myself up over and over and hate myself. The love of my life was gone forever and I had no idea how to heal my own heart, never mind the heart of someone even closer. Someone related by blood who felt the same pain I did—if not more.

From the day I met the handsome seventeen-year-old Joseph Delaney, my heart had been entirely his. As a sixteen-year-old girl falling in love for the very first time, it was one of those fireworks situations you see in romance movies. Our eyes met across the sandpit where his little brother was playing with a remote-control car.

Joe was every teenage girl's dream. Piercing blue eyes and light brown shaggy hair that reached his shoulders. He was tanned, despite the British weather, and his arms were very defined—thanks to the drums, I later discovered. That was another thing. He was a cool musician and he informed me he was going to be a famous rock star with his best friends and their band. I had no reason to disbelieve him; he was *so* sure of it. They had just settled on the name Sonic Idols and I remember thinking how professional it sounded. Looking at him back then, I could easily imagine him adorning the walls of girls' rooms everywhere.

When the band was signed by Blue Demon Records, Joe had celebrated by asking me to marry him. His words reverberated around my mind every single day from then.

"Allie, I can't imagine anyone who I'd want beside me on this crazy ride more than the woman who fills my heart with so much love and happiness. You ground me. You remind me of who I am. You love me so completely and my feelings for you are deeper than any ocean. You and me, we're destined to be connected. Two souls forever entwined. Say you'll make it official. Say you'll marry me?"

The tears in his eyes and the hope in his voice were something that will stay with me eternally. The simple aquamarine ring he bought me remains on my hand. He swore he would replace it with something bigger, bolder, and diamond encrusted with his first big pay cheque, but I didn't want that. I wanted the small, square cut stone that he had bought because he knew turquoise was my favourite colour. That meant more to me than any amount of diamonds ever could.

Standing in the kitchen of the Delaney's family home, I twirled the ring around my finger as tears trickled down my cheeks. I'd got to the point where wiping them away was a wasted exercise. They'd only be replaced by more, so what was the point?

A hand squeezed my shoulder. "Are you all right, love?"

I turned to see the red-rimmed eyes of my would-be mother-in-law and I placed my hand over hers and nodded. "Are *you* okay?"

Her lip trembled but she forced a smile. "Getting there. I'm so sorry about Simeon's behaviour. He's taken this all so hard. Understandably really as Joey was his hero. I'm not sure how he'll recover from this."

My stomach knotted with guilt and the physical pain of it, almost excruciating in nature, stabbed at every nerve and fibre inside me. I closed my eyes and whispered, "Please tell him I'm so very sorry."

After hugging Joe's mum tightly, I left the house where I had spent so many happy days, for what I expected to be the very last time. I was moving back to Scotland to be nearer to my parents and they had already found me a cottage to rent. I needed to be alone. And the little farm cottage near Kelso would give me what I needed. But I couldn't bear to say goodbye and so I would simply leave with my mum and dad after the service.

Hopefully, in time, I would figure out a way to make amends to Si for not being there to stop Joe making the worst mistake of his short life.

CHAPTER 3

Si

The funeral was unbearable.

So many people attended—including camera crews from MTV and other well-known music stations who were there to report on the premature snuffing out of a star on the rise. Joe was loved so much by so many and I had let him down. The atmosphere was thick with sadness and emotion.

But I was numb.

I couldn't handle it, and so I think my mind just shut the world out. My once happy-go-lucky attitude was irreparably damaged and my soul dented. I stood there at the crematorium staring blankly at the coffin as people around me sobbed and wailed. My broken heart was so shattered that no amount of crying would help. So I stared, willing him to burst out of the box and tell everyone the joke was over.

But, of course, it was no joke.

My folks had asked me to speak at the service. But how could my measly words make up for the loss of such a wonderful guy?

I took to the podium and cleared my throat. "Joe was the best. There's no other way to describe him. Instead of telling me I cramped his style like most big brothers do, Joe went out of his way to be there for me. He taught me about music… about life… and about love. I remember one conversation we had about death when we were kids. He insisted he wanted a joke or a silly rhyme on his head-stone when he was an old man, so people knew he was fun when he was alive. The rhyme went… Roses are red, violets are blue, I'm dead and I'm behind you… boo!" A small rumble of low laughter travelled the room. "But I have to say that now he's gone…and he wasn't an old man… I have no clue what wording would be a fitting tribute. How do you sum up in a few words the life of a man who achieved so much and touched the lives of so many? How do you say goodbye to your best friend? How do you move on knowing that every time you want to share good news, he won't be there to listen? I just… I don't know how. Joey… you were more than just a big brother… you were my hero. I'll never forget you or what you did for me. Rest in peace, big bro. Know that you're loved."

I crumpled the paper in my hand. Whatever I had written was forgotten as my emotions took over. Tears trailed down my face as I stepped away and glanced over one last time at the coffin. The opening bars to "Oceans" by Pearl Jam began to play and I was reminded once again of the fact that I would never lay beside my brother on his bed as he listened to the song that reminded him of Allie. I lost it. My legs buckled and I couldn't breathe. I heard a cry, and only seconds later—when Dad came to my rescue and helped me back to my seat—did I realise it had been me who made the anguished noise. Back in my seat, my body shook and my heart hurt as I gave in to my tears.

♫♫♫

As I left the building with my mum at one side of me and my dad at the other, Mum squeezed my shoulder. "Are you okay, sweetheart?"

Fighting to keep myself upright, and angry that I was the one being comforted when they had lost their son, I gritted my teeth to stop my jaw from trembling. "I don't think I'll ever be okay again, Mum," I told her honestly.

She reached up and cupped my cheek in her palm. "You *will*, Simeon. I promise we'll all get through this. Together. As a family," she insisted, and I smiled like a dutiful son.

The last thing I wanted to tell her was that I could have happily swapped places with my brother and that I had seriously considered joining him since he'd gone. The only thing stopping me from taking my own life was the thought that they had been through enough. I couldn't be so selfish.

Thankfully, our interaction was cut short when Mum was enveloped by family and friends, all wanting to do their bit to console her. Joe was her first-born son and I had lost count of the number of times she had sobbed, saying that no parent should have to lose a child this way. She didn't say she blamed me. But I was still alive and he was gone.

Guilt was crushing me from the inside out. And what guilt hadn't reached, anger at myself had begun to corrode.

I glanced over and saw Allie standing alone, her blood-shot eyes expressing the same emptiness that now lived inside me. I *should* have gone to apologise to her. I *should* have gone over and hugged her or at least said *something*, but what the fuck could I say? And why would she listen?

Everyone gradually left the crematorium and made their way to the venue where the wake was being held. I promised my dad I'd follow, but instead I went home and packed a bag then wrote an apology to my folks, asking them to let me have some time. I took a last look at the photos showing all the happy times I had spent with Joe, and then I left my home and made my way to the train station to catch a train back to uni. It was a cowardly thing to do but I had to leave. The crazy thing was, no one had told me they blamed me for Joe's death but *I* blamed me enough for everyone.

I needed to be out of the way so I could cause no more hurt.

♫♫♫

Back on campus, studying was virtually impossible. The fact I was studying English, my second passion to music, did nothing to ease my mind. I couldn't get lost in books the way I used to. Nothing would hold my attention. Not even my old favourites could distract me from the melancholy that had taken up residence in my head and heart, and so my assignments began to suffer.

Both Mum and Dad did their best to try and console me. They turned up at my digs several times over the weeks that followed, and after lecturing me on the fact I was getting skinny, they insisted on taking me out for food. But we'd end up sitting there in silence; that or the conversation would revolve around memories of Joe and I would slump deeper and deeper into depression. I got tired of hearing people tell me I needed to talk to someone about my grief when the one person I could talk to was no longer around. It was like rubbing salt in an open wound. So I stopped socialising too.

But one day changed it all.

There I was, sitting at my desk in my tiny room, staring at a blank page that had been open on my laptop for fuck knows how long, when someone knocked at my door. I fully expected to see my parents' worried faces when I reluctantly rose and opened it, but instead a familiar, bearded face greeted me and I was grappled into a bear hug that almost squeezed the life out of me.

"Jeez, Si. You look like utter shit. We're all worried sick about you, bud," my long-haired visitor informed me.

"Nick? W-what are you doing here? Why? I mean…"

Nick Dacre, the lead vocalist of Sonic Idols and one of my brother's best friends, had taken Joe's death hard too. The evidence showed in the dark circles around his eyes.

He pulled away from me and gripped my shoulders. His eyes were glassy but a line of worry formed between his brows. "Someone had to come and sort you the fuck out, mate. I insisted it was me."

I stepped back and scowled at him. "I don't need 'sorting the fuck out', Nick." I punctuated my response with air quotes. "I'm fine, so you can go back to London or wherever the hell you should be."

He shoved past me and stepped into my dingy box of a room. "Yeah? Fine, huh? You disappeared after the funeral with no proper explanation to your folks, just a letter saying you needed to be alone. You haven't been home in weeks. Your calls home last about ten seconds. You're clearly not eating enough and this room stinks of fucking B.O. But all that's completely normal, mate, so no worries, eh?" His voice dripped with sarcasm.

Evidently, he was on a mission from my mother.

I slumped onto my bed and heaved a sigh as I ran my hands through my lank, greasy hair. "I just couldn't hack the wake, that's all. All those people grieving. It just hurt too much. That's all it is. I feel like... like it's all my..." I was on the verge of admitting that I held myself entirely responsible for Joe's death, but didn't need to voice it so I stopped myself. Saying the words aloud would be too painful and would sound like a pity party.

He sat down beside me. "You feel like it's your fault, don't you?" His voice was low and I could feel his eyes boring into me.

I lowered my head further and rested it in my hands. I couldn't reply.

"I knew that's how you felt. Right from the first time I saw you after it happened." He fell silent for a moment. "But, do you know what? It's *not* your fault. If anyone's to blame, it's me. And I can't blame myself, Si, because if I let myself venture down that path, I'll have a nervous breakdown. Or jump off a fucking bridge." He gripped my arm and pulled it down, forcing me to sit up and face him. He squeezed my arm tight. "Blaming ourselves won't bring him back, Si. You *have* to stop. You *have* to move forward. And… that's why I'm here."

I shook my head. "What do you mean?"

"You have to finish off what Joe started."

I shrugged my shoulders in confusion. "And how the hell do I do that?"

Nick took a deep breath and let it out slowly, as if plucking up the courage to speak again. "Replace Joe in the band, Si. We need you."

I stood and held my hands up. "Whoa, whoa. Hang on. You can't be serious about that? How the fuck can you ask me to even *think* about replacing Joe? He's only been gone a couple of months, Nick. No fucking way. It's like… it's like I'd be pretending to be him. I can't do that. It's wrong."

He pleaded at me with his eyes. "It's not wrong. It's a perfect way to pay tribute to your big brother, mate."

I paced up and down the small confined space, feeling like a caged animal. "The fuck it is! Jeez, I can't believe you're even *suggesting* it. Are you mental? I think you should leave."

Nick held his hands up in a kind of surrender gesture. "Si, we need a drummer. You're a fucking brilliant drummer. You know all the songs. You're family. And what better people are there to spend your time with than with family, eh?"

I clenched my fists and my jaw simultaneously. I wanted to punch him. How dare he suggest that *anyone* could just step in and replace my brother? Let alone me.

I gripped the dirty strands of my hair to stop myself from grabbing Nick by the throat. "He's not a fucking dead plant, Nick. You can't just get a new one and hope it lasts longer."

"I'm in no way suggesting—"

"And even if I wanted to—which I don't—I'm not good enough. I'm *not Joe*. I'll *never* be Joe. I...I really think you should leave now before I lose my shit completely." I stepped towards the door.

Nick stood too but didn't follow me. "No. I won't leave. Not yet. You *need* to do this, Si. I *do* mean it. You need to carry on where he left off. It's catharsis. It'd help. He'd want you to do it and you know I'm right. He raved about your playing. Did you know he thought you were better than he was? And that he was gutted you didn't join a band? Did you know any of that?"

More than a little shell-shocked, I shook my head. He'd said words to that effect on many occasions, but I'd never taken him seriously, always figuring he was just being a good brother. A supportive brother. But... maybe he meant it after all?

Nick stepped towards me. "So, this is your chance. This is your opportunity, Si. Do it for Joe. Please?"

CHAPTER 4

Si

Walking in to the first rehearsal with Sonic Idols was bizarre. Blue Demon had booked us this plush studio in London, the likes of which I had only dreamed about. Nick had met me at my hotel so I wouldn't have to turn up alone. It was like he'd taken on the big brother role. It was kind of him and I appreciated having him beside me as I walked into the room, shaking like a leaf.

"Si, my old buddy!" Chris called as we stepped towards the guys who were tuning up. "I've got a great joke for you."

I turned to Nick, who rolled his eyes and placed his hands on his hips. "Fuck's sake, Chris. Give the guy a chance to settle in, eh?" he chastised his Aussie friend.

Chris waved his hands. "Nah, nah. This is a good one. Okay, so… how do you know a drummer's at your door?"

I scrunched my brow and folded my arms over my chest, waiting to see if it was one I'd heard before. "Go on."

He started laughing. "The knocking speeds up." He guffawed, throwing his head back and holding his stomach like some mental cartoon character.

I shook my head and couldn't help laughing at his reaction rather than the joke. I glanced at Nick, who had covered his eyes and was shaking his head too.

I gestured with my thumb towards Chris. "So, is this something I can look forward to now?"

Nick slapped my back. "'Fraid so, mate. 'Fraid so."

The initial rehearsals with Sonic Idols were nerve-wracking but great fun. I somehow felt closer to Joe when I played his kit and sat where he had once sat.

After the first session was over, the guys gathered around me and there was manly hugging and back slapping again.

"Fucking awesome, dude," Chris told me as he ruffled my hair.

"Oy, less of the head patting. I'm not a fucking dog." I threw my hand towel at him and it landed on his head.

"Aww, jeez. You'll be advertising hair products like Dacre soon. You blokes and your hair. Pussies." We all laughed in good humour.

"Chris is right, Si. Joe'd be proud, mate," Stig informed me. He was a man of few words, but I appreciated the encouragement.

"Same time tomorrow then, lads?" Nick interjected as he flung his guitar case over his shoulder.

I nodded eagerly. "Yeah. Can't wait."

"But tonight, we go get pissed!" Chris made a whooping noise and the other guys joined in. They all high fived and so I did the same. "Time to celebrate our arses off and drink to Joe's memory."

The management company was very supportive about me joining Sonic Idols, which was a relief, but I didn't care for being told how to behave. They wanted to coach me on being interviewed for TV and by the press. I told them in no uncertain terms that I was there to play drums and that was it. I had no interest in being on TV.

Yeah... that lasted a week.

After the first live show we played, I had voice recorders thrust in my face by five journos at once, bombarding me with stupid questions.

"How are you feeling about replacing your brother in the band that's tipped as the next big thing?"

"Do you feel like you're stepping into his shoes?"

"Do you miss him?"

"Would Joe approve of you being his replacement?"

"Do you enjoy playing?"

You'd think they would have come up with something a little more original, but no. I answered in as few words as possible then pointed them towards Chris. He was the one who loved the limelight, and he was the one who the camera loved in return. I reckon the Aussie charm won over every journalist he met, and some of the journalists— the female ones—got a little more *up close and personal* backstage, if you get my drift. The six foot plus blonde guitarist was a pussy magnet. To say he was a male tart would be a massive understatement.

Anyway, after that experience I succumbed to some

coaching by the management company. I had no idea being a rock star was so damn complicated. Here was I thinking I'd get up and bang a few song outs with my mates. But nope. There were countless things I could and couldn't do and say. Myriad ways I could give groupies the wrong impression and a gazillion things that could get me negative press. I considered myself severely schooled.

Not long after I joined the band, Blue Demon Records sent us off on a small UK tour. It wasn't said in so many words, but I got the impression the tour was intended as a test for me. I was younger than the other guys and I had just ditched my studies to become the drummer in a newly broken out rock band. You could say I was living every kid's dream, but I'm guessing the label had to make sure that a grieving, nerdy, nineteen-year-old lad was cut out for whatever the hell fame was about to throw at him.

Being on the tour bus was a little weird. I hadn't known what to expect, but being surrounded by four other burping and farting males—including Den—in a confined space was probably the worst aspect. Most of the time we sat around jamming and writing new tracks. When we weren't doing that, we retired to our respective shelves—aka bunks—to listen to music or sleep. Almost every day, Chris had a new drummer joke to tease me with. Apparently, he was the same with Joe, so at least I knew I wasn't getting special treatment.

The first night was in my home city of Leeds, and I think every person I had ever encountered showed up at the Academy to see us play. The venue wasn't the biggest in the city, but none of the planned dates were in huge places—another reason I presumed it was a test.

The stage was in darkness and covered in dry ice when we walked out and took our places. My heart was beating to a rhythm all of its own when I smacked my sticks together to the intro of the band's first single, "Hot 'n' Heavy". Next, the stage lights illuminated the place, filtering through the clouds of smoke, and a sudden rush of adrenaline coursed through my veins as I played the beat. Nick paced the stage like a pro and the piercing screams of hundreds of females could be heard over the music—I was pretty sure one of them was my mum—so the sound tech took this as his cue and bumped the volume higher still. My heart pounded and a feeling of euphoria gripped me. Joe was right all along. This *was* me. This *was* what I was meant to do. It was just gut-wrenching that it took Joe to die for me to realise.

Now, I've never been one to believe in ghosts or spirits or whatever, but that night—and every gig since—I've felt Joe's presence, spurring me on, pushing me to play harder. To put everything I have into my playing. That first night was like an out of body experience. I closed my eyes and let my breathing and heart rate calm as we took the tempo down for the band's ballad, "Don't Leave Me Alone". This was the one song I was dreading as Joe had written the lyrics for Allie. He wasn't known for song writing but this one had come from his heart and the other guys had loved it. As I played, I could imagine watching the band from somewhere above the stage, like I was watching with Joe, and for the first time since he died, I felt peace. Like everything was going to be okay. And I knew that was because I had made the right decision.

I was fulfilling my destiny.

The tour got better and better. Each night was a natural high that exceeded the night before. I didn't need drugs. I didn't need chemicals of any sort to get me there. Playing was enough. And as the tour continued, I slowly began to change my thinking. The songs stopped being 'the band's songs' and became '*our* songs'. I was one of them. We were a unit. And strangely, the guilt I thought I would feel in taking Joe's place became a sense of pride. I was being accepted, and I knew deep in my heart that Joe would love them all for that, and he would love me for continuing in his footsteps.

It was on that tour—admittedly spurred on by Chris the guitarist—that I underwent the needle gun and had my first tattoo. A set of angel wings on my back with Joe's name in the centre. A fitting tribute to the man responsible for my place in the band. And every night, Stig the bassist, Chris or Nick would make eye contact with me and grin like the Cheshire Cat, and I'd feel this thrill rise from my boots and emanate right to my fingertips. There was no other feeling like it. Not even sex.

Therein lies another story. The guys were hell bent on getting me laid. Believe me, it got old very fast. I was by no means a virgin, but I didn't sleep around. I'd always wanted what my folks had. What Joe and Allie'd had. But I'm a hot-blooded male after all, and the buzz of playing took a while to leave my system. The guys convinced me that sex was a great stress release. They also insisted the no strings attached relationships of the road made the guilt less.

So, the final night of our tour arrived and I hadn't plucked up the courage to sleep with anyone up to that point—to the utter disappointment of the other guys who bedded a different girl every night. I considered myself a bit of a geek with my floppy hair and beard, but the guys insisted that I was getting plenty of looks from the opposite sex, even though I was evidently oblivious. The last gig was at a venue in Nottingham. The crowd was awesome, and just under the glare of the lights, I could see a petite blonde wearing a low-cut top right at the front near the stage. Nick and Chris had both played up to her and she'd been lapping it up. But every chance she got, she stared in my direction, playing with her hair. From what I could see of her—and that was only from the waist up—she was cute, with a sexy figure and a nice smile. Although, I was at the back of the stage, so what did I know? At the end of the show, the other guys were signing stuff and posing for photos with the band's first groupies, and I was packing my gear away.

"Hi," came a voice from behind me.

I looked up to see the petite blonde smiling down at me. I nodded once. "Hiya."

"So… you're the new drummer, eh?"

I stood and discovered that I towered over her. She wore a black flared mini skirt and black combat style boots. Her arms were tattooed with skulls and roses and her blonde hair was around shoulder length. Quite pretty close-up. Just as I had suspected.

Remembering she had asked me a question, I shook my head. "Oh… drummer. Yeah. New drummer." I sounded like a total muppet. *Fucking hell, Si, you tit. Me man. Me hit things with pointy sticks.*

She giggled. "I suppose the sticks are a bit of a giveaway." She nodded towards my hand, and sure enough, I was gripping a pair of sticks I had yet to pack.

Heat flared up in my cheeks and I cringed. "Erm, yeah. Sticks." *Jeez, just stop talking, you dick.*

"Me and my friends have just invited the band back to our place. We're having a few drinks and they've all agreed to come, but the singer said I should ask you along as you're apparently shy. Do you fancy it?" the girl asked, playing with her hair again.

Great. Thanks, Nick. Thanks a lot. I scratched my back with the sticks. "Erm… yeah. Sure, why not?"

The girl smiled. "Great. We'll be waiting at the bar. I'm Tiff, by the way."

I held out my hand like she was about to interview me. *Again, dick.* "I'm… erm… Sim, I mean Si. My name's Simeon, but that's a bit of a mouthful, so people call me Si."

She licked her lips suggestively. "Oh, don't worry, *Si.* I quite like a mouthful." And with that, she turned, flicked her hair, and sashayed back towards her group of friends who were fawning over the rest of the band.

Fuck me. That was forward.

Against the better judgment of the guy who had apparently been assigned as our manager—an orange-faced camp bloke called Den—we all followed the girls and their friends to a house just on the outskirts of the city centre. It was a large detached building that had been sectioned into one-bed flats, rather like student digs, but the shared kitchen was the hub of the party. Tiff found me and handed me a can of cheap-looking beer. I cracked it open and took a long pull.

She dragged me by my free hand to the main staircase, up to the first floor, and in through a door which displayed a hand-painted, artsy sign that read, 'If the t-shirt's a-hanging, I'm probably a-banging.' *Tasteful.* And before I could speak, she whipped off the top she wore and stuck it on the outer door knob. *Well, at least I know where I stand.*

She dragged me inside and shoved me up against the wall. The next thing I knew, she had her legs wrapped around my waist and her tongue in my mouth.

Now, I know what I said before about wanting that perfect relationship and everything, but I also remember saying I'm a hot-blooded male, and when a sexy blonde girl with perfect tits wants to shag you… well, anyway, I'll leave it at that.

I was relieved that Nick had stuck a wad of condoms in my hand as we got out of the cab. The last thing I needed was to be discovering a few months down the line that I was about to be a rock star *and* a father. It wasn't something that had featured in my fantasies, that's for sure.

Tiff pulled away from me, her chest heaving and her eyes dark with lust. "I want you, Si. Get naked." She lowered her feet to the floor and shimmied out of her short skirt until she stood before me in lacy black underwear.

There was hardly any blood left north of my waist-band, but I managed to strip the clothes from my body. She raked her eyes up and down me, assessing what was on offer, but I was too aroused to care by that point.

A sexy smile tilted up her mouth and she shook her

head. "Boy, are we gonna have fun tonight." She unclasped her bra, slipped her panties down her legs, and crooked her finger at me. I quickly grabbed a condom from my jeans and followed her to the bed. She pulled me down on top of her and gripped my erection firmly, causing me to inhale sharply at the sensations of pleasure she created.

Suddenly she stopped, pushed me onto my back, and straddled me. "Si, I think there's something you should know before we carry on."

I opened my eyes and did my best to focus on her serious expression, rather than the pert breasts with tight pink nipples she had bared before me. What the fuck was she about to tell me?

I swallowed, trying to ignore the rising panic in my gut. "Oh yeah? What's that then?"

"I'm not looking for a relationship. As good-looking and nice as you are, I won't be contacting you again after tonight."

I laughed in disbelief. It was the opposite of what I expected. "You don't even know how good I am yet."

She shook her head and trailed her black painted nails down my torso, making me shiver. Her fingertips traced my abs with featherlight touches. "I'm sure you'll be good, Si. I have a sense about these things. But the thing is… I sleep with musicians." *Wow, okay. That was matter of fact.* She shrugged. "It's just what I do. I get slagged for it all the time, but at least I'm honest. I wouldn't call myself a slut. I'm always careful, but I like the thrill of it. I just thought you should know."

I bit the condom packet and tore it open, keeping my eyes locked on hers. "Don't worry, I promise not to propose marriage. Now, do you want to put this thing on me or should I do it?"

She giddily took the rubber out of my hand and stretched it on as I closed my eyes once more. Who the fuck was I? Where had the bravado come from? It had been a long time since I'd had no strings attached sex, so I let myself go, safe in the knowledge there would be no repercussions.

Just pure, unadulterated pleasure.

CHAPTER 5

Si

Time flies when you're on the road.

One place blurs into another and the view from the bus becomes one big cityscape. So much so that I've been known to ask Den what country we're in, never mind the city. I don't wish to sound ungrateful, because I love playing, but sometimes I wish I had a real home to go back to, instead of a crash pad in London—a city I don't even like.

The crash pad I bought was a two-bed apartment close to Nick's place—although mine was a hell of a lot more modest. I'd been saving money whilst simultaneously trying to convince my folks to let me buy them somewhere new, but they kept turning me down. I never gave up hope though. In the basement of the apartment block, in its own private spot, stood a Harley Davidson that I knew I would probably never get the chance to ride, but ever since being a kid, I had dreamed of owning one so it was the first big purchase I made. I was photographed for Rock Hard magazine sitting atop the beautiful beast out in the Cornish countryside, against an azure blue backdrop. It was a stunning little place they had chosen close to Crantock on the coast. I remember it well because I had the best Cornish pasty of my life there. Funny the things that stick out in your mind. Whilst I was straddling my favourite purchase, crowds of fans gathered to watch me pose like some wannabe catalogue model—except I wasn't quite so natural at the posing thing. The makeup artist had to continually powder my obvious embarrassment away. I cringed when the magazine came out and my mum told me she had framed the centrefold to put it on the wall in their home office.

So much changed so rapidly. I went from scraping money together from a bar job and my measly student loan to feed myself and buy text books, to having more money than any young adult would know what to do with. It was quite intimidating to begin with, but I loved the fact I could buy my folks gifts and send them on spa breaks together without worrying about the cost.

Winning a Grammy for best rock album two years after joining the band had to be one of the highlights of my career. We were up against Angel and the Fallen. I felt sure they would win, but hearing our name announced by a glamorous A-list actress almost knocked me from my chair. The occasion was one to add to the memory bank and never let go of. Talk about stories to tell my grandkids. I have to say that I look bloody good in a tux too. The whole band chose to take our dress code up a notch and it caused a media frenzy. The fans were so used to seeing us in denim and leather, that seeing Nick with his hair scraped back in a ponytail, Chris all clean shaven and suave looking, Stig with a shirt on, and me, well, looking like me in a tux, took our fandom to a whole new level. Pictures of us donned every magazine and tabloid. Even some of the broad sheets got in on the action.

Looking out from the stage at the myriad faces cheering for us, most of the folks on their feet, caused a lump of pure emotion to lodge in my throat. I was relieved not to be the band's spokesperson, as I'm fairly sure I would have just sobbed instead of delivering the articulate acceptance speech Nick gave. Sometimes being in the background has its good points.

When we weren't touring, we were recording. Blue Demon used only the best studios and top-notch producers. Getting to work with such talented people was mind-blowing and I had to remind myself not to gawp at these people in dumbstruck awe. The sessions were long and often repetitive, but I told myself over and over that I was fortunate to be in this position. Joe hadn't been lucky enough to see the band through to the top of every rock chart in existence, and so I was doing it for him as well as me.

And on top of that, there were the band photoshoots. I hate having to do the pouty face thing, but apparently, it's what the female fans—the record buying folks—love to see. So, we obviously obliged and still do. These events weren't all bad though, don't get me wrong. On one particular shoot in London, I got quite friendly with the photographer's assistant. Somehow, we ended up kissing and dry-humping in a broom cupboard at the end of the shoot. I was totally oblivious to the fact that the guys were waiting for me for half an hour until the photographer himself banged on the door and scared us half to death. Turned out the assistant was his twenty-one-year-old daughter and I narrowly missed a severe arse kicking. I apologised profusely and told him I really liked her and wanted to take her out on a proper date. But the girl said she wasn't interested in a relationship with a slutty rock star—apparently we're only good for one thing and I'll leave *that* to your imagination. Charming, eh? And there was another lesson learned—know who you're getting up close and personal with before the shenanigans.

After recording the next album, we were off again on the post production tour, and my life seemed to be whizzing past at a rate of knots. Another startling thing about being on tour is that something you'd never imagined yourself doing is suddenly second nature. Back at the start of my time with Sonic Idols, when I was a fresh-faced nineteen-year-old, the thought of multiple one night stands really didn't appeal to me at all. But by the age of twenty-four, I had notched up a fair few on my imaginary bed post, I can tell you. Language barriers didn't seem to exist. When a woman puts her hands all over you then gets naked and lays back, you kind of understand where you stand. And so long as the women and I were on the same page—i.e. one night stand, no strings attached— then why the fuck not make the most of it?

The problem is that touring and recording… recording and touring some more wasn't conducive to meeting my one true love, and so sex was just that. Sex. A way to relieve the stress and get my rocks off—if you'll excuse my crudeness.

I never slept with the same woman twice. Although, that was on the advice of Chris, who informed me that—regardless of what they make their mouths say—if a woman has sex with you twice, they see relationship potential there. I think he was kind of belittling the intelligence of his conquests, but in all honesty, there was no real need to shag the same woman twice anyway. We were never in the same place long enough and the buffet was always being replenished, if you get my meaning.

♫♫♫

The incident with Nick at the airport when we were due to set off for Germany was a huge shock. A wake-up call, if you will. None of us really knew what to do when it happened. Seeing him—a fit bloke in his late twenties—collapse, clutching his chest, was upsetting beyond belief, and we all wondered if he'd make it. After what happened to Joe, we had to face the fact that the band couldn't take another blow like that, and without Nick fronting us, the band would fold.

We all thought he'd suffered a heart attack as the symptoms seemed to point that way, but when he was rushed to the hospital, blue lights flashing and siren blaring, it turned out to be the culmination of anxiety and stress. Who'd have thought that could manifest itself so badly? The road and the crazed fans were really taking their toll on him and he finally reached his breaking point. It made us all think about how we dealt with the darker side of fame, and I resolved to make more time for relaxation. But then when he was supposed to be recuperating back at his place in London, Nick did a disappearing act and we were all stuck in some kind of limbo, wondering what the hell had gotten into him. He was obviously well enough to fuck off, but hadn't had the decency to tell us where to or why. It caused so many arguments and Den got paler and paler, which was worrying. We were all so used to his glowing orange hue that seeing the worry affect his desire for fake tan made us question everything.

All was so not right with the world.

What was worse, however, was we couldn't tour without our lead vocalist, and we couldn't finish recording either. Chris tried hard to locate his best mate, but Nick eluded him at every turn. Even Dacre's mum was in on it all and I think the guys resented that, but knowing my own mother, I could totally understand her reactions. She was protecting her son. She had seen what had happened when Joe died and how it had affected my family, and she simply didn't want anything like that for her son. Totally rational, if you ask me.

After two weeks of being unable to resolve the situation, and with the record company and venues breathing down his neck, Den did the only thing he could. He announced that we were to take a holiday until the whole shitty mess was dealt with.

You'd think that after being on the road for so long, I'd

jump at the chance to go home or go somewhere and see something other than a hotel room or a stadium. The opportunity to visit interesting places, museums, beaches should have been an exciting prospect to me. But the thought of not being on tour filled me with dread. It had been my life for so long, it was impossible to know how to cope without it. What the fuck could I do with all this unwanted free time?

My first instinct was to visit my parents. It was long overdue, after all. But everything had to be so cloak and dagger. Contrary to my wishes, my folks still lived in the house in Leeds where Joe and I grew up, and this meant that every single website, social media page, and jungle drum had the news of my return home before I'd even arrived there.

Blue Demon had assigned security detail to my mum and dad's address, and I was instructed not to go out unaccompanied, which really pissed me off. I'd be a prisoner on my bloody so-called holiday.

When I arrived home and was deposited inside the house by two huge bodyguards, my mum gripped me and clung on for dear life. "Oh, darling. We've missed you so much. How's the tour going?"

I shrugged. "Well, it was going great until… you know."

My dad slapped my back. "We heard about the whole thing with Nick on the news. They're saying it's connected to drugs, Si." A crease of disapproval furrowed my father's brow.

I shook my head fervently. "Nope. Not a chance in

hell, Dad. I know Nick. He wouldn't do that. Not after Joe."

My mum stepped back and cupped my face. "But stress does terrible things to a person, sweetheart. You never know what—"

I placed my hands over hers. "No, Mum! I *know* Nick. He may be stressed, but drugs? After everything the band went through with Joe?"

My anguish must have been clear on my face as both parents hugged me again. "We just worry about you, son. That's all."

I kissed them both on the head in turn. "I know you do. But I'm fine. I'm *better* than fine. I'm touring with a world-famous rock band, for Pete's sake!" I tried to sound excited in a bid to ease their worry, but I couldn't disguise the fact that I too was concerned for my surrogate big brother. I just hoped they located him sooner rather than later, and that he was safe and not being held against his will or something equally as horrendous.

Walking into my old bedroom after such a long time away filled me with emotions I thought I had long since learned to control. It smelled the same somehow. Not unclean, you understand, but… homely. Familiar. I could still close my eyes and picture Joe and me playing with building bricks on the carpet, trying to make the tallest tower we could until we ran out of blocks, or squabbling over whose turn it was to choose the next CD—Joe always seemed to win. It was in this very room where my musical education took place. I went from liking fluffy pop music to loving the likes of Nirvana, Pearl Jam, and Soundgarden. Joe's influence was strong and he was so right about the musicians being uber talented.

I placed my bag down and walked over to the notice board. There was a new photo in the centre. It showed Joe and Allie and must have been taken about six months before he died. God, they looked so fucking happy it made tears well in my eyes.

I placed my finger on the image of Allie smiling up at Joe as he gazed lovingly down at her. "I'm sorry I never said sorry to your face, Allie." I swiped at moisture as it escaped my eyes and I felt a presence in the doorway.

"Simeon? Are you okay, sweetheart?" I glanced over to find my mum there, her hands twisting nervously in front of her.

"Me? Y-yeah, Mum. I'm fine. Just… you know… coming back here…"

She stepped inside. "W-what did you mean?"

I frowned and cleared my throat. "About what?"

She glanced at the photo on the pin board. "When you looked at that photo you said, 'Sorry for not saying sorry'. I don't understand what you mean."

I heaved a sigh and ran my hands back through my hair. I shook my head, trying to find the words to explain, but they wouldn't come readily, so I went and sat on my bed.

"I never apologised to Allie for not being there when he died."

I glanced up to find a confused expression on my mother's face. "Why would you need to apologise? You did nothing wrong."

A lump formed in my throat and I swallowed in a bid

to dislodge it. "He asked me to go on the tour with them and I chose uni instead." I clenched my jaw as anger began to rise inside of me. "If I'd been there… if I'd gone on the tour, I could've stopped him taking the drugs. He wouldn't have done it if I'd been there, Mum. He'd still be here. Him and Allie would be married and you'd still have your son." I bit down on the inside of my cheek, desperate not to cry anymore.

She came and sat beside me. "Is that why you never come home? Is that why you struggle to talk about Joe? Because you feel responsible?"

"I *am* responsible, Mum. Didn't you hear what I just said?"

She gripped my hand, hard. "Now you listen to me. What happened was a stupid accident. Blaming yourself for what another grown man does is ridiculous. He was an *adult,* Simeon. And he made his own choices that night. You can't blame yourself."

I wanted to believe her. "But you must have thought it. You and Dad. You must have been angry with me for not going on the tour with him."

Her eyes filled with a combination of sadness and pain. "We have *never* blamed you. We have *never* been angry with you over it. Never. I can't believe you've been carrying this around with you for all these years. This is absolutely crazy." She cupped my face and her voice softened. "Please get that thought out of your head. *Please.* I promise you with all my heart that the thought never crossed our minds to blame you, sweetheart."

The sincerity in her eyes was so clear, and I pulled her

into my chest, holding her tight. Relief flooded my veins and it was as if a weight had lifted from my shoulders.

She pulled away and wiped at her eyes. "I know Allie didn't blame you either. She's kept in touch. That photo was one she found when she was going through some boxes ready for moving house. She sent us a copy as it was the most recent one she had of the two of them.

"Oh. How is she? Is she okay?"

My mum shrugged. "She's not great, to be honest. I need to tell you something. She blames herself too. She thinks you hate her because she was too ill to be there the night Joe died."

What? "But how… why would she…?"

"You didn't speak to her on the day of the funeral. You left without saying goodbye. She has always thought that was because *you* blamed *her*." She sighed and shook her head. "I really should bang your heads together."

♫♫♫

In bed that night, I lay awake, thinking about how I could possibly make things right. I decided the only thing I could do was talk to Allie face to face. Yes, it would mean heading off to the Scottish Borders on a bit of a whim, but hell, I had nothing else to do with my time until Nick was back in the fold. *If* he ever came back.

The next morning, I picked up my mobile and dialled Den's number.

Den sighed heavily in my ear before I even had a chance to say hello. "Ugh, for fuck's sake, Si. Don't tell me you're running away too!" The trouble was, his thoughts were a little too close to the mark for comfort.

Taking a deep breath for courage, I fessed up. "I do want to head off for a few days, but at least I'm telling you and not just taking off. *And* I'll be contactable so you won't need to fret. I just have some stuff to do. Some things that need to be said directly to someone."

He huffed again. "Bloody hell fire. And here I was thinking you were the reliable one."

I couldn't help laughing at the melodrama he created out of nothing. "Den, I *am* reliable. Like I said, I just need to take a few days out. A week maybe... two weeks tops."

"Next you'll be saying a month or a bloody year. I'm too old for this shit, Delaney. My poor heart can't take it, you know."

I chuckled again. "Come off it, Den. You're fitter than the rest of us. Stop being such a drama queen, eh?"

He made a snorting noise filled with disdain and frustration. "I want a bloody girl band next time. They can't be any worse than you lot. At least I could cope with expecting all the hormonal crap."

I sucked the air in through my teeth, mocking him. "You sure about that? They have so much more than that hormonal shit going on, you know? Bitchiness, drama, cat fights."

He fell silent for a moment. "Okay, fair point. But if you so much as *hint* that you're not coming back—"

"It won't happen, Den. I promise."

He sighed again, sounding utterly defeated. "Right. Well, I'm trusting you. Although God only knows why. I'll have a car with you for eleven." He hung up before I could thank him.

I stuffed my possessions in to my old duffel bag and made my way downstairs. The smell of bacon wafted through the air to greet me and my stomach rumbled.

"Ooh, someone sounds hungry," my mum said as she tiptoed up—spatula in hand—to kiss my cheek.

I patted my belly. "Yeah. Very. Look… I'm going away for a few days. I hope you don't mind."

Her happy expression disappeared. "But you've only just come home."

I nodded and cringed. "I know. I know and I'm sorry, but… I need to go and see Allie, Mum. I need to talk to her. To set things straight."

She began to serve up bacon onto two slices of bread which I presumed were for me.

After a few silent moments, she handed me the plate. "I understand. I'm just a little sad that we won't get to see much of you. You'll be back on the road before we know it."

I took the plate and pulled her to me with my free arm. "I'll be back before I go on tour. I promise, Mum. I wouldn't leave without saying goodbye." I kissed her head. "A car will arrive for me at eleven. The sooner I get there, the sooner I can come home to some of your steak pie."

I winked down at her and she smiled. "And you can't talk to Allie on the phone?"

I shook my head. "I need to speak to her face to face, Mum. I owe her that much."

♫♫♫

Bang on eleven o'clock, a black car with tinted windows pulled up outside my parents' home, where a crowd of fans—mainly female—and paparazzi had gathered.

Before opening the front door, I kissed and hugged my mum and dad. "Bye, you guys. See you in a few days."

My mum clung to me as she always did when it was time to say goodbye. "You've got the address?"

I held up the piece of paper she had given me. "Yes."

"Take care, son. Don't go getting in any trouble with the press, okay?"

I rolled my eyes. "Dad, I'll be fine. I promise."

My security guard, Steve—who was, I might add, built like a brick shit house—shielded me as he opened the door and we made our way out to the car. Keeping his eyes on the crowd, he opened the car door and, to a chorus of "WE LOVE YOU, SI!" and "THIS WAY, MR DELANEY!" and "IS NICK REALLY DEAD?" I climbed in, unscathed, and fastened my seatbelt as the door was closed.

Steve climbed into the passenger seat and turned to face me. "Everything okay, Mr Delaney?"

I nodded. "Fine, and please just call me Si. I hate all that formal bollocks."

He nodded and his mouth formed a line, which I guessed was his way of smiling. "Very good, sir. Si it is. This is George and he's driving us up to Kelso today."

"Great to meet you, George, and thanks. Do you chaps mind if I have a nap? I didn't sleep much last night."

"You don't need to ask permission, Mr D—Si. We work for you, remember?"

I felt my face warming. "Oh, yeah. Okay, well I'm going to stick my headphones in and listen to some tunes and have a sleep."

Steve gave a single nod and turned to face front as a black screen rose between me and the front of the car. I knew I'd never get used to the whole fancy chauffeur driven car thing. I stuck my earbuds in and hit shuffle before resting my head back and closing my eyes.

CHAPTER 6

Si

I must have really needed the sleep as Steve woke me up to tell me we had arrived at the address I had provided. Knowing that the journey was a fair few hours, I was pretty disappointed that I hadn't been awake for at least some of it. I sat there for a moment and rubbed my hands over my face.

I didn't really think this through. What if she tells me to piss off? I have nowhere to sodding stay. She might be married or something, and her bloke might not want me there. In fact, if he knows anything about me, he'll probably tell me to fuck off. Maybe a little more research and a few more questions would've been a good idea, Si, you muppet.

Steve's voice dragged me away from my thoughts. "Si, sir, it all seems quiet out there but would you like me to accompany you to the door?"

So, I was still *sir*? I guessed the informal thing wasn't going to work. "Erm, no thanks, Steve. No one knows I'm here so it's all good. Thanks though."

Steve left the car and opened my door. When I stepped out, I found myself on a lane outside a little stone cottage that sat in what appeared to be the middle of nowhere. There was a distant bleating of sheep and I could hear birdsong, but other than that, and the wind in the surrounding trees, it was so peaceful. There was a little white Fiat parked at the side of the house which I took as a good sign of someone being home. But who was it? My heart skipped at the thought of having to defend myself against some huge, brusque Scotsman.

I grabbed my duffel bag and suddenly remembered I hadn't arranged accommodation. "Shit. Hotel," I cursed.

Steve chipped in from behind me. "Don't worry, sir. Den has arranged a room for you at the Roxburgh Hotel. From the pictures I've seen, it's very nice." I turned to face him, relieved. "George and I are instructed to stay there too, until you're ready to leave. Here's a card with our mobile numbers on, so you can give us a call if and when we're needed to collect you."

I took the card from his hand and closed the car door. With a deep breath for courage, I turned and walked up to the sage green painted front door and knocked.

Within a minute or so, it opened, and a woman I recognised immediately stood there, drying her hands on a tea towel. She wore jeans and a pale blue fitted shirt. She looked just as I remembered.

She frowned but then her eyes widened and she shook

her head in what looked like disbelief. "Yes? Can I help you?"

I swallowed and blinked, suddenly overwhelmed with a flood of memories bombarding my mind. "Allie. Allie, it's me, Si. Si Delaney?"

She gasped and flung her arms around my neck. "Oh my God. I thought it was you but then my head said it couldn't be! But it really is!"

Her warm welcome was a surprise, and as we stood on the doorstep, I heard the car pull away, leaving me there to face the music, no matter the tone of it.

Allie let me go and wiped at her eyes. "Come in, come in," she said as she stepped aside, tugging my sleeve.

I smiled nervously and walked into the small lounge of her cottage. "This is a cute place."

She gestured to the sofa. "Have a seat, please." I did, and she sat opposite me on the other two seater, leaning forward eagerly.

Her gaze didn't leave my face. "It's rented but I do love it here. Great for painting."

Nerves were getting the better of me and I began to tap and drum my fingers on the armrest. "I can imagine. Very inspirational." I glanced around my surroundings, looking for hints as to whether she was married or living with someone.

She laughed quietly. "You're such a typical drummer. Just like Joe."

I stopped tapping and cringed. "Sorry. Nerves."

"I'm so glad you're here." Her voice wobbled a little and that brought my attention back to her. She looked great. Her once long auburn hair was now shoulder length and in a choppy kind of style. Her make-up free face was fresh and she looked so healthy. Clearly the Scottish air of home agreed with her.

She carried on talking, seeing as I had apparently lost the ability to form a decent sentence. "So, what brings a famous rock star to the Scottish Borders?"

I scratched the back of my neck. "The band's taking a bit of a hiatus from touring just now and I had some free time…so…"

She cringed. "Oh, God. Yes, I heard. Is Nick okay? I've tried to find out but things have seemingly been put on lockdown. That's not why you're here, is it?" Her eyes widened and I was a little confused. Her hand came up to her mouth. "He's not… he's not *dead* or anything, is he?"

Whoops! I held up my hands. "Nick? No. No, nothing like that. I think he just got to the point where he had to take a break. The band's been touring pretty much non-stop for five years and I think it just took its toll."

She heaved a huge relieved sigh. "Thank goodness. I was really worried for a minute there."

"Nah. No need. I reckon we'll be back on the road before we know it." I noted the hope in my own voice.

I watched as she fiddled with the towel still gripped in her hand. "So, what *does* bring you here, Si?"

I inhaled deeply, vying for time to form what I wanted to say. As usual, I failed. "Look, I've been on the road ages today and I'm parched. Any chance of a brew?"

She smiled warmly. "Sure. I'll put the kettle on. Come keep me company?"

I followed Allie through to the kitchen at the back of the little cottage, and again, assessed my surroundings.

Through the window I could see nothing but countryside from the small hedge that skirted the garden. A clump of trees stood swaying in the distance, and beyond that, a range of hills rose from the horizon.

"You've got a great view, Allie."

She came to stand beside me as the kettle began to hiss. "You see those trees? There's a family of deer that plays around out there at dusk. I've taken some fantastic photos of them."

"Ah. So, you're a photographer now too?" I remember her always being very creative. She made her own clothes, designed fabrics, and painted when I knew her before.

I glanced to find her cheeks had tinted pink. "I wouldn't call myself a photographer. I mean, I dabble, but nothing serious." *Modest as ever.*

Taking the bull by the horns, I blurted out without really thinking, "Allie, I came to say I'm sorry. That's the reason I'm here. I'm so, so fucking sorry for everything. It should have been said a long time ago but..." I shook my head.

She turned to face me, a mask of confusion now in place. "Sorry? I don't understand, Si. What do you have to be sorry about?"

I lowered my chin and closed my eyes. "I'm sorry I wasn't there on the night he died. I'm sorry I couldn't stop him making that stupid decision. And I'm sorry for not being there for you in the days before the funeral. I was a total bastard to you back then. I should've offered more support. Huh, who am I kidding? I should've offered *some* support. That would've been a start. Instead, I let you deal with all that shit on your own. He was my brother, and the only other person who really knew how I felt, apart from my folks, was you. I failed you, Allie. And I'm so, so sorry. I hope you can forgive me."

When I lifted my head again to look at her, tears were trickling down her face, leaving glistening trails on her skin.

Her lip trembled. "You're wrong, Si. It was *me* who failed *you*. *I* should've been there that night. He was my fiancé. I should've been the one to stop him from being an idiot. I lived with him, for goodness sake."

I turned towards her, shook my head, and placed my hands on her arms. "You know, I thought for all these years that you must hate me for all the same reasons. I wanted to talk to you but I couldn't face you after his death. Too much guilt. I was scared you'd tell me what I was thinking was true, and hearing it directly from your lips would've crushed me. I only found out last night how you truly felt. My mum told me you thought I blamed you and I was so shocked. So I came straight here as soon as I could. I was horrified that you could even *think* I'd be angry with you, Allie. I've *never* blamed you. I've only ever blamed myself."

A sob broke free from her chest and she collapsed into me. I pulled her into my arms and let her cry as I stroked her hair. She released all the pent-up sadness she had been carrying around for the years since Joe's death, and I just held her. It was a battle to stop my own tears from falling but I had to remain strong. We'd both been through hell and needed each other but hadn't dared to ask. I was angry at myself. Bitterly fucking angry. Joe would've been so damned disappointed in me and that hurt like hell.

She eventually pulled away and wiped at her damp face. "Ugh. I'm sorry, Si. You didn't need that. Anyway, I don't know about you but I feel like coffee just won't cut it right now. Fancy something stronger?"

Her words were music to my ears and I laughed lightly. "Yeah, whatever you've got. I'm having a gazillion different emotions right now and I think this is one of the times when only alcohol will suffice."

She walked over to her wine rack and grabbed a bottle from it. "Rioja okay?" I nodded, and she grabbed two glasses from a cupboard. I made my way back through to the lounge with Allie close behind me.

I watched as she opened the wine with shaking hands and poured two full glasses. She handed me one and picked her own up. "Cheers."

"Cheers," I replied, before taking a few gulps of the red liquid. The slight acidic tang made my mouth water. I knew nothing about wine but I liked this one.

"So, what's been going on in your life, Si? It's been so long."

I shook my head. "Oh, you know… touring, playing, recording… touring some more."

"Ah, the hectic life of a rock star, eh?"

I chuckled. "Yeah, something like that. There's nothing else to tell really. You probably know more about me than I do if you read the newspapers."

She raised her eyebrows. "Hmm, yes. I heard that you're gay now and living with that guy from that other band… I forget the name."

I rolled my eyes. "Jeez, that one made me laugh. You go for one night out with another band and you're photographed speaking directly into someone's ear because of the loud music in the club, and all of a sudden two and two make five."

She laughed heartily. "I must say, it was a shock. Can I take the revelations as falsehood then?"

"You can take it as utter bollocks. He's a great guy and I have no problem with people thinking I'm gay, but his boyfriend is built like a fucking out-house and I'd rather not get on his bad side."

We laughed for a while about how the tabloids had made up stories where there were none.

She wagged a finger at me. "Oh, that was a good one about Nick and his hair. I bet that brand of shampoo has rocketed lately."

"Yeah. I was once asked what product I use. I think I told them camel snot or something like that."

She burst out laughing. "You didn't?"

"I did. It stopped them from writing a bloody article about me and my hair care routine anyway."

"Ah, yes. Good point." She raised her eyebrows. "And I have to say, there have been lots of photos of you with random women too."

My stomach twinged with shame and my face became warmer. "Hmm. The paparazzi always seem to be at the ready to mark me as a womaniser."

She tilted her head and eyed me with suspicion. "So… no long-term girlfriends or wives in your life yet?"

I huffed and took another gulp. "Me? Nah. The chance would be a fine thing. No bloody spare time to fit a relationship in. What about you?" I wasn't sure I wanted to hear the answer seeing as she had been my brother's girlfriend, and the thought of her with someone else just felt weird.

She laughed. "No girlfriends or wives, that's for sure." Then her smile disappeared. "But in all honesty, no. There's been no-one. Friends have tried to set me up with guys and one even tried to get me to register on that *Made For Each Other* dating site but I just haven't wanted to." She dropped her gaze to her wine glass. "No one has compared to Joe."

I knew exactly how she felt. He was pretty irreplace-able. Although, maybe therein lay the problem. Comparing one person to another probably wasn't the best way to find love. But how the hell would I know?

As if snapping herself out of a trance, she sat bolt upright. "Hey, I found some old photos a short while ago. I sent one to your mum. It was so good to look back… but so hard at the same time, you know?"

I nodded and took another mouthful of my nectar-like drink. "I'd love to see. If they're to hand, that is. Don't go clambering in to the loft or anything."

Before I finished my sentence, she was on her feet and disappeared upstairs. She returned a few moments later with a shoe box. "Tadaaaaa!"

I lowered myself to the floor and she joined me. "Pre-pare to be totally embarrassed. There are some *great* ones of you in here."

I laughed and shook my head. "I spend my life embar-rassed, Allie. I doubt you could make things worse."

She grinned. "Just you wait."

CHAPTER 7

Si

Three bottles of wine were almost done but the trip down memory lane was far from over.

I laughed hysterically as Allie passed me another photograph. "Fuck! Look at my cheesy grin on that one. And what's with the hair?"

She rested her head on my shoulder as she looked at the image I held. "Aww, you look so cute. It's the way you're grinning up at Joe that gets me every time. Your face… so sweet."

"Yeah. I worshipped him. He was so… *good* with me. And with my mates too. He never seemed to get fed up of me hanging around."

"That's because he worshipped you right back," she whispered. "He missed you like crazy, you know, when we moved to London. He was forever looking over his shoulder as if he expected you to show up. I've never known brothers who were so close. You may as well have been twins."

"Except we looked nothing alike."

She lifted her head and regarded me. "You look just like him now. Your features are the same. Same eyes, same nose, same mouth."

I smiled. "Same beard."

"Ah, well, *that* was why I didn't recognise you straight away, standing there on my doorstep all manly like. You were very... *smooth* when I last saw you." She pointed at me, wine glass in hand, and almost sloshed her drink on the floor. "Whoops!"

I couldn't help laughing. "I was *smooth*? I hope you mean my skin and not my pick-up tactics." *Okay, so the wine's going to my head a bit now too...*

"I wouldn't know about that. I only had eyes for Joe..." Her words trailed off and she took another large drink of her Rioja. "Ooh. Top up needed." She scrambled to her feet and went to grab a fourth bottle from the kitchen. I knew we'd both regret this in the morning but I made no attempts to stop her.

Rifling through the box, I came across a photo I had never seen before. It appeared to have been taken around the same time as the one Allie had sent to my mum—roughly six months before Joe died. As I stared at the image, the occasion came drifting back. We were in the back garden at my house. Joe and Nick were playing a version of Bon Jovi's "Wanted Dead or Alive"—Nick on Joe's scratty old acoustic guitar and Joe tapping on an upturned bucket like a bongo. Allie was watching Joe, of course, from where she sat on a low-slung branch of the apple tree, her hair scooped around over one shoulder and glinting red in the sunlight. What concerned me was the expression on *my* face. I had been snapped with my eyes transfixed on her. But the way I was looking at her was disconcerting.

I looked head over heels in love.

She appeared from the kitchen and took her place on the floor beside me again. "Ah... you found *that* one. I meant to hide it away to save your embarrassment." She nudged my shoulder with hers.

How the fuck do I play this? "My embarrassment?" *Okay, so feigning ignorance it is then.*

She took a drink from her freshly topped up glass and nodded slowly. "Joe said you fancied me. That you had a huge crush on me." She playfully held the word 'huge' on for longer than necessary and her words slurred slightly. Under normal circumstances, I would've found that amusing, but not on this occasion.

I scrunched my face and threw the photo down so it skimmed across the table and fell out of sight. "What? I hope you ignored him. Jeez, he was a bloody wind-up merchant that guy." I shook my head vehemently and reached for my glass. I finished off the contents in one go and topped my glass up again to the brim.

She placed a hand gently on my arm. "Si, it's fine. Kids get crushes. It's not like you're in love with me *now*, for goodness sake. You've nothing to be ashamed of."

Oh, God. If you only knew the truth.

I couldn't look her in the eye. "Pfft. Ashamed? Why

would I be ashamed? It's bollocks. I hope you *know* it's bollocks?" *Okay stop protesting, you dick. Let it go.*

She fell silent and stared into her glass for a few moments.

I was just about to say something to fill the quiet void when she spoke. "I miss him so much. The way he used to look at me. The way he made me feel... the way he loved me."

I watched as tears cascaded into her wine glass and the urge to comfort her was too strong to fight. "Hey, come on. Don't cry." I took her glass from her hand and placed it alongside mine on the coffee table. "Maybe we've had enough wine, eh?"

She lifted her face and the pain in her eyes would have floored me if I hadn't been sitting down there.

She wiped at her eyes. "Why did he have to die and leave me all alone? Why did he have to be so stupid and try drugs? Was being with me not enough? Was I not exciting enough for him?" Once again, she lowered her gaze as more tears came.

In my alcohol-addled brain, I knew they were rhetorical questions. Questions she had no doubt asked herself many times before. And still I felt compelled to answer.

I tilted her chin up with my finger. "Hey. Stop that, Allie. You were perfect for him and he adored you. We all did. What happened that night was nothing to do with you. He made a stupid mistake. We all make them. But it's not a reflection on how he felt about you, you hear me?"

I wanted to convince her although I knew my words would do little to alleviate the agony she still carried inside. But as I sat there and thought about the conversation we'd had moments before—the one where I had tried to shrug off my adoring gaze in the photo—all the feelings I'd kept locked deep inside for years began to bubble to the surface. Feelings I had *almost* forgotten. Feelings I had desperately tried to ignore and hide.

I was drunk and I should've stopped. I should've got up and walked away. I *should've* called my driver to pick me up.

"Allie, you're the most amazing woman I've ever known. You're funny, intelligent, and talented. It's so obvious why Joe loved you so much. I totally understand why he wanted to be with you every moment of every day." *Stop it, Si. She doesn't need this. Stop talking. You're drunk and she's broken-hearted.* My heart pounded at my chest, playing its very own drum solo, and my breathing rate increased. Adrenaline or alcohol—I wasn't sure which —coursed through my veins and emboldened me. "I mean, look at you. You're so, so beautiful. Who wouldn't be crazy about you?"

She gasped and I should've taken that as my cue to leave, but I didn't. Instead, I lowered my face until my mouth hovered dangerously close to hers and I closed my eyes. *Just one kiss for comfort. One light kiss. One friend to another. That's all.*

I expected her to slap me or scream at me. But when that didn't happen, I threw caution and sensible thought to the wind and took her mouth with my own.

Her lips were soft and yielding, and I could taste the remnants of her tears mixed with the wine we'd been drinking. I slipped my arm around her and pulled her into my lap. Her legs straddled mine and the friction of her pressing down on me sent shivers darting through my body. Sweeping my hands up her arms and into her hair, I kissed her with urgency as she gripped my shoulders and kissed me back with just as much.

What the hell's happening? Why the fuck are you doing this? She was Joe's, not yours.

Never yours.

I chose to ignore the voice of reason niggling at the back of my brain as I caressed her face and arms and she held onto my shoulders. She began to move her hands and I felt sure at that point she was going to push me away, but instead, her hands slipped into my hair and she moaned. I moved my mouth down to her neck and she lightly grazed my scalp with her nails.

Whatever the hell this was, I needed it. I needed to make her forget the pain, and I sensed she wanted that too. I dared to slowly trace from her waist up to the side of her breast with my thumb and she gasped again.

She pulled away and rested her forehead on mine. "I want you to love me, Si. Please will you love me?"

You can't do this. It's wrong. You're betraying your brother. Just stop.

No matter how loud my subconscious screamed at me, I somehow managed to ignore it. She reached down, gripped the hem of my T-shirt, and dragged it upwards and off before tossing it aside. The ghost of a smile graced her lips as she traced the tattoos on my chest and bent to kiss them. First the skull, then the dragon. I closed my eyes and let my head roll back as she moved her mouth across my heated skin.

Opening my eyes once more, I gripped her arse and

lifted her as I stood; my gaze locked on hers. I walked towards the staircase and hoped I was heading in the right direction for her bedroom. She continued to kiss and nibble at my bottom lip. Once at the top of the stairs, she reached to her right and shoved open the door to my left. I carried her in and laid her down on the bed. I unfastened my boots, kicking them aside before removing my jeans. All sense of reason had long since gone, and all that filled my heart and mind was the need to be inside her. She lay there, pleading at me with her eyes, and I suddenly felt very sober.

But I didn't stop.

I lowered myself to my knees on the bed beside her and reached to unbutton her shirt. She lifted to allow me to remove it and she unclasped her bra, letting that fall too. Her breasts were just as beautiful as I imagined. Pert but real, and I longed to feel them in my hands. I traced the waistline of her jeans and flicked the button open as I lifted my gaze from her flawless, pale skin to her vivid blue eyes that were now darker somehow.

My hand hovered just inside her panties and I paused. I needed to stop. *We* needed to stop.

But she slipped her jeans and panties down her legs and reached up to pull me towards her again. This kiss was deeper. I slipped my tongue into her mouth and couldn't help the gravelly moan that left my own throat as my fingers glided lower and found her arousal.

Sheer bliss.

Kissing and touching her was the most sensual experience I'd ever had. I'd wanted this for so damn long, but I wanted more. I *needed* more of her.

My fingers toyed with the sensitive flesh at the apex of her thighs and she closed her eyes. "Love me, Si," came her whispered command again. I stood, discarded my boxers, and grabbed a condom from the wallet in my jeans pocket before climbing onto the bed again and resting myself between her silky-smooth thighs. She opened her eyes and her gaze was once again locked on me. She lifted herself up and tangled her hands in my hair again. "Please, Si. I need you." Last time she had needed me, I had let her down, and I had no intention of doing that again.

Once I was sheathed, I lowered myself until I was poised at her entrance, and she lay back again, lifted her legs, and wrapped them around me, pulling me, willing me closer. I hesitated again. We'd drunk almost four bottles of wine. This was crazy.

It's just sex. Just a release, that's all. You've had no strings attached sex plenty of times before. That's all this is. Just sex.

Who was I trying to convince? I was the only one who could hear my inner voice and I was blatantly ignoring it.

I sank myself deep into her and nuzzled her neck as she shivered and scratched at my back, willing me deeper still. Her body enveloped mine and I closed my eyes, relishing the sensations of pleasure deep in my groin and the adoration filling my heart. I lifted my head to gaze down at her beneath me and she pulled me down to kiss her again, our tongues tangling together, our teeth nibbling and our hot, panted breaths mingling.

I moved inside her and all cognitive thought left my head. I was simply a mass of pleasure and sensation. I had *never* felt this way with a woman before and it scared the hell out of me, but yet again, I pushed away the niggling fear and concentrated on giving pleasure to Allie. I teased her nipples with my tongue and teeth and she gasped, moaned, and writhed beneath me.

Pressure began to build and my breaths came faster as I moved in time with them. I reached down between our bodies and connected to the nub of nerves between her thighs again and she cried out, tightening around me and moving her hips in perfect synchronisation with mine. I buried my mouth between her neck and shoulder and found my own incoherent, growled release.

I lay there for a few moments, not daring to move, and enjoying the feeling of her heart beating rapidly against my bare chest. I placed a gentle kiss on her cheek and held her to me briefly before moving away to clean myself up.

When I stood from the bed with my back towards her, she gasped and then cried out, "Your tattoo. Oh my God, Joe. What have I done?"

CHAPTER 8

Si

Allie locked herself in the bathroom and I could hear her pained sobs vibrating through the walls.

It was official.

I was the biggest bastard on the planet.

Once I was dressed, I dolefully walked down the stairs again and sat on the sofa. I made a quick call to Steve and asked to be picked up as soon as possible, and he confirmed he'd be there. I hung up the call, suddenly feeling so alone it hurt.

With my head in my hands, I whispered, "Sorry, Joe. I'm so sorry, Joe," over and over, as if doing so would erase or undo the colossal mistake I had just made.

It's one thing to realise you're in love with your brother's nineteen-year-old girlfriend when you're sixteen, but a whole other thing to have sex with her when you're an adult who should know better. And even though Joe wasn't around anymore, that fact somehow made it worse. Like I'd tarnished his memory. Defiled it in the worst possible way.

Betrayal. That was the word that fit what I had done.

And I had ruined my relationship with the most special person tying me to my brother's memory. How the *fuck* could she ever forgive me now?

I smacked myself in the head, hard, and cursed aloud. "Fucking stupid idiot, Delaney. Stupid, stupid, stupid." The pounding in my head was nowhere near the punishment I felt I deserved.

"A-are you okay, Si?" came a whispered voice from behind me. I hadn't realised the sobbing had stopped, nor had I heard Allie enter the room.

I turned my head but didn't look directly at her. "No. No, I'm not okay. I've called my driver. As soon as he gets here, I'll be leaving. You won't hear from me again."

She sniffed and cleared her throat. "I... I see. Erm... okay. But you don't have to go."

Confusion clouded my head and I couldn't think straight. "Allie, the way you cried out when you saw my ink tells me I *do* have to go."

She stepped around the sofa and stopped in front of me. "I'm sorry about that. It's just... I just..."

"You realised we made a mistake of fucking epic proportions. And you were right. Because right now, I feel like utter shit."

"Si, you have to understand that you were my first since Joe died. I have all these warring feelings inside and I don't know what to do with them. How to react. I feel safe with you because I know you. I needed you and you gave me what I needed, but—"

Anger bubbled up from deep within me, and for the first time in my life, I felt used. But not just used. Used *and* discarded. The only woman I had ever loved had just used me to get her out of a fucking dry spell. Not in all my years of meaningless one night stands had I felt so utterly pathetic and stupid. Stupid for hoping that maybe one day she could fall for me the way I had fallen for her all those years before. Okay, so it was a dumb bastard of a dream. But it hurt like a bitch.

I stood and towered over her. "Oh, well, I'm glad I could be of fucking service."

She gasped and reached out to slap me but I flinched out of the way.

Rage and hurt flared in her eyes. "How *dare* you? That's not what I meant and you know it. That was such a cruel thing to say when you know I'm not that kind of woman. All I meant was—" She was interrupted by a loud, insistent knock at the door.

We both glanced at the inanimate object as if expecting the owner of the knuckles to burst in. When they didn't, I turned to face her.

The pain evident in her eyes twisted at my heart, and I hated myself for saying something so crass. "Look, Allie... I don't know what to say to you, and quite frankly, anything I do say will no doubt make this whole thing even worse. But... this should never have happened. I know you feel the same and I know it's too late to realise that now, but I'm so sorry if I hurt you. The last thing I would ever do is hurt you." I gazed into her vivid blue eyes and clenched my jaw, fighting the onslaught of more alcohol-fuelled emotion. My hand itched to touch her, but instead I balled my fist, digging my nails into my hand. "I swear it would be the last fucking thing I would ever knowingly do." My voice broke and I turned and walked away from her as fast as I could, opening and closing the front door without looking back.

Steve greeted me and opened the car. "Good evening, Mr Delaney. I hope your visit went according to plan. I took the liberty of ordering a snack to be left in your suite and—"

"I told you, my name is Si. Now, can you just get me the fuck back to the hotel as fast as possible... *please*." I was aware there was no need for my shitty attitude, but I slammed the limo door behind me and sat with my head back, eyes closed, head still pounding.

♫♫♫

Back in the unfamiliar setting of my hotel room, sleep evaded me.

Alcohol had soaked up every last drop of water in my body and my brain rattled around in my head like a loose crate in a lorry. My mind's eye assaulted me with images. First it was Allie beneath me, touching me and crying out in ecstasy, and then in quick succession, there were images of her running to the bathroom, sobbing and slamming the door. The only thing that would have made the whole thing worse was if she'd thrown up too.

It had been my tribute ink that had hammered the final nail in the coffin. Angel wings and Joe's name emblazoned on my skin. She had seen that and completely lost it. I understood. I mean, who in their right mind sleeps with their dead fiancé's brother? Oh yeah, that's right... the same type of person who sleeps with their dead brother's fiancée.

♫♫♫

I must've fallen asleep eventually as the sound of my mobile woke me. I contemplated ignoring it. But the fact it may have been Allie struck like lightning and I fumbled for my phone.

Please be Allie... please be Allie... please be Allie. "H-hello?"

A loud belch reverberated over the airwaves. "G'day, little drummer boy!" *Chris. Great timing as always.*

I rubbed my hand roughly over my face. "Hi, Chris. What's up?"

He snickered like a teenager. "Got a joke for you, dude."

Here we go. I rolled my eyes. "Oh yeah? This should be good."

"Yeah, it's a corker. Okay... so... why is a drum machine better than a real-life drummer?" I remained silent and waited for the terrible punchline. "A drum machine won't shag your girlfriend." He proceeded to guffaw loudly in my ear, but after the events of the previous night, I wasn't in the mood for his piss-taking and the joke hit a little too close to home for my liking.

"Was there a reason for your call, Chris? I've got stuff to do, mate."

He fell silent for a few moments. "Okay, what's up? I know you've gone up north for a fricking holiday, mate, so I know you don't have shit to do."

I pinched the bridge of my nose, hoping it would ease the pain in my head. "I don't want to talk about it, Chris. Can you just tell me why you called and then I can go back to feeling like the scum of the earth?"

He sighed heavily. "Look, Si, we've almost lost a second member of the band this month and I don't want to have to worry about you too, so just spill it, eh?" His tone had morphed into big brother mode.

How do I say this? "I made a huge mistake last night. I'm such a fucking idiot, Chris." I fought the urge to smack myself in the head again.

I heard a noise that sounded like Chris had slumped onto a chair or bed. "Okay, spill it. What've you done?"

I sat up and shook my head. "I can't believe I'm actually going to tell you this. But you *must* promise not to judge me, okay? I'm beating myself up enough for both of us."

"Go on. I'm listening." I could sense a combination of worry and intrigue in his voice.

I cleared my throat. "I... erm... I went to see Allie yesterday."

"Ah, great. How's she doing? I've been meaning to get in touch. Oh, but hang on... what did you say to her? Did you fucking upset her?"

I closed my eyes. "I kind of did."

He heaved out a frustrated huff of air. "Okay. What did you say?"

"It's not what I said. It's more of what I… erm… we kind of slept together."

Silence.

The pain in my head increased and my empty stomach lurched. "I didn't mean to… I mean… we drank a lot of wine and—"

"Fucking hell, Si. I knew you were in love with the woman, but fuck." *Shit. So everyone knew all along? And no one admitted this to me? Just fucking great!* His voice lowered. "How was it then? I mean, judging by how you sound it wasn't that great. Was it…you know… totally shit?"

Annoyance niggled at me and I snapped at him. "Hey, I'm not going into fucking details with you. Jesus, what do you take me for? And why would you even ask such a thing?"

"Okay, okay. Calm down, mate. I just meant… you know… sometimes we want something so badly that when it happens it doesn't live up to expectations. That's all I meant, dude."

"Yeah, well for your information it was in no way shit. Far from it. Let's leave it at that, okay?"

"So if it wasn't shit, why the hell do you sound so pissed off? Shouldn't you be planning the next time? Or did she think *you* were a shit lay?" I sensed a hint of humour to his tone and chose to ignore it.

Instead, I cringed as I remembered the events of the evening. "When I stood up after we… you know… she saw my back tat and freaked out. Started to sob. Locked herself in the bathroom."

"Oh, fuck. That'd do it. It's a pretty damn big reminder of what she lost, mate."

I dropped my gaze and rubbed my temple. "It must have been like a slap to her face. Anyway, then I turned into Needy-Mc-fucking-Arsehole and said a few things I maybe shouldn't have. We didn't really deal with the issue and I left before we could talk about things. I figured she'd want me gone. But now I feel shitty. Like I should have done something else. I don't know."

"Look, Si, get your driver to take you over there and tell her you need to talk. You can't leave things like this, dude. She's still in contact with your folks. What the hell will they say if she tells them? You can't have this hanging over you. It needs dealing with."

Shit. I hadn't even thought about my folks. He was right. And I hated when Chris was right.

When I had been thoroughly chastised for my behaviour like an errant fucking schoolboy, I hung up, never discovering the real reason for his call. I showered and dressed, ordered room service, and then called Steve to ask him to take me back to Allie's house.

CHAPTER 9

Allie

I heard Si's car pull away, its tyres spinning on the gravel of the lane outside my house. My head pounded and my heart ached. So many damned emotions swirled around inside of me that I didn't know which to address first.

The sex had been amazing, and it had been so long since I had allowed anyone to touch me that I was completely and unexpectedly overwhelmed by not only the sensations, but the emotion too.

Sex with Joe had always been sensual and meaningful, and I missed that so much. Having Si here and drinking too much alcohol had led to reminiscing about happier times, and then the rest. It shocked me how much he reminded me of Joe initially. His mannerisms, his voice. All I wanted was to feel close to someone again. To close my eyes and pretend Joe was back in my life. It was wrong and so twisted that I was ashamed of letting things go as far as they had. But ultimately, Si had given me what I needed. A release. A sense of being wanted. To know that I wasn't some frigid woman destined to be a spinster.

What Si had given me was hope.

Seeing that tattoo on his back, however, brought me back to earth with a resounding thud. He wasn't Joe. And he was missing his brother just as much as I was. What I *had* done, in fact, was take advantage of Si's grief. And seeing that inked tribute was like a bolt of electricity straight to my heart.

The guilt was back.

Of course, Si had seen my reaction, heard me crying in the bathroom, and presumed I was repulsed at myself for having sex with him. He was so wrong. I was angry with myself. I had no right to do what I did.

The one thing I couldn't deny, however, was that when he was making love to me, I wasn't fantasising about Joe as I had expected I would—or worse still—as I had *intended* to. When I looked up into those azure blue irises, it was very much Si and me making that connection. I was so present in the moment with him that I forgot about Joe and how he had made me feel. Instead, it was Si touching and kissing me. Si making me moan and bringing me to climax.

Again, however, once it was over, I was struck with an immense guilt for the whole thing. How the hell could I have attempted to replace Joe with his brother so easily? What kind of bitch was I? A renewed hate for myself was building, and when you added that to the way I had taken advantage of Si's alcohol-fuelled lust and the old crush he'd had on me as a kid, it made me some kind of black widow predator.

I really wasn't nice to be around.

Once he had left, I stood there for what seemed ages. And the more I thought about it, the angrier I got. Not only at myself, but at Si too. His reaction to what we'd done hadn't exactly been a pleasant one. Slapping himself in the head and apologising to Joe's ghost repeatedly wasn't what I had expected. He also could see it had been a mistake. But why did that hurt me so much?

After standing there in a trance, I grabbed my mobile. I was going to message and demand he came back so we could deal with this like the human, mistake-making adults we were. Only I stared blankly at my phone as it dawned on me that the only way I could contact him would be to ring his parents or Nick. And for obvious reasons, I couldn't and wouldn't do either.

So, basically, I was stuck in my own little version of hell, reluctantly replaying the images and sensations in my mind that Si had created throughout my traitorous body.

CHAPTER 10

Si

There was the risk she wouldn't be home, but there was a greater risk she may not let me in if she was. But I knew I had to at least try seeing as I had neglected to ask for her number after I'd slept with her and abandoned her. I had treated her like a quick shag. How much more disrespectful could I have been?

So, on the day following my first visit to Allie's and only a few hours after being told off by the biggest womaniser the rock world had ever known, I was back on the doorstep of the little countryside cottage.

I knocked on the door and waited... and waited. Her car was by the house so she was either in the shower or she was ignoring me.

I closed my eyes and shook my head as I crouched to

the letterbox and flipped it open. I couldn't hear the sound of water running but I *did* hear someone shuffling around.

She was avoiding me.

"Allie. Allie, I'm guessing you're in there and that you just don't want to talk to me. I can understand that after the way I behaved yesterday. And the things I said." I peered around me to check no one was watching me talking through the letterbox. Seeing the coast was clear, I continued. "I wanted to say I'm sorry. Not... not for sleeping with you. I know you may be sorry about that part, but for me... for me it was amazing. Y-you were amazing. But I wanted to say sorry for hurting you. For leaving and not talking things through. It was cowardly and I'm truly sorry. But you were right... about what Joe said about my feelings for you. I thought I'd hidden it well." I remembered what Chris said. "Clearly, I didn't hide it as well as I thought. Anyway, it's out there now, but I want you to know I never meant to hurt you. You mean far too much to me for that." No reply came and I realised my actions were futile. I had a sinking feeling inside and I fought to keep my emotions in check. "Anyway, I'll go. Take care of yourself, Allie, and please... please don't blame yourself. You were emotional and I... I took advantage of that. I'm to blame. I let my feelings get in the way and it was stupid. I need to ask one more thing. Please don't let what happened last night ruin things between you and my folks. I would hate that. They love you. Remember that, okay?"

I stood and turned towards the car, ready to leave, when the door opened behind me. My heart tripped over itself and I swung around to find Allie standing there.

Her eyes were bloodshot and ringed with red. "I think you'd better come in, Si."

CHAPTER 11

Si

I nodded to George and Steve and the car pulled away, leaving me on Allie's doorstep once more. I slipped my hands into my pockets and stepped inside the cottage again, only this time I was nervous for a whole different reason.

I cleared my throat and asked the most ridiculous question. "Are you okay?"

She shrugged. "Do I look okay?"

"Look, Allie—"

"Can I get you a coffee? Tea? Are you hungry?"

I stepped towards her and placed my hand on her arm. "Stop, okay? Let's just sit and talk. I think we need to clear the air."

She nodded and moved over to the same sofa she had sat on the day before. I followed suit and sat opposite her again, lowering my gaze, unable to deal with the hurt in her eyes. In one way, it felt like we were starting over again, but deep down, I knew we couldn't.

"What did you want to say?" she whispered.

I lifted my face and locked my gaze on hers. "I want to say I'm a prick. And I'm sorry for being that way. I hate that I made you cry, Allie. I wouldn't hurt you for the world. I hope you know that."

She smiled. "We're not the best communicators, are we, you and I? And you're not a prick. I was just shocked. Seeing that tattoo with *his* name on was just a little overwhelming. Poor timing, I guess. I think I may have overreacted, but then again, alcohol played its part. When I came out of the bathroom and you were hitting yourself in the head, I realised you regretted what happened and then you left. I felt cheap. *And* foolish." She shrugged.

This was a shock to hear. "Cheap? Foolish? Fuck, no!" I shook my head and stood to join her on the other sofa. Once seated, I took her hand in mine. "You're misunderstanding everything. Allie, I've liked you since I was sixteen years old. But you belonged to Joe and I was a kid so I presumed back then that I'd just grow out of it. I was realistic. Like you said yesterday, kids get crushes and then they fade away. I knew that. But you were so… vibrant. So beautiful, and you had no idea just how stunning you were." I smoothed my thumb over the soft skin of her hand. "The guilt was horrendous. I almost confessed to Joe on so many occasions, but I was terrified I'd lose him if he knew. Turns out he knew all along. Turns out everyone knew." She remained silent and so I continued. "When you left to go to London, I thought I'd finally get over you. I was eighteen but still a kid really, and I presumed out of sight meant out of mind and all that, but... it didn't happen. When he died, not only was I riddled with guilt about not being there, but I was carrying the guilt around about the attraction I'd had to you for all that time. I tried so hard to switch it off. When I got to university and then when I joined the band, I slept around. I'm not proud of it. But I felt sure I could get you out of my system that way. And anyway, I thought you hated me for Joe's death. But then I spoke to my folks and they said you'd been carrying guilt around too. I couldn't believe it. I had to come and see you. To let you know that I didn't blame you. But I *never* expected us to end up... I just never expected it, Allie. And I'm sorry it was so horrible for you. I didn't mean to take advantage like that." I reached up and stroked her face, hoping the depth of my sincerity was evident.

She shook her head and sighed. "You didn't take advantage, Si. I distinctly remember asking *you* to make love to *me*, not the other way around."

I shook my head. "But I should've said no."

She shrugged. "Why? Why should you have said no?"

"Because... Joe. I'm his brother, you're his fiancée."

She gritted her teeth. "*Was* his fiancée. *Was*. He's gone, Si, and he isn't coming back. And as much I hate that fact, as much as I wish it wasn't true, it is. Am I supposed to remain celibate forever now? To never have sex again?" I didn't know how to answer that. "I've been grieving for so long that I've forgotten how to live. I've forgotten what it feels like to have a man want me so desperately. Yesterday, with you... I felt cherished again. It's been such a long time since I've felt that. I felt *safe* with you. I felt desired. It was so good to feel that way again. To just forget…"

I furrowed my brow. "So… so you weren't disgusted about what we'd done when you were locked in the bathroom?"

She smiled briefly. "Far from it."

I let out a relieved sigh. "That's… that's good."

"But it can't happen again, Si." Her words cut like a knife but I don't know what I expected.

I dropped my gaze again. "I understand. I'm just not Joe."

She lifted my chin and forced me to look at her. "Simeon, stop that. It's got nothing to do with you not being Joe. You're you, and that's a good thing. You don't have to live your life forever in the shadow of a ghost." She closed her eyes and let go of my chin. "But anyway… I'm not looking for another Joe. I'm not really looking for another relationship. It's too painful to lose someone and I can't let myself go through that again. Sex is one thing but love…"

"Just because you lost Joe doesn't mean you'll lose everyone. You can't go through life fearing that. You're too young to give up on love and I think you know that really. You said you'd forgotten how to live, but it sounds like you're afraid to *let* yourself."

She stood and paced around but didn't make eye contact. "I know it doesn't make sense to you, Si. But… *this*… us… we wouldn't work. You'd be on tour and I'd be at home hoping you came back alive. Hoping you too hadn't made a stupid decision. And that's just too much to deal with." She ran her hands through her hair. "And anyway, we had sex *once*. That doesn't mean…"

Ah. I smiled without a shred of happiness. "That doesn't mean we have a future, I get it."

"I'm sorry, Si, but it doesn't. How can it?"

Regret at allowing myself to appear so vulnerable knotted my insides and I stood to face her. "I'm not stupid, Allie. I may not always act like it, but I'm an adult. I know the difference between sex and love. The two aren't mutually exclusive. And I didn't expect you to fall head over heels in love with me after one fucking shag." *Harsh, Si. Harsh.*

She raised her arms and let them fall heavily. "But what *did* you expect? The sex was great… really great. But I can't give you anything else."

I shrugged and shook my head. "I have no idea *what* I expected! I didn't expect we'd have sex in the first place so how the hell should I know what to say?" I was beginning to wish I hadn't returned to see her. The last thing I wanted was to argue and end up making things worse. "I think I should go. This isn't helping either of us."

"No, don't leave. Stay a little longer. We can sort this out, I know we can."

"But if I stay, it won't make a difference. Things will still be strange. We crossed a line and I don't know how we come back from that. But now I've made love to you and I know what that feels like, I can't forget that feeling, Allie. And I don't want to. But I think I maybe need time to try and get back to where we were before. Just friends. No strings. No complications."

Her lip trembled. "But if you leave now, that'll be it. I

know you'll feel awkward around me and you won't want to see me again. And I've only just reconnected with you. I don't want to lose that. You do mean a lot to me. You always have."

Sadness descended over me. "I don't want to lose it either. But maybe we should have thought about that before we had sex. Sex complicates everything. Especially when one party wants more." I watched as tears escaped the corners of her eyes and I stepped closer to kiss her forehead. "Let yourself fall in love again someday, Allie. Otherwise I'm not the only one living in the shadow of a ghost."

And with that, I left.

CHAPTER 12

Si

The journey back to my parents' house later that same day afforded me far too much time to think. I tried to eradicate the images in my mind of Allie naked beneath me by listening to music through my earbuds. But every song seemed to taunt me. When it came to "From Where You Are" by Lifehouse, the lyrics seeped deep into my heart and all at once reminded me of happy times I had spent with Allie and Joe over the years. The way I had loved her from afar but been so happy for Joe at the same time. Knowing now that Joe had known how I felt and had still included me in their lives made me love him even more. I thought back to the smiles on the photographs Allie and I had looked at; ones that had brought back so many memories, and although they were difficult to see, they were harder to let go.

The lyrics made my eyes sting and a painful lump of emotion lodged in my throat. I was sad before, but that sadness had been compounded during a visit that was supposed to heal wounds and repair friendships. That one passionate time Allie and I had shared was beautiful, but how could something so good have ruined everything? I tugged the earbuds out and threw them aside.

I had to formulate a plan of what I could say to my mum and dad so they wouldn't suspect anything. I hated lying. But this would be more like a lie by omission, which I justified in my mind as being acceptable on this occasion. What the hell would they think of me if they knew the truth? God, they'd be so disappointed, and I couldn't cope with that.

I spoke to Chris when we were almost back home and the news wasn't great. "Nick needs a bit longer. Den's pissed off but I think we should give him the time, Si. He's the backbone of our crew. I for one want him back on board with his head on straight. So, sit tight and we'll be back on the road soon, okay?"

I sighed heavily. I just wanted to be busy again. "Yeah. Sure, Chris. Whatever Nick needs."

"How are things with you and Allie? Did you sort it all out?" I sensed the hope in his voice.

"Not exactly. But give it time."

"Are you okay, mate? Your heart still intact?"

I laughed. "Oh, yeah. Intact like a mosaic. The cracks are visible but it still functions. Barely."

"Wow. Deep. Take care, okay? Speak to you soon."

The call ended as we pulled through a crowd of paparazzi waiting at the edge of my folks' driveway.

Fucking vultures. There's no wonder Nick ended up like he did.

As Steve walked me up to the front door, I was greeted by two further guards who had been placed there for our protection. Clearly the reporters had nothing better to do with their time than to harass someone as boring as me and as ordinary as my family. They'd no doubt be going through our rubbish bins if they could get access.

Some of the reporters shouted out at me, blatantly ignoring the fact I was wearing shades—which I presumed they would take as an indication I wasn't in a talking mood.

"Si! Over here, mate!"

"Si, are you gonna pose for a piccy?"

"Si! Is it true Sonic Idols are going back on the road next week?"

I laughed and made an exception to the silence I usually kept. "You seem to know more about that than I do." A rumble of excitement travelled the crowd, who had clearly taken my ambiguous answer as affirmative. I couldn't be arsed to correct them. The truth was I had no clue when we'd be back on the road again.

Life back at my folks' slowly returned to normal. Whatever normal is. We ate family meals together, played Scrabble, and watched movies. It felt a little like old times and there was some comfort in that. However, boredom was setting in and I was checking my phone so frequently that my mum began to get suspicious.

"Are you that fed up of our company, Simeon?"

I glanced up from the little screen in my hand. "Huh? Sorry, what did you say, Mum?"

"You do nothing but check that thing every five minutes. Are you bored of me and your dad already?"

I slid over to my mum on the couch and draped my arm around her shoulder. "Never. You know you're the best mum anyone could wish for, don't you?" I kissed her cheek and she grinned.

"What are you after? More of my steak pie, no doubt."

I patted my expanding belly. "Ugh, I'd love to say yes but all this slacking off has given me a podge. I'm going to have to do some serious exercise before we go back on the road."

My dad chipped in, "You could always work out in the garden. Or find something musical to do to keep you occupied and out of the biscuits."

He had a point. And I remembered Joe's old guitar from the photo I had found at Allie's.

I knew I hadn't seen it in my room. "Do either of you know where that old guitar is?"

My dad laughed. "You mean that grotty old thing Joe bought from a charity shop?"

"Yeah, that's the one. It may have been grotty looking but it played well."

"It's in my shed. Easy enough to find if you want to get it out tomorrow. You might need to tune it though."

I knew there was a tuner in my room in one of Joe's bedside drawers. So, a plan began to formulate in my mind of how I could spend at least some of my time until Den or Chris called about the tour.

A week passed and I had taken to writing songs in my room on Joe's old guitar. I was nowhere even close to the talent of Nick or Chris, but I had to do something to keep me occupied. I was scribbling some melancholy lyrics down when I heard a knock on the front door and rolled my eyes. The security guards were vetting every single person that came to the door, and for some reason, we'd had the milkman, a florist delivery, the postman, and someone who said they knew us but didn't—all in the same bloody day. Each time the guards would knock and consult with my folks so they were up and down like a fecking yo-yo. It was driving me mad and I wasn't the one having to deal, so goodness knows how fed up they were.

I heard my mum's voice and the sound of laughter and presumed it must have been someone they knew or Dad would have been tearing a strip off the security guards. Hoping it was maybe Chris or Den arriving to collect me, I eagerly made my way down the stairs. Maybe they didn't call in advance in case it sparked a media frenzy. Who knew? Adrenaline flooded my veins and as I walked into the living room.

But I stopped dead in my tracks as our visitor gasped. "Oh. Si. I… I thought you'd gone back on tour. The newspapers said—"

My mum laughed. "No, Allie, love. They always speculate and get their facts wrong about this bloomin' band. Drives you potty, doesn't it, Simeon?"

I nodded. "Erm…yeah… H-hi, Allie. What are you doing here?"

Mum slapped my arm. "Simeon! That's a bit rude. I invited her to stay for a while as a surprise. I thought maybe you two could carry on catching up now things are all sorted between you."

Fuck. If only she knew.

Allie shook her head. "I'm so sorry, Maggie, but when you invited me, I presumed it was because you had the space. I hadn't realised Si was still in his room."

My dad chimed in, "Simeon can sleep on the sofa, can't you, son?"

Knowing I was frowning, I shook my head as if it would somehow straighten my expression. "Erm... sofa... yeah. Yeah, fine."

Allie's cheeks coloured pink. "No, no. It's okay. I'll go to a bed and breakfast. I don't want to put you out."

My mum glared at me and it was clear she wanted Allie to stay. "It's no trouble, is it, Simeon? Tell her."

I forced a laugh. "Oh, sure. No, it's fine. The sofa's comfy. When you've slept on a tour bus and in numerous hotels, you can sleep pretty much anywhere." I was trying to convince myself as well as Allie.

She chewed on her lip and nodded. "Okay, if you're sure."

I reached down and grabbed her small suitcase. "I'll take this up to the bedroom for you." It was a good excuse to leave the room and I stomped up the stairs like a sulky kid. Why the fuck did my mum have to interfere? I mean, I know she didn't have a clue what had happened between us, but still...

I opened my bedroom door and walked in to drop the case by Joe's bed. I glanced up and caught sight of a photo of him grinning out of the paper.

"Yeah, I'm sure you'd think this was fucking hilarious."

"I don't actually. This wasn't planned. Well, not by me, anyway." I swung around to find Allie in the doorway, twisting her hands in front of her. "I didn't want you to think I'd come down to cause trouble for you."

I heaved out a long puff of air. "I don't think that."

She stepped further into the room and stopped by Joe's old guitar. "You're writing?" I wasn't sure whether I should be affronted at the surprise in her voice.

I scratched my chin, embarrassment heating my cheeks as I grabbed and closed the notepad before she could read my crappy attempts. "What was it you said about your photography? Dabbling? Yeah, well that's me. It's just a way to pass the time."

She smiled and tilted her head to one side. "You could play me something maybe?"

Knowing the content of the lyrics and how much related to my feelings for a certain unattainable Scots lass, I quickly tucked the pad in a drawer. "Erm… no. I don't think so."

She sighed and closed her eyes briefly. "Look, Si, I'm happy to go and stay elsewhere. If this is going to be awkward for you, I—"

"No, Allie. It's fine. My mum would be pissed off with me if you left. She obviously wants you here."

"But you don't." It was a statement, not a question.

I didn't reply.

She fidgeted awkwardly. "I'll keep out of your way. I'm so sorry about this."

I shrugged, trying to appear nonchalant. "No big deal."

♫♫♫

That evening, I took the coward's way out and only came downstairs to eat. An awkward atmosphere descended over the table, and the sound of cutlery clanking against ceramic was all that could be heard.

Mum did her best to pour oil on troubled waters. "So, what are you two going to do whilst you're here? It'd be nice for you to spend some time together like old times, eh?"

Allie and I glanced at each other but she spoke first. "I'm sure Si has lots to do. He doesn't need me cramping his style."

My dad snorted. "Pfft, yes, he'd absolutely turn down the chance to spend time with a beautiful young woman... not! Eh, Simeon?" He laughed and I waited for the tumbleweed to blow in.

Mum glared at me. "You're not too busy, Simeon, are you?"

In a bid to give myself thinking time, I made a big deal of chewing the fork full of food I'd just placed in my mouth.

I swallowed. "I... erm... actually, I'm writing and I need to get some practise in at some point. You know. Keep things fresh in my mind and all that."

Something hit my leg with force under the table. "But you can spare some time for Allie, can't you?" I turned to find my mum's eyes so wide that I worried her eyeballs might pop out.

Allie interjected, "Honestly, it's fine. I came to see you two. I didn't even know he'd be here."

Mum was on the point of spontaneous combustion so I shook my head and cleared my throat. "Oh, no. Of course I have the time. Absolutely loads. Tons of it." She kicked me again. I had evidently gone too far.

♫♫♫

When it was time for bed, my mum brought me all the things I needed for my makeshift camp on the sofa.

She kissed me on the cheek. "Try and make more of an effort tomorrow, love, eh?"

I flared my nostrils and tried to keep my cool as I whispered, "I *am* making an effort. It's just... it's strange having her here, Mum."

Mum shook her head. "Well, I don't know why. You went all the way to Scotland to sort things out. You said it went well. So, what's the problem? Is it just because I'm forcing you to do the gentlemanly thing and sleep down here? I know it's annoying that the spare room is an office now, but your dad wanted a bat cave."

I laughed. "I think you mean a man cave. And hasn't he got his shed for that?"

"Yes, but you know what he's like for hobbies. Anyway, I'm sorry you don't have somewhere better to sleep. I don't think I thought this through."

"Pfft. Don't be daft. Anyway, I'm tired. Night, Mum." I kissed her on the forehead and hoped she'd leave.

She patted my cheek. "Think on what I said, okay?" I nodded and she turned to go at last. "Night, love. Sleep well."

I glanced down at the sofa. "Yeah, I doubt that," I mumbled, not loud enough for her to hear.

Once I was alone, I stripped down to my boxers and

clambered onto the sofa, covering myself up with the duvet. I tossed this way and that, but no matter what I did, my six foot one frame and the sofa were not a great combination. If I laid one way my neck hurt, but the other way my feet stuck up in the air. I was definitely in for a shitty night.

I heard soft footsteps and then, "Si? Si, are you asleep?" Allie whispered from just inside the lounge doorway.

"Funnily enough, *no*," I hissed back.

She padded over and crouched down beside me. "Look, why don't you come and get in your own bed?"

"Well, why do you *think*? We're adults and sharing a bedroom is something members of the opposite sex apparently don't do unless they're married."

She giggled. "You're so funny." I had no clue why she thought so. She nudged me. "Come on. It's silly you being squished up and uncomfortable down here when there's a spare bed upstairs in my room."

I huffed indignantly. "*Your* room? I think you'll find it's *my* room." Okay, now I got why she found me amusing. I sounded like a sulking toddler, and in the dim light of the moon shining through a gap in the curtains, I could see her lips pursed. She was trying not to laugh at me.

Cheeky cow.

She poked me again. "Come on. I insist you sleep in *your* room. In *your* bed. I'm at the opposite side so I promise not to hassle you."

I glanced at the door. "But what about my folks?"

"I think they'll be perfectly fine with it. It's a logical

solution, after all. And like you said, we're adults. We don't have to see each other naked. We're just sleeping, Si."

I must admit, the thought of snuggling down in my own bed with my own comfy mattress was far more appealing than waking bent double and seizing up. But the thought was fleeting and quickly replaced by conjured images of Allie naked.

"Okay. So long as you're sure." I stood and followed her towards the door. "And thanks."

Her night shirt only just covered her arse, and I wondered if I should mention the fact before following her up the stairs. Although, she was wearing panties, so I decided not to bother and just enjoyed the view.

CHAPTER 13

Si

By the time I came downstairs the following morning, Allie had dealt with the sleeping situation. It turned out my folks were surprisingly fine about us sharing a room. All of a sudden, it was the most logical solution in the world, and Mum couldn't figure why she hadn't thought of it sooner. They were oblivious to anything that would lead them to feel otherwise.

And so it went on. It was a little strange to begin with, and I couldn't sleep properly. My biggest fear was me kicking my covers off in the night and Allie being subjected to the sight of my morning wood. Thankfully, it didn't happen—or not that I'm aware of, anyway. Some nights, I would just lay awake and listen to her breathing. It sounds kind of creepy, but I found it soothing. The next few days were a little more relaxed as we got into a kind of routine.

Early mornings, we sat up in bed and chatted about anything and everything. It was as if we had put what happened up in Scotland behind us, and that was a double-edged sword for me.

One particular morning began much the same. My mum had brought us both a cup of coffee in at nine and we were sitting on our respective beds, chatting away as usual. Allie eyed me with suspicion for a few moments and I could tell she wanted to say something.

Sure enough, she eventually spoke. "You must love all the attention you get from girls. So much sex blatantly thrown in your face all the time."

I almost choked on my coffee and snickered. "I don't think I want to have *this* conversation with *you*."

She gave me a wave of her hand in encouragement. "No, come on. I bet you love it. It was the one thing I used to hate about Joe being on tour. I knew he loved me but the temptation must have been hard to resist sometimes."

I stared into my mug and inhaled the steam. "If we're talking about Joe, I can honestly say, with my hand on my heart, you had nothing to worry about on that score. Joe was one hundred percent yours."

"What about you now you're in the band?"

I shrugged as an uneasy tension knotted my stomach. "That's different. I'm single."

I could still feel her eyes on me. Assessing me. She wasn't going to give up. "But what about when you meet Miss Right one day? What then?"

I lifted my chin and focused on her, fixing her with my gaze. "If I meet Miss Right one day then I'll be Mr Right. All my attention will be hers. As will my heart and my body. *If* I meet Miss Right, I have no intention of being unfaithful. My time, my love, and my soul will be entirely hers." She swallowed hard and fidgeted a little. I got a small amount of pleasure from watching her squirm and so I continued. "If she's Miss Right, I'll only *want* her. Only *crave* her. No one else will even register on my radar. When I'm in a serious relationship, I'm a one-woman man, Allie." It was true. Well the *intention* was true—although I hadn't really had a serious relationship to speak of.

She stared at me. Her nostrils flared and her lips slightly parted. I wasn't sure what was going on in her mind but I would've given anything to know.

Suddenly, as if coming out of a trance, she shook her head. "Whoa, we got a bit intense there."

She'd broken whatever spell had been cast and disappointment washed over me. Something had crackled in the air between us and I know she felt it too.

I expected her to make her excuses and leave the room. But instead she took a sip of her coffee and carried on like nothing had happened. "Can I ask you something?"

I shrugged. "Sure. Go ahead."

"How come your mum and dad don't live in some huge swanky house now you're famous?" Wow. That was what you call a massive change of subject. "I mean, don't get me wrong, this is a lovely family home. But knowing your relationship with them, it surprises me you haven't bought them somewhere bigger." She cringed. "Shit, sorry.

That sounded so judgmental and nosy. I didn't mean it that way."

I laughed. "Don't worry. It's not through want of me trying, that's for sure. I've offered to buy them the house of their dreams but they won't hear of it. This house is who they are. Joe and I were born here and they love this place. So many happy memories, I guess. They just don't want to leave. I did pay their mortgage off and buy them each a car but that's all they'd let me do. Apparently, it's *my* money for me to spend on what *I* want. I did tell them I *wanted* to spend my money on buying them a new house but..." I rolled my eyes. "So, I just keep paying for weekend breaks to the best spa hotels and treating them to meals out as often as I can. They always try and pay me back but I won't accept it."

She cocked her head to one side. "Aww. You're so sweet."

I shook my head. "Nah. I adore my parents. I'd do anything to make them happy. It's the least I can do." I dropped my gaze briefly as thoughts of Joe tripped through my mind, and I didn't want to elaborate on the meaning of my comment.

It was as if she got the message loud and clear. "So, tell me, what's it like being on tour? And on stage? Is it scary? Is it exciting?"

I scrunched my face. How the hell do I put that into words? "It's like sex." *Okay, a little blunt, but true nevertheless.* "Euphoric. Like a natural high. One that doesn't fade quickly. And there's the travelling. A new city every day, new scenery, new venues, new people. The adrenaline rushing through your veins as you look out at the crowd knowing they're there just for you. They came to see *you* play. They love *you*. Or rather the idea of you." I laughed. "I've had so many marriage proposals you wouldn't believe it. And not just from young women either. I've been offered money for a night of sex. I was once offered money to date this woman's daughter. Suffice it to say, she wasn't my type." I raised my eyebrows but let Allie interpret that as she saw fit. "The whole thing is a total buzz. It's addictive, I think." She listened intently, hanging on my every word. "And the best part about it is I get to be there with my best friends doing what I love. And I get paid. It's a no brainer, really. I just wish I could sing like Nick. That dude's voice is incredible." I shook my head in awe. "And Stig, crazy bloke that he is. The energy he's got. Man, I honestly don't know where it comes from. He leaps around the stage like a bloody kangaroo on springs and he's a vegetarian for fuck's sake. Who knew tofu and lentils could give you such vitality?" I laughed and Allie joined in. Her laugh was a sweet sound that I realised I hadn't heard enough of. "And Chris, obviously, he's the babe magnet of the band. It's at his feet the women fall willingly. I think it must be his Aussie charm. Women just can't resist it." I laughed and shook my head. "Tell you what though, I feel sorry for the woman he marries. Although, I can't ever imagine him actually settling down. I think he'll be the eternal bachelor of the band unless hell freezes over or some miracle occurs and he really falls in love. And, of course, then there's Den. He's like the fifth member. As gay as the day is long, bloody good at his job and fierce with it. He knows what he wants for his boys— as he calls us—and he makes sure he gets it for us too. He drives us all mental mostly, but I don't know how we'd cope without him."

I realised I'd been rambling on and on and snapped my attention back to her to find her smiling at me with a wistful look in her eyes.

I cringed. "Shit, sorry. I got a bit carried away there."

She shook her head, her sweet smile still in place. "No, that was so lovely. You talk about them like they're family."

"That's because they are."

Her smile faded a little. "It's funny. Joe used to be the same. You're like him in so many ways... but so different too."

I smiled and lowered my gaze to my mug of coffee again. "Yeah... so I've heard."

She placed down her mug and walked over to my bed, taking a seat on the edge. "When you talk about the band and about playing, you... you just light up. It's clear you love what you do."

Having her so close to me again was a little unnerving and butterflies took flight inside me. "I do. I really, *really* do. And I finally feel like I'm supposed to be there. For ages, I felt like an imposter. Like Joe was the drummer but I was temporarily in his place, you know?"

She reached over and placed her hand on my arm. "You *are* supposed to be there, Si. And Joe would have been so proud of you. But sometimes it's as though you think you've got be *like* him or... or to compensate for him not being here. And that's sad. You're a lovely guy and you're so, so talented in your own right. You should embrace that. Don't feel the need to apologise for the fact that you're here and he isn't."

Without thinking it through, I said, "But you'd rather be sharing this room with him right now."

She sighed. "You're doing it again. This isn't about Joe anymore. Of course I'll always keep him in my heart. And I'll always love him, as will you. But... step out of his shadow. You're not in *his* place. You're in your own, Si. Remember that."

Her gaze was fixed on me and her words made my heart soar. Hearing that, especially from her, meant so much. I leaned forwards to hug her as a thank you, but as I moved, she connected her lips with mine and slipped her hands into my hair as she pulled herself closer. She was kneeling above me and I encircled her in my arms. Her tongue slipped into my mouth and tangled with mine, and for a few moments, I lost myself in the pure sensuality of the kiss.

But confusion washed over me and sensibility reigned so I pulled away. "Whoa, sorry. I shouldn't have done that."

She touched her lips with her fingertips. Her cheeks were flushed. "No, *I'm* sorry. That was all me. I just... I can't explain what happens to me when I'm around you." She closed her eyes briefly and then peered at me with a questioning expression, as if I had the answer. "I shouldn't be attracted to you, Si, but I am," she whispered.

I stood and grabbed a T-shirt from the end of my bed. "We're in Joe's old room and we were just talking about him. I'm just a reminder of him. That's all it is. Don't sweat it. I'm off to take a shower."

I left and quickly made my way to the bathroom where I locked the door, stripped out of my clothing, and turned the shower to hot until I was embraced in a cloud of steam. I stepped under the molten cascade and closed my eyes, willing my body to calm the fuck down. But it wouldn't co-operate, so I did the only thing I could. I got myself off with the memories of that kiss.

CHAPTER 14

Allie

When I arrived at the Delaney's and realised Si was still at home, I was ready to turn around and leave, but his mum clearly wanted me there. I wasn't sure if she was testing us to see if we really had sorted our issues out like Si had told her, or if she was just so keen to spend time with us both that she saw my visit as killing two birds with one stone.

After the kiss in his bedroom, Si made excuses and left the room like it was on fire. I mentally slapped myself. *Seriously, what the hell is wrong with me?* But, oh my word, his kisses were enough to melt my underwear and I couldn't help craving them. But I definitely should have left at that first instant and then none of this would have happened.

Everything I said had been sincere. He *was* meant to be in the band. He wasn't simply some kind of Joe replacement. But although he said he felt settled with Sonic Idols, something told me he was still trying to convince himself.

After that kiss, he began to avoid me. He spent a lot of time hidden away in the garden shed, and I desperately wanted to get things back to normal with him. I would have to figure out a way of controlling myself around him. It was as though my body was drawn to him against my mind's will. Like he was a drug and I was okay so long as I got a little fix every so often. There was no doubt in my mind that he had awakened a long dormant sexual appetite, but the way I was behaving was incredibly stupid and I knew it. What kind of person did it make me? A bad kind; that one thing was certain. Of all the men in the whole world, the last one I should be fantasising about was my dead fiancé's brother.

I had to take things back to how they were before. Well, before we slept together for the first time, at least. Things between us should have been light and breezy. Fun and uncomplicated. Sex shouldn't have entered into it with us.

But then again, he was single and so was I. Nothing would bring Joe back. And as much as I missed him, I had a life to live. Everything had been on hold for so long. Like I had taken a break from life in general—afraid to move on in case I sullied the memory of the one good thing I'd had. But this thing with Si had gone beyond sullying Joe's memory. And that was the thing I couldn't bear to think about.

CHAPTER 15

Si

Like a total coward, yet again, I avoided Allie at every opportunity for the next few days. Our morning conversations stopped too. Mainly because I was up before her and out in my dad's shed with Joe's old guitar, trying to put some order to the feelings inside me. I figured it helped Nick and Chris to write it down, so why couldn't it be cathartic for me too? It was no doubt clear to Allie that I was keeping away from her, and I only hoped she didn't take it the wrong way. But the more we chatted, the closer we got, and the closer we got, the more I wanted her. It was futile. So, I did the best thing I could. I hid.

The paparazzi presence had dwindled to almost nothing too. The novelty of Sonic Idols' troubles had worn off, thankfully, and it was beginning to feel like normal life. Like it was before I took Joe's place in the band and

Sonic Idols whisked me off to the dizzy heights of stardom. It was strange but quite comforting at the same time.

The security guards had been relieved of their posts at the front door, and the little cul-de-sac once again resembled a run of the mill residential street. I'm sure the neighbours were relieved. Bless them; they put up with a hell of a lot without much complaint.

Tuesday morning of the following week and the weather was great. A cheerful blue sky formed a canopy and backdrop for the birds which were in full song. I had already been in the shed with a coffee and the guitar for around an hour and my song was *still* utter garbage. I could strum a tune, but I wasn't up to the standard of my contemporaries. I was thinking that maybe I should leave it to the professionals. After all, there's the joke Chris told me about a drummer informing his bandmates he'd written a song, the punchline being they were the last words he uttered before the door hit him on the arse on the way out.

I stepped out into the garden to stretch my legs and I heard a cacophony of noise at the front of the house. Voices shouting… so many voices I couldn't make out a familiar one. Filled with dread and panic, I ran to the house and in through the conservatory.

My mother was standing by the front door, peering through the glass panel with her hands over her mouth, sobbing her heart out, and in another room I could hear my dad's strained tone speaking loudly, demanding someone get here as soon as humanly possible.

Mum turned when she heard me.

Tears were streaming down her face and all the colour had drained from her cheeks. "Oh, Simeon, you've got to help her!" she pleaded, gripping my arm. "Your dad's on the phone with the police and I'm too scared to go out there. Please do something."

I yanked the front door open, and to my absolute horror, Allie was surrounded by hordes of reporters and fans all screaming at her. Camera flashes were going off left and right, and Allie stood there with her hands over her ears and her head bowed.

She was being bombarded by painful questions. "*Just tell us if it's true, Allie. You know what it feels like to lose someone to drugs. If it's drugs, will the band fold?*"

"*You bitch! Joe died because of you!*"

"*Allie, are you going to pose for us, love?*"

"*Allie, how to does it feel to lose a loved one to an overdose, only to find his best friend has gone down the same path?*"

The whole scene was reminiscent of the one that caused Nick to disappear. My heart plummeted in my chest. Allie must have been terrified.

I ran down the path towards the crowd, flailing my arms like a mad man, and screamed, "Get the fuck away from her!"

Suddenly the attention was on me. The camera lenses were thrust in my face, and even though it was daylight, I was dazzled by flashbulbs too close for comfort, causing spots before my eyes. I shoved my way through the crowd to get to Allie, not caring if I felled a few reporters in the process.

Once I reached her, I shouted above the noise of the crowd into her ear. "Allie, it's me. I've got you. Come on."

She slowly lifted her chin and fixed me with a blank stare. Her eyes were bloodshot and her pale face was wet from the tears she had shed during the melee. As if only just recognising me, her eyes widened and she flung her arms around me, sobbing. My heart almost shattered into a million pieces as I clung to her and she shuddered.

I lifted her into my arms and turned to head back to the house. "Get the *fuck* out of my way, the lot of you. *NOW!*" I roared. Some of the crowd moved and I managed to take a few steps.

They began to ask me questions, clearly ignoring my furious state. "*Is it true, Si? Is Nick Dacre in rehab for drug addiction? Is that why the band has split?*"

Turning to the reporter who had asked the question, I sneered. "I will only say this once. Nick Dacre is no drug addict. *You've* caused this. All of YOU! Now get out of my fucking way. You've caused this poor girl enough stress to last a fucking lifetime. LEAVE!"

At that moment, police sirens could be heard, along with the screeching of tyres, and the crowd began to disperse. Police in riot gear appeared and grabbed at the scattering hordes, making several arrests.

One of the officers escorted me inside the house and met my parents in the hallway. Dad and Mum went into the kitchen with him and I took Allie into the lounge, where I placed her carefully on the sofa.

My heart hammered at my chest as I swept the hair away from her face, checking for bruises. I looked directly into her eyes. "Are you okay? Did any of them touch you? Hurt you?"

She shook her head slowly as more tears came. "I'm okay. Just shaken up. Thank you. I was so scared, Si, but you… you saved me," she whispered.

I rested my forehead on hers. "God, if anything had happened to you, Allie… I'm so sorry. I'm so, so sorry you were mobbed like that. This was all my fault. I shouldn't be here thinking I can be some normal bloke living a normal fucking life. How stupid am I?"

She shook her head. "It wasn't your fault. They're just greedy for stories. Every single one of them wants to get their hands on the next big scoop. It was stupid of me to head out alone and expect to be okay."

"Not at all. Jesus, you were only a hundred yards from the door. Where the hell did they come from?"

She shrugged. "I don't know. It was surreal. One second I was heading out for a jog with my headphones in, and the next, they just appeared, coming towards me like a pack of zombies with their arms outstretched."

The police officer arrived in the doorway. "Miss Kendry? May I have a quick word?"

Allie lifted her face and smiled briefly at the officer. "Sure."

"I'm Officer Benson of West Yorkshire Police. I wanted to check that you're okay. I need to take a statement from you and ask if you wish to press charges at all."

I stood. "I'll leave you to it."

Allie grabbed my hand. "No! Si, don't leave. Please?"

I squeezed her hand and crouched down beside her once more. "Okay. I'm here for you."

♫♫♫

Once Officer Benson had recorded statements from Allie and me, he left us alone with the assurance that there would be a police guard on the property for the foreseeable future. As much as I had hoped to get back to a semblance of normal life, I appreciated the fact that they were so concerned.

After a long call with Den, in which he panicked and turned the air blue with expletives, I hung up and went to sit beside Allie once again on the sofa. My parents had joined us in the living room and my mum had handed out glasses of brandy, strictly for medicinal purposes, of course. Bless her heart.

As I sat on the sofa, Allie snuggled into my side and fell asleep. The ordeal had exhausted her. Thinking nothing of her actions, I sat and watched TV, where the local news reported the horror that had occurred on my street.

I could sense my parents watching me, and when I glanced over, they pretended they were watching TV too.

I scrunched my brow and whispered, "What? What's up?"

They glanced furtively at each other and my mum said, "Nothing, love. Nothing at all."

A while later, Allie awoke and excused herself to go take a bath, and I went into the kitchen to make coffee. My mum followed close behind, just as I suspected she would.

She reached into the fridge for the milk and placed it

down next to the mugs I had prepared. "She thinks a lot of you."

I smiled. "Well, the feeling's mutual, Mum. She's… erm… like a sister to me."

My mum reached up and cupped my cheek. "Simeon, I'm your mother. Don't try to kid me. You've been in love with that girl since you were sixteen years old."

I rolled my eyes. "You as well? Oh, for f—"

"Language, Simeon. And anyway, it's sweet the way you went to her rescue. You're like her hero." She placed her hand over her heart. "The way she looked at you earlier…"

Trying to remain calm, I turned to my mum and forced a smile. "Don't go thinking anything's going on. Okay? That'd just be… *weird*. She was Joe's. Not mine. My feelings don't count."

She snorted derisively. "Poppycock. Utter twaddle. She's not a ragdoll. She's a human being and it's up to her who she loves. And your feelings *do* count, you silly thing. Of course they count. And what exactly is weird? You're two single adults." She paused and appeared thoughtful for a moment. "And Joe's gone, love."

With that comment, she left the kitchen and me reeling in it.

What the hell just happened?

CHAPTER 16

Allie

All I wanted to do was take a little time out to think. To come up with a plan to get things back on track with me and Si. I pulled on my running leggings and jacket and stuck my earbuds in. A run would surely help. When I stepped out the front door, a strange uneasiness niggled at the pit of my stomach. It was too quiet. I was trying to decide whether I should retreat inside and maybe ask if I could use the running machine in the garage instead, but like a pack of wolves who had been stalking their prey, the crowds appeared out of hiding and pounced.

The niggling became terror as the baying creatures began to yell in my face. There was no space between them, and their aggressive faces blurred into one menacing monster, seemingly ready to rip the flesh from my bones.

It was a nightmare, only I couldn't wake up. I had no choice but to stand there, lights flashing in my face and verbal abuse battering me from all angles.

I *knew* it was my fault Joe died. I didn't need to have it spat in my face by total strangers. And what was it they were saying about Nick? How did that have anything to do with me? I began to question myself. Had it been some kind of domino effect that, unbeknownst to me, I had created with the smallest of ripples all those years ago?

I was frozen to the spot with fear. It was as though I had stepped into some modern version of Dante's Inferno and I was about to be eaten alive by demons, and I realised that stepping out of the house on my own had been a mistake of gargantuan proportions. I hadn't expected them to be around, let alone to be interested in a nobody like me. But where were the security guards? Why was no one coming to my aide?

Suddenly, like a light in the darkness of the moment, the crowds parted and I tilted my chin to see the concerned blue eyes of Simeon Delaney staring down at me. Had I passed out? Was I dreaming? I honestly couldn't tell.

But then he leaned in and told me, "Allie, it's me. I've got you. Come on." Suddenly, I was floating in his arms as he carried me back to the safety of the house. All I could hear was the whooshing of blood in my ears, and all I could feel was the angry thundering of Si's heart against my cheek. I think I must have blacked out at that point. Probably with relief. The next thing I knew, I was being placed gently down on the sofa.

Si had saved me. He had come to my rescue and

scared away the wolves. I was a shaking, sobbing mess, and he could've been seriously hurt out there, but all he was concerned about was my wellbeing. He smoothed the hair back from my face and wiped the tears away. My heart ached and the tears came again.

CHAPTER 17

Si

Allie was quiet for the rest of the day. Understandably so. She had never experienced the crazy, dark side of fame before, and I think it had been quite the eye-opener. She had retreated to the bedroom after her bath, and Mum had checked in on her several times throughout the afternoon but Allie had insisted she was fine.

Eventually, when I went up to go to bed, the room was in darkness and I presumed she was asleep. After brushing my teeth and showering, I went back to the room and climbed into bed as quietly as I could. My mind was still whirring from the events of the day and I was trying to process everything. It had been the first time I had been truly angry at the press and fans. Admittedly, that was probably due to the fact they had accosted Allie, and a protective streak had reared its head from within me. But my mum's words were what foxed me the most. Had she, in a roundabout way, given me her blessing to pursue a relationship with Allie? Not that it made any difference because Allie had made it clear that any attraction to me was purely physical. And as much as I would have loved to have taken advantage of the fact, I told myself that to do so would be stupid and harmful to both of us in the long term.

And, anyway, my feelings for her were deeper than that.

I was just about dozing off when I heard sniffing and quiet sobs.

Concern gripped me and I sat up. "Allie, are you okay?"

The noises stopped completely, as if she was holding her breath.

"Allie?"

She sighed heavily. "I'm so sorry, Si. I didn't mean to wake you. I just… I keep replaying the whole of today's debacle in my mind and I can't believe how stupid I was to go out without checking with someone first. I should know these things happen. I should have been prepared."

"Hey, you weren't to know that the vultures were hovering. This isn't something you're used to and it's been so quiet for the last few days, so how could you know? Don't be so hard on yourself."

Silence again.

"Si?" Her voice croaked.

"Yeah?"

"Can I sleep beside you? I think I'd settle better." I clenched my jaw. Of course I wanted to help her, but to be in the same bed? She must have sensed my trepidation. "Don't worry about it. I shouldn't have asked. I'm sorry."

Guilt niggled at me for being so selfish. *Come on. Step up, you fucking loser.* "Hey, no. Come on over, Allie. It's fine."

The next thing I heard was her footsteps padding across the dark space and then the mattress dipped as she climbed into the single bed beside me. It was a tight squeeze, so I lifted my arm and she settled into my side with her head on my chest. This was the one place I had wanted her to be for God knows how long. Only I'd dreamt of it being under better circumstances.

After a few moments, Allie whispered, "Are you sleeping?"

"No. Not yet."

"I just wanted to say thank you for today. You were amazing. You were like some superhero out there, and I'm so grateful to you for saving me like that. I really mean it. The way you carried me back to the house when I was frozen and couldn't move. I was… floored."

I shrugged. "It was nothing. I hated that they did that to you and I wasn't going to stand there and let them harass you."

She stretched up towards me and placed a gentle kiss on my bearded chin and my heart began to hammer at my chest. It was a simple, sweet gesture, but being in such close proximity to her was messing with my head.

Before she could retreat, I slipped my hand into her hair, smoothing my thumb over her cheekbone. "I want to kiss you. But I know I shouldn't," I whispered.

I could feel her warm breath increase in speed as it met my lips and she replied, "Who says you shouldn't?"

Tentatively, I leaned towards her once again and found her lips parted in readiness. I kissed her tenderly at first, wary about taking advantage of her fragile state, but when she increased the fervour of the kiss, I was swept along on a wave of deep lust and the love I had harboured for her for so long. A little voice in the back of mind told me I would regret it, but I swatted the thought away as she pulled her body flush with mine—my arousal no doubt evident to her between the two thin layers of fabric acting as a barrier.

She moved away, and for a moment I expected her to go back to her own bed, but instead, when she lay down in my arms once again, I felt the heat of her bare skin against my chest. Her breasts brushed against me and her thigh hooked over my hip. She wanted me as much as I wanted her—well, physically, at least.

I moved my mouth to her neck and nibbled on the soft skin there, eliciting gasps and whispered moans from her throat. Her hand slipped down my back, creating a trail of shivers, and my erection flinched. She pushed me onto my back and began to slip my boxers down my thighs. I knew I should've stopped her but I really didn't want to.

After a little fumbling, I felt her stretching a condom onto me and I clenched my jaw at the pleasurable sensations of her hands touching me so intimately. The bed dipped again and she straddled my hips, sinking down onto me and sighing as she took me in. As she began to move on top of me, I lost myself in her body and the way she made me feel; like every nerve ending was alight with electricity and pleasure. I couldn't get close or deep enough. I wished I had turned on a lamp so I could watch her... watch our bodies where they joined, and see her face flush and her pupils dilate.

I pulled myself up so I could take her mouth with my own. Our tongues caressed each other's as our teeth greedily nibbled and our skin heated to almost combustion. Toying with her nipples with one hand, I gripped her with my other and thrust up into her with urgency as my climax began to build, and I could feel her tightening around me. The only sounds in the room were those of our bodies connecting and our heavy, pleasured breaths.

She gripped my shoulders and buried her face in the crook of my neck as her orgasm hit, and I followed soon after, trying desperately not to cry out my release.

She sat there in my lap and held on for a while until our breathing calmed, and then she moved to my side. Once I was rid of the condom, I laid back and wondered what to expect. Would she bail? Would she stay? To my surprise, she snuggled into my side again and pulled the duvet over to cover our damp bodies.

I slipped my arm around her and kissed her forehead. "Goodnight."

She made a sweet contented noise and nuzzled closer. "Mmm... night."

I laid awake for a while, trying to memorise everything that had taken place. It had felt different than the first time and I couldn't quite put my finger on why. But something had shifted between us and I hoped to God this hadn't been her way of saying thank you for coming to her rescue. She owed me nothing. I lazily ran my fingertips up and down her arm and relished the feeling of her naked skin next to mine, and only when her breathing had levelled and it was clear she was asleep did I whisper, "I love you so much. I just wish you loved me back."

CHAPTER 18

Si

When I awoke, Allie was propped up, watching me, with her head resting on her hand. I smiled and rubbed my blurry eyes. "Good morning, sunshine." I couldn't help the grin that stretched my face. To say I was ecstatic to find her still in my bed was an understatement.

"Good morning. Your mum knocked earlier to say she and your dad were going out for a walk."

I lurched to a sitting position. "Fuck! Did she see...? Did you...? Were you—?" I gestured between us and at the door like a nutter.

She giggled and shook her head. "Your face. Silly Si. She didn't come in, you daft thing. She just knocked on the door and I answered her through it, telling her you were still asleep."

Thank fuck for that. And then a fresh horror hit me.

"Oh, bollocks! They went out alone? But yesterday? What about—?"

Allie placed a finger over my lips. "They have a body-guard with them. It's all fine. You can stop panicking now. And you can come and make me some breakfast." She climbed out of bed and I watched her gorgeous naked arse as she walked across the room to pull on some clothes. I realised I was staring at her and lifted my gaze to meet hers. She licked her lips.

"I'm ravenous this morning. Can't think why." There was a rush of blood south of my waistline at her sultry intimation and I swallowed hard. She smiled seductively. "Don't get any ideas, Mister. I'm hungry for *food*." Now fully clothed, she walked back over to me and bent to kiss my head, but I grabbed her and pulled her down on top of me.

"I could make you forget all about breakfast if you'd let me." I tucked a strand of hair behind her ear and looked longingly at her lips.

She raised her eyebrows. "I'm sure you could. But seriously, come on. I really am hungry."

I closed my eyes briefly, and when I opened them again, her expression had changed. Gone was the playful smile she had worn only moments ago.

I sighed. "What the fuck are we doing, Allie?"

She shook her head. "I… I don't know." Her voice was small and quiet. "I just know that I don't want it to stop. Not yet."

I clenched my jaw and chose my next words carefully. "I don't want it to stop *ever*. But I get the feeling that it will."

An air of melancholy began to descend and I decided to lighten the mood. If there was only to be an 'us' for a limited time, it needed to be fun and memorable. I would deal with the sadness on my own time.

I reached down and smacked her arse. "Last one to the kitchen cooks."

She yelped and shoved herself out of my embrace. "Not fair! I wanted *you* to cook."

I leapt to my feet, naked as the day I was born, and tried to swat her gorgeous backside again. "You know what to do then."

She giggled and tried to dodge me. "You'd better put some clothes on! You can't be walking around starkers, Delaney."

"Nah. It's only my folks and you!" I teased, and her eyes widened.

"You wouldn't!"

I burst into laughter. "Your face. Of course I wouldn't. There could be bloody paps out there with zoom lenses. I don't want my junk all over the tabloids!" I bent to collect my joggers from the floor.

"Well, I'm off down to the kitchen right now so it looks like you're cooking." She smacked my arse this time before dashing out the door, laughing her head off.

I rubbed the bare skin where it smarted but I was still grinning like an idiot. "Oh, you'll pay for that, Kendry! Just you wait!"

♫♫♫

Knowing full well breakfast was on me, I took a

shower, figuring there was no point rushing to get down-stairs. I decided I'd make her wait for her food and I grinned at my sly, devious plan. Once I was dried and dressed in my joggers and a ratty old Sonic Idols T-shirt, I went down to the kitchen.

Allie had started to make breakfast for *me,* in spite of her earlier protestations.

I smiled and shook my head as she handed me a mug of freshly brewed coffee. "You're too sweet, you know that, Kendry?"

She put her hand over her heart. "Aww, Delaney, you'll say anything to get your hands on my bacon."

I chuckled. I slipped my arm around her waist and nuzzled her ear. "Is that what we're calling it now?"

She whacked my chest with the spatula. "Cheeky." But then her attention darted to the back door. "Ooh, shit. I think your folks are back."

Getting the hint, I stepped away quickly as my mum and dad walked into the kitchen.

"Hey, kids. What've you been up to?" Mum asked as she removed her coat.

Allie's cheeks tinged bright pink and I had to stifle a laugh before informing her, "Erm, not much. Just cracking the whip so this woman here would make me some breakfast."

Mum rolled her eyes. "Oh, I bet you did no such thing. Allie wouldn't stand for nonsense from Joe, so she certainly isn't going to stand for it from his baby brother."

I glanced over at Allie again, just in time to see her skin pale and her expression change. And with that one jokey sentence from my mum, my bubble was burst.

After breakfast, I once again retreated to the shed with the old guitar and the scraps of paper tucked inside the notebook I'd been scribbling in. I'd been sitting there for around twenty minutes when there was a gentle knock on the door. I lifted my chin to see Allie, arms folded across her chest, leaning on the open doorframe.

"Hi, Allie. What's up?" I turned the paper over and put the pen on top of it.

"Just wanted to check in on you. Are you okay? You went quiet when your folks arrived home."

"Yeah, yeah. I'm fine. Just figured I'd leave you to chat with them for a bit. It's a nice sunny day so I thought I'd come in here."

She scrunched her face and giggled. "*In* here where the sun *isn't*?"

Okay, so she had a point. I laughed and nodded. "Yeah, it does sound a bit daft, I suppose. I just… aww, nothing."

She stepped inside. "You just what? What's up, Si?"

I waved a hand dismissively. "Like I said, it's nothing. What're you up to?"

She pulled her lip between her teeth briefly and I watched, mesmerised, until she snapped me back to reality. "Isn't it obvious? I'm spying on you. What are you writing? Am I ever going to get to see?"

I felt my cheeks heating up and I glanced down at the paper. "Nope. Not a chance."

She stepped closer still and touched the tip of her tongue to her teeth. "Oh, come on. How will you know if it's any good if you don't give it an audience?" She pouted and I was momentarily distracted again by her sensual mouth.

I reached and scratched the back of my neck. "It's not worthy of an audience, that's why."

She lurched forward before I could react and grabbed the piece of paper.

I stumbled to my feet and the guitar fell to the floor with a clanging thud. "Give me that back, Allie. I mean it now. Come on."

She held the paper aloft and giggled. "Nope. Not until I've read it."

I jumped towards her but she ran out of the shed and towards the back of the garden where the old tree stood. I followed in hot pursuit. I had to get that paper back before she read it.

She could bloody run and dodge like a professional footy player, and I couldn't get my hands on her. After what felt like an age, I bent double to catch my breath and then the worst thing happened.

She climbed up onto the lowest branch of the tree, cleared her throat dramatically, and began to read aloud. "*Your heart beats next to mine but I wait for you to leave, I've wanted for so long to wear my heart upon my sleeve. I want to see you laugh, to see the light upon your face. The one he used to put there, that no one could erase. I've loved you for so long now and you don't even know, how much my heart will break when it's time for me to go. I want to see you laugh, see the light upon your face, and I wish that I could put it there, but I can't be in his place.*"

I watched in painful silence as her teasing, mocking

smile rapidly faded and she lifted her gaze from the page and locked it on me.

She shook her head and confusion creased her brow. "This is… it's…" She glanced at the paper again in disbelief. "You wrote this about… it's about me, isn't it?"

I closed my eyes and let my face tilt towards the sun. The rays warmed my skin but I could take no pleasure from it. Lowering my head once more, I looked across at her with a heart full of deep sadness at her reaction and I nodded.

She rested her palm on her forehead. "But… it's not *true*, is it? It can't be true. It's got to be a joke, Si. I mean, okay, so you had a crush on me when you were sixteen and we… we slept together… but… *love?*"

Her eyes pleaded with me, and for a split-second, I considered forcing a loud guffaw and saying *"Haha! Got you! That'll teach you for being so nosy!"*

Instead, I rubbed my hands over my face and shook my head. "I couldn't tell you, Allie. It wouldn't have been right. You were Joe's girl. But yes, I'm afraid it is true. I've been in love with you for a very long time. It wasn't just a crush or some sexual attraction bullshit. It was and still is bone-fucking-deep love, Allie. And the worst part is, I know you'll never feel the same. Because I'm not him."

Her nostrils flared and she pointed at me accusingly. "But you slept with me, knowing that your feelings were one-sided. And knowing that I was oblivious. That's really not fair, Si. To either of us."

I nodded again and roughly ran my hands back through my hair. "Yes, and it was stupid. But you needed me. You needed to feel wanted and safe and desired. *I* wanted you to feel all those things too. Because… because you *are*, Allie. You're wanted and desired. By me. But you're loved too." My heart pounded inside my ribs and the urge to hold her, to kiss her to show her just how I felt was almost overpowering me. But I clenched my jaw and stayed rooted to the spot.

Her lip trembled. "I can't believe this. It can't be happening." She threw the piece of paper to the ground and ran towards the house.

"Allie! Please don't go." My words fell on deaf ears and she disappeared into the house.

♫♫♫

As I stood there in the garden, hoping my parents and the neighbours hadn't witnessed what had just happened, my mobile rang and I took it from my pocket. It was Den.

"Hey, Den. What's up?"

"Good news, Si. The Germany tour is back on! Your car's ordered for tonight to bring you down to London. Then that's it. Life goes back to normal." There was real joy in his voice. If only I felt the same way. The thought of leaving Allie when things were so tense between us made my insides ache, but I knew deep down that I would have to leave anyway at some point. I would just have to resign myself to the fact it would be sooner rather than later.

"Si? Did you hear me? We're back on the road, buddy!"

"Shit, sorry. Yeah. Yeah, that's great news, Den. Great."

He huffed. "Well, you could sound a bit more bloody

enthusiastic. It's not too long since you were telling me you were bored out of your fucking skull. What changed?"

"Nothing, mate. Nothing at all. It's all good. What time is the car coming?"

"It'll be with you around five o'clock. So say your goodbyes and get yourself ready to rock!" He screamed and I held the phone away until he had finished.

I grimaced as I tentatively put the phone back to my ear. "Okay, fine. I'll go and pack."

"Bloody hell. You'd better cheer the fuck up, Delaney. We don't want any sour pusses on the bloody tour. Sour pusses don't get sweet pussy, don't forget that!" He cackled and I rolled my eyes as he sang, "Toodles!"

The line went dead and I stuck my phone back into my pocket.

With a heavy heart and unwilling footsteps, I went back into the kitchen. My folks were, thankfully, nowhere to be seen and Allie was seated at the breakfast bar, waiting for me.

She nodded at a plate in front of her. "Your mum made sandwiches."

I scrunched my brow. "You not having any?"

She shook her head and crumpled her nose. "Kind of lost my appetite."

I sighed. "Because of those song lyrics?" I sat down beside her.

She rubbed at a ring of coffee on the counter top. "What do you think?"

"That's why I was being so secretive. I didn't want you to see them. They were just a way for me to get the words out of my system. A kind of emotional release. No one was supposed to see. Especially not you. While ever you thought this was just a physical thing, I knew it'd be easier. For both of us."

She shook her head. "I still can't believe it, Si. All these years?"

I sighed heavily. "Please, can we just forget it? Get back to how things were and pretend the last hour didn't happen?"

She shook her head. "I don't think we can. At least not how we've been since we reconnected. We should never have crossed that line. I'm so sorry."

My heart sank. All my hope shattered. "It's probably a good thing I'm leaving then."

"What do you mean?"

"Den just called when I was outside. We're going back on the road."

She nodded but didn't make eye contact. "Oh, right. Great... great. When?"

"Five o'clock."

Her head snapped towards me. "Tonight?"

I turned to meet her eyes. "Tonight."

She twisted her fingers together in her lap. "I see."

"I'm sorry it's such short notice, Allie. I hadn't seen it coming. Well... I mean, I *knew* it would happen, obviously, but just not yet. Not *now*."

She smiled sadly and shook her head. "But... it's maybe not a bad thing. Maybe we do need time apart to remember how things were before. You said yourself that you knew this would end."

My stomach plummeted towards my boots and my appetite vanished. "Yeah. I just didn't want to be right." I pushed myself away from the breakfast bar. "I'd better go and pack."

I left the room, fearing that if I stayed a moment longer, I would beg her not to end this and to give us a chance. And I *had* said to myself I would deal with the sadness in my own time.

It turned out my own time had arrived.

CHAPTER 19

Allie

Si was leaving to go back on tour and I had no clue how to react. Discovering he was in love with me had muddied the already cloudy waters of whatever our bizarre relationship had become. My head was telling me this was most definitely a good thing. We needed to be apart and let this thing between us fizzle out. Sex wasn't love. And I *couldn't* love him. It was too weird. Too taboo. What the hell would people think? His parents? The band? My parents? I shivered as I imagined the expressions of disgust on their faces if they discovered what had happened up to now. And I seriously questioned my sanity. Who the hell was I becoming?

What had started out as a need to sate repressed sexual desires had become an ugly farce. And now *love* was involved? My stomach roiled and I was sure I was going to be physically sick.

I left Si to pack and kept my distance.

I made my way outside to the beautiful old tree at the bottom of the garden that we had always congregated around. The vast garden was so disproportionate to the petite house, but I guess when the Delaney's had purchased it all those years ago, the garden and their two small boys had been what they had considered. Now the tree was older, but just as wonderful with its wizened bark and low slung branch. I pulled myself up to sit in peace and quiet with my thoughts, but a deep, unrelenting sadness descended over me. I couldn't quite put my finger on what was making me so emotional, but nevertheless, tears streamed from my eyes as I sat on my favourite spot in one of my most treasured places on Earth.

It was a little like losing Joe all over again. I had conjured up this ridiculous situation and dragged poor Si along for the ride, and now he was going to get hurt. Joe would be looking down on me and hating me. Blood is thicker than water, after all. Why was my heart aching so much? Why was the thought of Si leaving hurting me? The sex was great, admittedly, but I was behaving like he had broken my heart and not the other way around.

I resolved to try my best to remain stoic when it was time for him to get in the car and go. I had to let him believe that he could move on. Because he would have to. And so would I.

CHAPTER 20

Si

I knew saying goodbye to Allie was going to be one of the hardest things I had ever had to do. Especially considering the way things had ended with us earlier. Before the incident in the garden, I had foolishly begun to hope that there was an actual possibility of an 'us', but then she had discovered my true feelings for her by reading my crappy song lyrics out loud. Now she knew this was more than just sex for me and had reacted so negatively, the 'us' bubble had burst spectacularly, taking my heart down with it.

By inadvertently expressing my love for her, I'd discovered that she—in all certainty—didn't feel the same and never would. Now I was leaving and there was a distinct possibility that this situation would never be resolved, and everything would now become a painful memory. Something to look back on and cringe about.

After all, I would find it so hard to look back and smile.

Packing and preparing to leave was rushed, meaning there was no time to prepare for my goodbye. There had been calls to make to Den to ensure extra security detail to the property, thanks to the media frenzy that had spread like wildfire. If I didn't know better, I would think Den had instigated it all to create a buzz about the band going back on tour. But maybe I *didn't* know better. It *was* the kind of thing he'd do without really thinking of the consequences. "All's fair in love and rock" was one of his favourite phrases, after all.

The excruciating thing was, when Mum, Dad, and Allie stood at the door to say goodbye, I had no time to say *anything* to Allie.

My mum clung to me. "Safe travels, sweetheart. Let us know when you land in Germany." She pulled away and fixed me with a stern but teary-eyed look. "And I don't want to be hearing about you with lots of girls over there, okay? You've already got a reputation from what I've seen, and no girl will love you if you're a dress-catcher, you know."

My dad laughed. "The phrase is 'skirt-chaser', love. But your Mum's right, son. Keep it tasteful, eh?"

I nodded as a furnace glowed under the skin of my face, and I scratched my beard. "Well, I'd better be off. Germany awaits. Auf Wiedersehen, folks." I hoped I sounded happier than I felt. The heaviness of a reluctant goodbye was weighing me down.

My mum's face contorted in disbelief. "Simeon Delaney, aren't you going to say a proper goodbye to Allie?"

I rolled my eyes. "Well, *duh*. I wouldn't forget that, would I?" I feigned incredulity and stepped towards Allie. *How the hell do I do this?* All I wanted to do was pull her into my arms and kiss her. Tell her that no girl could compare with her and that any stories in the press about me with other girls would be based around how I'd bored them rigid telling them stories about a certain Scottish lass I had always loved. But of course, none of that was possible, and no doubt she wouldn't want to hear it anyway, so I awkwardly pulled her into a hug.

She squeezed me to her and I chewed the inside of my cheek in a bid to stop me from saying something in front of my parents that I'd no doubt regret.

Allie patted my back like a normal old friend would. "Take care, Si. Look after yourself, okay? And you never know, you might meet that *Miss Right* we talked about."

Well, if ever there was a fucking brush off, that was it. My heart sank further and I forced a smile as I pulled away from her. "Yeah. You never know."

A huge security guard I didn't recognise opened the door and nodded at me. "Ready to go, Mr Delaney?"

I gave a tight-lipped smile, put on my shades, and stepped outside. With long strides and my head lowered, I headed for the waiting limo to screams of my name and camera flashes firing off left and right. I didn't look back. I couldn't. Seeing a definite expression of goodbye on Allie's face would have been too final.

Once the car door was closed, I glanced briefly

towards the house to find only my teary-eyed mother and proud father waving.

Allie had gone.

♪♫♪

Life on the road was the same old, same old. Great, but no surprises. Since arriving in Germany, Nick had been in a constant daze. Something had clearly gone horribly wrong for him whilst he was on his recuperation break. It turned out he'd ended up in Scotland too, and had apparently had his heart broken. The coincidence hurt like hell, but thankfully, he hadn't been in the mood to talk much, so I was spared the rehashing of something that would've hit too close to home.

The guys had organised a party for Nick, and while we were all together, Den launched into a lecture about the upcoming dates.

"Just so you know, we have a whole new crew for this leg of the tour. Thanks to things being postponed, the other crew have moved on. Now, I want you to be on your best behaviour, okay?"

Stig gasped. "Whatever could you possibly mean, Den?" He glanced at the rest of us and winked before taking a swig of his beer.

Den wagged his finger. "You know very well what I mean. Don't any of you be playing the diva card. No sending the runners on stupid tasks. I want this crew to stick around for the duration of the European tour. And I know what you lot can be like."

Chris burst out laughing. "Yeah, Si." He nudged me. "No getting the runners to de-bubble your champagne."

I couldn't help laughing at that memory. "Come on! That was a classic! He tried as well, poor kid."

Nick joined in with the laughter and it was great to see him smile. "And what about the time you cling wrapped all the toilets backstage, apart from our dressing rooms."

I slapped his leg. "Oh, yeah! That was fucking hilarious, mate."

Den rolled his eyes and sighed. "The fact that you all find these things so funny is what worries me. I'm being serious. We can't lose this crew."

Nick held up his hands in a kind of scout salute. "We promise we'll be on our best behaviour, Dennis. Cross our hearts."

We all saluted in unison and tried in vain to keep straight faces. But it didn't last, and before I knew it, we were concocting new ways to catch out the new crew.

The night was great fun, and of course, we all got steaming drunk. Nick drank way more than he usually did and puked his guts up once before drinking a bit more. Den was trying his best to get our leader to sober up, but Nick was hell bent on getting wasted.

"I fucking love you all. Every last one of you. You know that?" Nick slurred.

Den thrust a drink at him. "Yeah, and we all love you, Nick. Now can you please drink this pint of water?"

Nick waved a finger at him. "You're a top bloke, Den. You should find yourself a nice lady and settle down."

"Make that a handsome bloke and you may tempt me. Water, Nicholas. Now."

"Oh, fuck. Yeah. You're gay. I totally forgot." Nick burst out laughing. "How daft am I?"

Den glanced at me and rolled his eyes. "Do you believe this guy? How long has he known me, Si?"

I laughed. "I think the alcohol has addled his brain, Den."

Nick's attention returned to me. "Ah, Si. My sud... pus... pesurdo... my pretend little brother." He grabbed for me. "You're brilliant, you know that? And I love you, mate. I do. Not in a Den kind of way. You know. Just to be clear. But I love you. You're not a patch on Cat. But I still love you." I wasn't sure whether he meant the animal or a person called Cat, but I was too pissed to ask.

"Aw, thanks, Nick. I like cats too. But I think I might be allergic."

He scrunched his face and tilted his head. "Eh?"

I laughed. "Never mind. Drink some fucking water or you'll be as much use as a handbrake on a canoe tomorrow."

♫♫♫

The following day, we arrived to soundcheck. Nick was wearing dark glasses and not speaking to anyone. We all kept out of his way as he sat on a box out in the stadium, drinking water.

The first night nerves jangled, and I wished so much that we were back in the UK. At least that way there was the slimmest chance that Allie would be there. It was a stupid, futile wish, and the band huddled for our group hug. I tried to put all thoughts of Allie to the back of my mind.

I grabbed a towel from my bag and made my way onto the stage to find a woman sitting at my kit, fiddling around with the mics. Her mostly blonde hair was streaked with red and it was long at one side and shaved at the other. She was wearing a black vest top and her left arm was covered in tattoos.

I approached her with caution in case she was a crazed fan. "Erm... can I help you?"

She glanced up and smiled. "Oh, hi, Si. Ooh, that rhymes!" She laughed and stood up from the stool, holding out her hand. "I'm Bobbie."

The American girl was quite pretty, really. I shook her hand firmly. "And you're at my kit because...?"

She curled up her lip at me as if it was obvious why she was there. "Drum tech?"

"Right. Of course. I didn't realise I was getting a new tech. What happened to Andy?"

She placed her hands on her hips. "Didn't Den tell you? The other crew bailed to tour with Angel and the Fallen."

I nodded. "Well, yeah, he said the crew had gone but I didn't think Andy would go too. Shit."

She pursed her lips and glanced at the floor. "Sorry to disappoint. But I'm good. Worked with a few tribute bands back home and then got this gig on the back of my recommendations. I won't let you down, Si. I promise."

I held up my hand as guilt needled at me. "No, no. I don't mean anything by it. It's just me and Andy go way back. Change is a bit of a pain. Shit, that sounded awful. I didn't mean *you* were a pain. I mean, I don't know you yet. You might be really great. You probably *are* great. I just…" I rolled my eyes. "I should stop talking, eh?"

Her cheeks coloured bright red and she nodded. "Probably." She laughed. "We'll be fine. I know what I'm doing. Been playing since I was ten so I'm up to scratch. And I've chatted to Andy via email so I know what you like and don't like. Although… he did say I should watch out for you playing tricks on me. He said something about you asking me to get champagne for you and that I should refuse?" She tilted her head in confusion.

I laughed. "Don't worry. I've been given a lecture already about playing tricks on the new crew. I think you're safe." She grinned and nodded. I stepped forward, raised my eyebrows, and whispered. "Or *are* you?"

The soundcheck went well. And just as she had insisted she would, Bobbie had got the kit just right. I was impressed. I didn't tell her that though. I needed her to be on top of her game the whole time and not slacking in any way. A little too much encouragement could instigate complacency, after all.

♫♫♫

Later on, with the Arena Halle, Berlin full to capacity, we gathered backstage as we always did, and Chris growled out his motivational speech as we huddled. "Listen to that fucking crowd, guys! Let's go and remind them why we're fucking number one in the fucking world!"

It may have been a bit cheesy but it always did the trick. We all whooped and cheered, slapped each other on the back, and made our way to the stage with huge grins and took our places before the lights went up.

The tour began with a bang.

The crowds loved us and greeted us like long lost friends. Being on stage and feeling the thud of the base drum vibrating throughout my whole body was like coming home. It was a familiar feeling I could cling to, and I knew it would cause me no pain. I knew where I was with the band and my skins. No judgement. No unrequited feelings. Just rhythm, sweat, and adrenaline.

Night after night I sat there, shirtless and wet through, beating the hell out of my kit and just loving playing again. It was in those moments that Allie's memory let me be. For the most part, anyway. But then, back in my hotel room or on the tour bus, thoughts of her crept back in. I had no right to miss her. None. In fact, I should have counted myself a lucky bastard. Let's face it, it's not every day you get to experience being with the one you love and never thought you could have. That brief glimpse of hope is something often totally missed by those in my position. But thinking about it, maybe that actually made it worse. The problem was, I *had* tasted her lips and that meant I now knew what I was missing.

Thankfully, Chris had left me alone and hadn't bombarded me with questions about Allie, and I was relieved for that fact. I didn't need to keep rehashing it out loud. It was bad enough living with the thoughts in my head.

One particularly restless night, I ended up in the basement gym of the hotel, pumping iron in the hope that I'd release some of the tension I'd been carrying in my shoulders.

A familiar voice startled me. "So, how did you end things?"

I dropped the bar back into the holder and sat to find Chris, arms folded, standing before me with a furrow of concern on his brow.

Ugh. Here we go. I thought his silence was too good to be true. I shrugged. "It was over before it started, mate."

"How many times did you shag her?"

I winced at his choice of words. "*Fuck*, Chris. She's not some tart for God's sake"

He stepped towards me. "I'm well aware of what and who she is, Si. She was *Joe's* woman. You need to leave well alone or you'll end up getting hurt. Just fuck some other babes and you'll soon forget her. That's what I do."

I laughed derisively. "Yeah. Because *you've* loved and lost, eh?" I shook my head. "Chris Malham, the great fuck 'em and forget 'em king."

I watched as a distinct appearance of hurt temporarily clouded his eyes. "Hey, you know fuck all about my love life, Delaney. Maybe we've all loved someone we shouldn't."

His almost admission took me by surprise. "You've *loved* someone?" *Oh, fuck.* My heart leapt in my chest and I swallowed down the nausea that had ridden up my gullet. "Did... did you fall for Allie too?"

He held up his hands and scrunched his face. "No. Jeez, Si, Absolutely not. Forget I said anything. But move on, mate. It was never going anywhere with you and her."

I nodded. "You're right. I thought I could get her out

of my system though, Chris. But she's still in here." I pointed to my head. Then, after a pause, I pointed to my chest. "And here."

He sighed heavily. "Shit. You really do love her, eh? It's not just you coveting something Joe had and you didn't?"

Sadness weighed heavily on my shoulders. Heavier than any of the weights I had just been lifting. "No. I really do love her."

He plonked himself down beside me on the bench and slapped me lightly on the back. "And I'm guessing it's all one-sided?" I nodded. "That's fucking shit, mate."

"You got that right."

CHAPTER 21

Allie

I had never been one for keeping up with the news—especially the gossip pages. But since Si left for Germany, I had watched like a hawk. Something inside me just needed to know if he was okay. But secretly, I think I was keeping an eye open for photos of him with other women. Why the hell that was of interest to me, I have no idea. But every time Sonic Idols popped up on the news or anything connected to them showed up on my social network feed, I had to click on it and read. It was a little disconcerting—my new interest in the love life of my deceased fiancé's younger brother—but it didn't stop me looking.

The German Music Awards took place whilst the guys were on tour over there and Sonic Idols were up for best rock video for their single "Who's Loving You Now". I watched the following afternoon when the show was repeated and I was so excited that they won. I watched with pride as Si walked up with the rest of the band to collect the award. He looked so shy and a sense of melancholy descended over me. I had never really paid much attention to the lyrics, but for some reason, everything now reminded me of him. Crazy, I know.

When it was his turn to speak, he leaned down into the mic, his cheeks aflame. "Erm... cheers, guys. This really does mean a lot. Especially seeing as I'm the Neanderthal who bangs about on stuff at the back whilst the talented blokes do all the work." A rumble of "*Awwws*" and laughter traversed the audience at his self-deprecation. He waved and nodded. "Oh, and hello Mum and Dad!" Another laugh followed by a loud raucous cheer and applause.

The MC announced the video and the lights went down as the huge screen at the back of the stage sprang to life. The song was a little different to their usual stuff, being a rock ballad. The arty black and white video showed the guys on stage, playing in slow motion. A shirtless Si's biceps bulged as he hit the snare drum and flung his head back, his wet hair arcing above him. Loud whistles and screams could be heard over the track.

I was mesmerised.

There were some shots of them interspersed into the film where attractive actresses were playing their girlfriends. Oddly enough, Nick was the only one of the band who didn't have a female companion, and I couldn't help wondering why. But for some reason, the fact that Si had some scantily clad blonde draped all over him made me angry. She was beautiful. Slim, with perfect breasts, full lips, and long legs. Pretty much everything I wasn't.

Urgh! Stop it, Allie, for goodness sake!

Insecurity was something I had never suffered from. Possibly because I hadn't been close enough to anyone for it to be an issue since Joe. So why the hell I was suddenly very self-aware, I had no idea.

Deciding I needed respite from myself, I changed into my jogging gear and stuck in my earbuds. I scrolled right past the Sonic Idols albums on my playlist and settled on The Prodigy's "The Fat of the Land" and headed out for some much-needed fresh air.

My feet pounded the hardened soil in time with "Breathe", and I lost myself in the rhythm of my own quickening breaths. I rounded the corner of the tree-lined lane and suddenly I was flying through the air with a panicked scream as my earbuds were yanked from my ears.

"Fuck! Fuck, Tyler, no! You stupid dog!" A voice I didn't recognise shouted from close by. "I'm so sorry! Are you okay?"

I looked up from my position on all fours in the dirt to see a horrified expression on the face of the voice's owner—a tall, blonde, clean cut man. A giddy chocolate-coloured Labrador skipped around, trying to lick my face.

My heart thumped at my ribs and the smarting in my knees became evident as I tried to stand up. "Erm... I think I'll live," I replied, out of breath.

"Here, let me help you. He's such a bloody excitable thing. He slipped his lead again. I was chasing him when he legged you up. I'm really, *really* sorry." The man gripped my hand and helped me to my feet. I winced as the dirt from the track scratched into the grazed skin of my palms. "Oh, shit. You're bleeding. And your leggings are ripped. Jeez, I feel so awful. Do you live nearby? Can I help you home?"

I shook my head and waved a bloody hand dismissively. "Don't worry, it's fine. I'll be fine. It's not far."

"No, come on. It's the least I can do. Where do you stay?"

I nodded toward my cottage. "Just back along the track. I can manage though. Honestly."

He reattached the dog's lead and held his arm out. "No, I insist. Come on. Let's go get those cuts cleaned up. I'm Evan, by the way."

I glanced up at the man who I guessed was a few years my senior and smiled briefly. "Allie."

"Good to meet you, Allie. Although, I wish it hadn't been down to my stupid dog almost killing you."

CHAPTER 22

Si

Berlin, Frankfurt, and Munich were all absolutely amazing. Sell out arenas with thousands of happy faces all wearing our band T-shirts, singing our songs, and screaming our names. The tour bus already stank like a sweaty jockstrap and sleeping on my rock-hard bunk was playing havoc with my shoulders. But I was somehow happy.

Late nights on the bus consisted of dirty stories, Chris's drummer jokes, too much beer and junk food, with a little song writing and jamming thrown in for good measure. It was hard to believe we were coming to the end of the German leg of the tour. It would be on to Belgium next, although there had been a whisper about a headlining gig at a big Scottish festival. My ears had pricked up when I heard Den on the phone. Scotland would mean we'd be in the same country as Allie. Excitement and a little fear were building in my stomach at the mere thought of it. But nothing was definite so I would have to try and put it out of my mind. Yeah, right. 'Cause that would be easy.

By the time we arrived in Cologne it was like we had never been away from touring. Chris had racked up his usual bevy of beauties, and Nick was finally beginning to smile more often. Den was getting on remarkably well with Roger, the new head lighting tech, and I had caught him blushing as they spoke, despite his orange hue. Maybe there was a possible romance on the horizon between the two fifty-somethings. I hoped so. Den deserved to meet someone who understood the demands of his job.

Stig had taken a shine to Den's new assistant, Nelly, and they had been spending a lot of time together, chatting in corners. She was very tactile and was forever stroking his arm. It was quite cute but served to remind me of the fact I was currently alone.

And me? Well, I'd been having a whale of a time. I'd hardly thought about Allie. Okay, maybe that last part is a lie. But I was *trying* not to think about her and that counts, doesn't it?

♫♫♫

We had a rare free day to ourselves and a night when we weren't playing, so Den had checked us into a plush hotel the night before and the guys had all gone their separate ways to do some sightseeing. Chris and Nick had gone to find the chocolate museum, and Stig and Nelly were going shopping. Den and Roger had arranged to go out for lunch, and I was left to decide what I would do with my own free time. I had just showered and was contemplating calling home when there was a knock on my hotel room door.

I opened it to find Bobbie, the drum tech, standing there, hands in the pockets of her leather bomber jacket and shyly stepping from foot to foot.

She was the last person I had expected to show up. "Hi, Bobbie. What are you doing here? I mean, h-how are you doing?"

She smiled and nodded. "Good. Great. Everyone has gone off to do their own thing, so because I didn't see you at breakfast… I was… um… just wondering what *you* were doing today. Thought maybe we could grab a bite to eat and go see the Ludwig Museum or a movie or something if you're not busy."

Shit. What do I say to that? "Ah, right. Erm…" I cringed. "Actually, I was just going to call my folks back in England and then maybe catch up on some reading. I'm knackered and I think I might just have a day of chilling."

Her smile faded. "Okay, sure. Whatever. Well, if you change your mind, I'm in two seventy. Just holler." Her cheeks coloured bright pink. "Or, you know, call me. Or… or stop by my room. That'd work too. I mean, seeing as I'm on a different floor I maybe won't hear you if you holler." I grinned and shook my head at her and she covered her eyes with her hand. "I should stop talking, huh?

Remembering my bumbling attempts at conversation when we first met, I laughed. "Probably."

She raised her hand. "Okay, well… see ya." She turned and walked away, chuntering to herself about being a dumbass.

I chuckled. "See you later, Bobbie." I closed my door and walked over to the phone to call my mum and dad.

"Hello?" My mum's familiar singsong voice made me smile. I realised how much I missed her.

"Hi, Mum. It's me, Si. How are you?"

"Simeon, love. So good to hear from you. We're all fine here. How are you? How's Germany? Where are you now?"

I nodded even though she couldn't see me. "Yeah, I'm good. Things are going really well. We're in Cologne just now. We've got a free day today so everyone's gone sightseeing."

"Oh, how lovely. I've seen Cologne on the telly. It looks gorgeous. What are you planning to do then? Why haven't you gone sightseeing too?"

"I'm shattered to be honest, Mum. Den booked us a hotel for a couple of nights so I might just have a lazy day of reading. Get some room service and catch up on sleep in a proper bed. The bed here is so bloody comfy and it's a super king size. I can spread out like a star fish and my feet still don't dangle off the end!"

She laughed. "Well, you have to make the most of that then."

"Yeah, my thoughts exactly. Anyway, how's dad? Keeping out of trouble?"

"Oh, he's fine. He's been decorating his office. He's painted it grey. Can you believe that? Of all the lovely colours he could've chosen. I think it looks like the inside of a battleship, but he insists it's manly." I could imagine her rolling her eyes as she spoke.

"Maybe you could put some flowery cushions and a fluffy rug in when he's not looking. Soften it up a bit," I joked.

"Ooh, now there's an idea." I wouldn't put it past her, that's for sure.

Knowing what I wanted to ask next, I took a deep breath. "So... have you heard from Allie at all?" I tried to sound nonchalant and failed miserably.

"As a matter of fact, she phoned yesterday. She's doing really well, love. She's... erm... met someone, actually. Isn't... isn't that lovely?" I could sense the trepidation in her voice.

My stomach plummeted to my feet but I feigned as much positive enthusiasm as I could muster. "She has? Erm... yeah. That's... that's great. So, who is he?"

"He's called Evan McHugh and he's an accountant. He's just opened his own business in Kelso. He's moved there from Dunbar, apparently, after a messy divorce."

A fucking divorced accountant. Jeez. She couldn't get much further from a drummer if she tried. "Ah, right. Where did she meet him?"

"Well, there's the funny story. She was out jogging when a silly dog ran at her and sent her flying. It was *his* dog. Evan's, I mean. Chocolate lab, apparently. Anyway, this Evan was a real gent. Helped her home and made sure she was okay. They had coffee and got on really well, as it turns out. Then, just as he was leaving, he asked if he could take her for a meal. They've been out a few times now." She fell silent for a moment. "Oh, I'm sorry, love.

Listen to me going on. You probably don't want to hear all this, do you?"

I swallowed a ball of sadness down and forced a smile that I hoped reached my voice. "No, don't be daft, Mum. I'm glad she's happy. That's all I ever wanted for her."

She sighed. "You're so sweet, darling. I'm sure you'll meet someone too. In fact, I just know you will." There was another long pause. "Are you okay, Simeon? I mean *really* okay?"

Trying to sound as bright and breezy as I could, I replied, "Oh, God, yeah. Absolutely fine. Listen, I'll have to dash. My mobile's ringing and it might be Den about tomorrow's gig. I'd better go," I lied.

"Okay, love. Call soon, okay? Love you."

"Love you too, Mum. Bye."

I hung up and stared at the wall for a few moments, trying to process the fact that Allie had moved on so damn fast. Then I reminded myself she had nothing to move on from. This whole thing had been one-sided from beginning to end. Anger mixed with sadness and disappointment inside me, but before I could let it reach boiling point, I picked up the phone again and dialled reception.

A sweet German young woman answered. "Hallo, Mr Delaney, this is Mia. How can I help you today?"

"Hello, Mia. Could you put me through to room two seventy please?"

CHAPTER 23

Si

"So, what changed your mind? You seemed pretty set on chilling out today," Bobbie asked, before taking a lick of her vanilla ice cream cone as we walked along Heinrich-Böll-Platz towards the museum.

I shrugged. "Oh, you know, I figured it's not that often I get a day off." *And I need to get back at the woman I love for moving on so fucking quickly.*

She grinned up at me. "Well, I'm glad you changed your mind." I finished my ice cream and tilted my face upwards. She gave a contented sigh. "Beautiful sky today, huh? Such a vivid blue."

I readjusted my woolly slouch hat. "Yeah. I think I underestimated how warm it is. Although, I was ordered by Den not to leave the hotel without a bodyguard or a disguise. Or preferably both."

She laughed. "I like your hat. Although, you're pretty distinctive, you know? I doubt a beanie will stop the fans from recognising you. And I can't profess to be much of a bodyguard."

I tugged the hat further down over my ears, made sure my shades were pushed up my nose, and grinned. "Nah. I reckon we'll be fine." I glanced around nervously as I remembered my last brush with crazy fans on my own doorstep. "So, how did you get into drumming then?"

She gestured to a bench outside the Ludwig and I nodded, so she sat. "My journey into music started with my folks. They were crazy about the music of the fifties and sixties and played it all the time at home. In fact, I was named after Bobby Vinton and my older brother was named after Dean Martin. Music has always been a big part of my life. My dad played guitar and my mom played piano. But they were never really my bag." Her cheeks coloured as she admitted, "I was always a tomboy. Drumming was more my thing... well, it was all thanks to my brother. He was in a band when I was little and I always thought he was *so* cool. As I got older, I figured I'd follow in his footsteps. Make him proud."

The similarity of our situations struck a chord with me. "Wow. Your brother too, eh? That's how I got into drumming. What does your brother do now? Is he still in a band?"

She lowered her gaze to the floor. "He... um... he died."

I was *not* expecting that. I swallowed hard and puffed the air from lungs. "Fuck. I'm so sorry, Bobbie."

She sighed. "Yeah. He fought a long illness but in the end, it won out."

I shook my head as memories of the pain of losing Joe bombarded my mind. "Jeez. I had no idea we had so much in common. How old were you when you lost him?"

She dropped the remainder of her ice cream into the dustbin beside her. "I was just fifteen. It was tough going there for a while but I figured getting into the music business somehow would help. Honour his memory and all that."

I nodded emphatically. "Shit, yeah. Me too. Do you have any other siblings?"

She shook her head. "Just me and Dean. My mom and dad have never really gotten over it."

I glanced over at her as she wiped her eyes. "Oh, God. I'm sorry. I've made you cry." I handed her the unused napkin from my ice cream.

"No, no. It's not your fault. It's just still hard to talk about. Even seven years on."

I nodded. "Tell me about it. So many things remind me of Joe. And then there'll be the times when something will happen and I'll think, 'I must tell Joe about that' and then I'll remember he's not here anymore."

She nodded and reached out to touch my leg. "I know. That happens to me all the time. I think that's what drew me to this gig with Sonic Idols, you know? Empathy."

I placed my hand over hers in what I hoped was a comforting gesture. "Well, look, if you ever need to talk…"

She smiled up at me, her green eyes glistening with tears. "Same goes, Si."

We sat in silence for a short while, surrounded by people walking around, getting on with their lives, oblivious to our shared grief.

I turned to find Bobbie watching me, her eyes filled with sadness, and I realised the conversation had caused a dark cloud to hover over us. "Hey, do you want to head back to the hotel? I totally understand if you don't feel like going into the museum."

She stood and held out her hand to me. "Nah. Dean loved art too. I feel close to him in places like this. Let's go get our culture on, huh?"

I slipped my hand into hers and let her pull me to my feet. I stepped closer and connected with her gaze. She really was pretty. Not stunning, but pretty and quirky. And *genuine*. That was the main thing. She was *real*. There was nothing fake or plastic about her personality. Okay, so she had emotional baggage, but luckily, I had a matching set. And the best thing? She wasn't my dead brother's fiancée.

♫♫♫

After a really pleasant day mooching around the Ludwig Museum, staring at pictures I didn't really understand whilst Bobbie talked about light and texture, I found myself sitting across from her at the small dining table in my room. A room service meal was laid out before us and a bottle of red wine open.

"What did you think of the art on display today?"

Bobbie asked as she tucked into her posh-looking chicken dish.

I took a long gulp of my Pinot Noir. "Erm... yeah. It was... interesting."

She laughed and eyed me suspiciously. "So, art is *totally* not your thing."

I cringed and chewed my lip. "Shit, sorry. Was it that obvious?"

"The blank expression on your face when I was droning on and on about my favourite pieces was kind of a giveaway."

I pretended to smack myself in the head. "Fuck. Must try harder, Delaney."

She waved dismissively. "Hey, don't sweat it. We can't all like the same things. I have to say, I just loved it though."

"Don't get me wrong, I really liked *some* of it. But a lot of it just looked like blobs of colour on canvas. Like someone had spilled paint and tried to clean it up. I really didn't get those ones."

A wide smile spread across her face. "I'm not sure whether to be disappointed or flattered right now."

I scrunched my brow. "How do you mean?"

"Well, either you really don't care about trying to impress me, seeing as you haven't pretended to understand the art, *or* you're so comfortable with me that you feel able to be completely honest. I'm not sure which it is."

I laughed. "Ah. Well, in all honesty, I could've tried to fake knowing what I was talking about but you'd have seen right through me, so let's go with the comfort thing, okay?"

She giggled. "Agreed."

The rest of the evening slipped by in a mix of chatter and jokes, and before I knew it, she was getting up to leave.

She stepped towards the door. "Thank you for a great day, Si. It's been really special. And I hope the art gallery didn't bore you too much. Well, not enough to put you off going out with me again, anyway."

I stood before her. "Nah. It takes more than that to put me off."

Her cheeks coloured pink. "Great. Well, I hope we can do this again sometime soon."

"Yeah. Me too." And I really meant it.

She opened the door and then stopped. She turned to face me and reached up to kiss my cheek. "Goodnight, Si. Sweet dreams."

"Goodnight, Bobbie. See you tomorrow."

Once she was gone and I had closed the door, I huffed the air from my lungs. I hadn't expected to get along so well with her. I suppose the fact that we shared common interests and our route into music was very similar gave us a base to work from. And for the first time in a while, I wondered what it might be like to be with someone else. But not just a quickie. No, a meaningful relationship, like the one I had dreamed of having with Allie.

CHAPTER 24

Allie

So, the rumours were true. Sonic Idols were playing the biggest music festival in Scotland. I had discovered the fact when I was watching the news whilst Evan was cooking a meal for us in his kitchen.

My heart leapt at the thought of the band being so close. Well, not exactly *close,* but in the same country at least. Inverness was bloody miles away.

I distinctly remember going there with my mum and dad when I was around fourteen and absolutely loving the atmosphere. Some really big names had played there in the past and I was so proud of Si and the guys for landing the headline spot. I knew it must have been a big deal to them but I didn't want to bother Si by texting to congratulate him. After all, I hadn't heard from him since things ended between us. Not that they ever really started.

"You're looking deep in thought, gorgeous. Are you okay?" Evan asked, as he placed his knife and fork down beside his plate. The meal he had cooked was delicious and it only served to make me realise how perfect for me he was. Financially stable, good-looking, good cook. What was there not to love? Well... *like*.

I shook my head. "Ugh, sorry. I drifted off there for a wee while. What were you asking me?"

"I asked if you like camping. Or are you more of a luxuries kind of girl?"

I scrunched my brow. "Camping's good fun. Why do you ask?"

His cheeks flushed red. "Well... it may be a bit too soon in our relationship, but I wondered if you fancied going to Belladrum? It's good craic and there are usually some great bands on."

Okay, this was so spooky. "Oh... I... erm..."

He cringed. "Look, don't feel pressured to make a decision yet. I just thought I'd ask seeing as tickets are on sale and they usually sell out quickly. Although, that bloody terrible rock band are headlining so we have to use that time to our advantage. Sonic Idols... more like Sonic Racket if you ask me. All they're missing is a bit of lip gloss and they'd be great in the nineteen eighties." He laughed before stuffing another fork full of food in his mouth.

Affronted by his comment, I scowled at him but then remembered he had no clue about my connection to the band. "I happen to love Sonic Idols, actually."

His eyes widened. "Shit. Sorry, Al. I didn't mean to

offend you. They're just not my cup of tea, but you're enti-
tled to your own opinion, of course."

Gee thanks, pal.

The truth was that Evan and I had been taking things
very slow. He had just experienced a nasty divorce and I
wasn't willing to dive head first into a serious relationship.
We'd talked about superficial things, but thanks to the
situation with his crazy ex and my last relationship being
ages ago, we both seemed reluctant to talk about our pasts.
We'd spent time together, but in all honesty, I couldn't
remember what we'd talked about other than our hobbies
and favourite TV shows. There had been a little kissing
but nothing more. We never really got—to quote a Sonic
Idols track—'hot and heavy'. It was a little as though we
were still in the friend zone.

I wasn't sure if sharing a tent with him would be
awkward, and the fact that he didn't like Sonic Idols
shouldn't have been such a big deal, but it made me question everything.

"You've drifted off again. Is my cooking so hypnotic?"
I lifted my chin again and he was watching me, head
tilted.

I sighed deeply and closed my eyes. "I'm so sorry,
Evan. I think maybe I'm not really in the right frame of
mind for company tonight."

His smile disappeared and he nodded. "I took it too
far, didn't I? Asking you to go away with me was a
mistake."

I held up my hand. "No. No, honestly, it's not that.
I'm just... I'm tired, I think. That's all."

He pushed his chair away from the table and stood. "I know it's more than that, Allie. Jen used to drift off like that when she was pissed off with me talking about work." He frowned and stared into space momentarily. "Tell you what, why don't we take the food into the living room and watch a movie? We don't have to talk if you're not in the mood."

Guilt twisted my insides. He'd made such a lot of effort, and there I was spoiling everything. I had no clue what the matter really was. I wasn't tired at all. Just over-thinking.

I picked up my plate and smiled. "Sure. Let's do that."

I stood, followed him through, and sat beside him on the sofa. He picked up the remote and switched on the TV. "So, what do you fancy? Horror, drama, romance?"

"Ugh, anything but romance."

He raised his eyebrows. "Like that, is it? You surprise me. Jen was crazy about romance movies. The sicklier and sweeter the better. She could cry at the drop of a hat. All it took was some romantic gesture on the part of the hero and I virtually had to swim out of the room." He laughed and shook his head at some apparent memory, a distinct look of melancholy in his eyes. As if realising he had said too much, he slapped his hands on his legs. "Ugh, enough of that. So, okay then, horror it is. And you can protect me at the scary bits."

He selected a movie and grinned at me before carrying on eating his food.

I stared blankly at the TV as the opening credits played and the eerie music kicked in with a thudding drum beat for dramatic effect, and I immediately wondered what Si was doing right at that moment.

Was he with someone?

And why the hell did I care?

CHAPTER 25

Si

The disappointment at Allie not being at our Scottish festival headliner just made me more determined to move on. It had been epic. The crowd loved us and I fully expected her to be there. But I guessed she was too busy getting it on with her divorced fucking accountant to give a crap about me.

Nick's shit was coming together with his Scottish woman, and even bloody Den and Roger were getting closer. Chris and Stig were the same as ever. Nelly the assistant had gone. Offered a job with her favourite band and off she went. Not a second thought for the man whose heart she had broken. Stig lost his bounce for a while, and seeing him change like that reminded me that love sucks. Maybe it's better to be with someone who loves you but maybe you don't love quite as much if it means companionship and not being hurt.

I think that was where things were going with me and Bobbie. I really liked her, don't get me wrong. But I didn't get butterflies when I saw her. Although, maybe I was putting too much store in the whole love at first sight thing. She was fun to be with. She was pretty. And we had *so* much in common that I never felt alone or awkward with her. She totally got me. Our relationship was growing from something bigger than lust. It was growing from a steady foundation based on solid common ground. And okay, that sounds dull as shit, but maybe… just maybe it was what I needed. I had spent so long pining for my brother's woman that I had no idea what being with someone who actually wanted me for *me* was like.

Nick had announced to the band that he had made a very special purchase which involved him being in Scotland for a while and we were on a short break from our European tour so it seemed the perfect time to take a little holiday.

Den called a meeting and we all met at a pub in Northumberland. Alnwick was a quaint little town with a pretty big castle, and the pub Den had chosen was just as nice. I figured I would ask Bobbie to spend a couple of days with me on the Northumberland coast after the meeting. The nerves were jangling and I hoped I wasn't about to make a total idiot of myself.

But anyway, back to the meeting. The majority of the crew and band had crammed themselves into the pub and were all waiting, drinks in hand, to see what the hell all the cloak and dagger shit was about.

Den stood and clinked his glass to get our attention. He was grinning like the bloody Cheshire Cat. "Thank you all for being here. I've already spoken to Nick and he's been sworn to secrecy until now as he can't be here tonight."

Chris rolled his eyes. "Oh, for fuck's sake, Den. If you're pregnant, I swear to God I'll scream." A rumble of laughter travelled around the room and Den whacked him on the head.

"I wish, Chris. No, anyway, this news may come as a bit of a shock to you all as things have moved quite fast but..." He closed his eyes and held up his hand to fan his face. He was getting emotional and I was getting worried.

Stig teased, "Bloody drama queen. Get on with it."

"All right, all right. I'd tell you to keep your shirt on, Stiggy, but we know that would be a waste of my breath." Stig burst out laughing and the rest of the crew joined in.

A terrible thought crossed my mind and I had to speak up. "Den, you're not... you're not *leaving* us, are you?" The laughing subsided and I watched as Chris and Stig gaped at Den, evidently hoping his answer was no, just as I was.

Den shook his head. "Not a chance. My boys are stuck with me. No, it's nothing like that. It's good news. Well, I hope it's good news, anyway. I certainly think—"

All of us shouted in unison, "GET ON WITH IT, DEN!"

"Okay, okay! Good grief. The thing is, Roger has asked me to marry him. And... and I've said yes!" He squealed and Roger stood up to hug him.

A raucous applause erupted and the whole crowd

jumped up at the same time to envelope Den and Roger in a group hug of mammoth proportions.

Bloody hell. My fifty-something gay manager was going to be a married man before me. That sucked. But in the best possible way. Den looked happier than I'd ever seen and his orange glow was tinged with a rosy tint of love. Okay, so I was a tiny bit jealous of his happiness, but he really deserved it.

Roger and Den had been inseparable since they met and it was evident from the start that they were destined for forever. So what if it had happened fast? Love is love, after all.

Once the excitement had died down, Den announced that he and Roger were having a ceremony up at Gretna Green and that we were all invited. Ugh, more of bloody Scotland. Why was everyone hell bent on torturing me with that place? Thanks to our gruelling touring and recording schedule, the ceremony was happening very soon. There was going to be a huge party and we were told we would get all the info by email or text just as soon as they had selected a venue.

At the end of the evening, I was sitting on a bar stool when I felt a tap on my shoulder. I turned around to see Bobbie smiling up at me.

"Hello, stranger. Are you avoiding me?"

I hadn't really seen much of her but it wasn't intentional. At least, I don't think it was consciously such. "Hi, Bobbie. Nah, not at all. It's just been a crazy night, hasn't it?"

"It sure has. I'm so happy for Den and Roger. I haven't

known them for long but they both seem like really great guys."

"Yeah. Well, Den is. I don't know Roger that well really."

She placed her hand on my thigh. "Sweet how they fell in love so fast, huh?"

I nodded. "Yeah. They're very lucky."

She leaned in and whispered, "Want to get out of here? I have a room upstairs if you want a little peace and quiet."

I glanced around to see what everyone else was doing. Chris had his tongue down the throat of some random woman. Stig was sitting in the corner nursing a beer, and Den and Roger were holding hands and chatting at one of the tables. Many of the crew had left and it was getting close to closing time.

Returning my attention to Bobbie, I nodded. "Sure. Why not?"

CHAPTER 26

Allie

Another date with Evan had ended in him talking about Jen. It was as if a floodgate had been opened up and he couldn't stop. I learned all about her favourite foods, favourite books, favourite designer labels. Jeez, I felt like I knew more about her than I did about my date.

We sat in the pub as Evan told me about the time he had found a bag of designer clothes in the wardrobe with labels still attached. Apparently, she had tried to hide them from him and he presumed they were clothes she had bought to impress another man. To me, it sounded like the kind of thing every woman does when she's trying to hide a spending splurge from her other half.

It got to the point where I switched off and started thinking about Si. I hoped he was okay and having fun on his tour. I wondered if he was thinking about me at all and if he was missing me.

Evan interrupted my self-destructive train of thought. "Sorry, I keep hogging the conversation, don't I? I think you drifted away a little there. No wonder really. So, anyway, do you like designer clothes?"

I glanced down at my high-street jeans and top and felt like responding with sarcasm but chose to be an adult. "Not really my style, if I'm honest. I'm a down to earth girl. Simple pleasures and all that."

"I bet you'd look good in some of the designers Jen loved. I have to admit, she did look great in her clothes. She's one of those types who suits anything."

I took a large gulp of my red wine, suddenly wishing I had ordered something stronger. "Lucky woman."

My morning run had been an emotional one. For some damn reason, every song I listened to reminded me of Si. Each lyric seemed to say, 'I told you so' or, 'It's your loss' and I was beginning to get rather paranoid that my playlist was out to get me. I hated that images of him above me in bed were playing over in my mind as I listened to the music that was meant to be a distraction. Instead, the memories played out like a music video, and at several points, I had to stop to skip tracks or simply to catch my breath. What the hell was going on?

I showered and called Si's mum for a chat. It always seemed to help. I made excuses as to why I hadn't attended the music festival. In actual fact, I blamed my relationship with Evan which was horrible as it wasn't that at all. I avoided asking much about Si and she didn't offer much either.

The call had just ended when there was a knock at my door and I sighed. I was still sporting the towel wrapped around my head after showering and hoped it wasn't anyone important.

I pulled the door open and Evan stood there, red-faced and frowning. "Oh, hi, Evan. I wasn't expecting you as you can probably tell." I cringed and pointed to my makeshift hat.

"It's okay. Can I come in? I didn't know where else to go."

I stepped aside, wondering why he looked so fraught, and gestured into the house. "Sure. Come on in."

We went into the lounge and he slumped like a rock onto my sofa with his head in his hands.

"Can I get you a coffee?"

He lifted his head and nodded. "Yeah. Coffee would be good. And drop some whiskey in there too."

I cringed. "I'm sorry, I don't have any—"

"It's okay. It's too early anyway. Just ignore me. I'm stressed."

I sat opposite him and watched him intently as he rubbed his bloodshot eyes. Something was clearly very wrong. "Evan, what's happened? Why are you so upset?"

He sighed heavily and shook his head. "It's Jen. She's a fucking bitch."

We appeared to have gone from not discussing his ex to me being some kind of sounding board for his trouble with her. I wasn't sure I liked the fact.

Trying to be a good friend, I pushed my annoyance aside. "What's she done?"

"She wants Tyler, *my* dog. She wants him to go live

with her. Says he belongs up there. But I can't let him go, Allie. I'd never see him."

"Ah. Could you maybe have a kind of joint custody situation?"

He huffed. "And have to see her smug fucking face every time I picked him up? Oh, yeah. She'd love that. She'd probably take great pleasure in making me jealous of her fantastic new life and how she's over me."

I frowned at his comments. "But you didn't want to be with her anyway. Isn't that why you divorced?"

"We divorced because she was unfaithful, Allie. It doesn't mean I don't still have feelings for her."

Oookay. That's a bit of a kick in the teeth. "I see."

"Don't get me wrong, I made her pay. *I* divorced *her.*"

"Was it a long affair?"

"I don't know. I found text messages on her phone from some guy telling her how sexy she is. How he wished she'd change her mind. Her replies were hilarious." He spoke the words with a curled lip.

"In what way?"

"*Oh, Michael, if things were different, I would have been happy to go away with you. That kiss was a mistake. I love my husband. Please don't contact me again.*" His mimicking voice was quite amusing and I had to try not to giggle.

But when I thought through what he had said, I was shocked. "That doesn't sound like an affair, Evan. It sounds like one kiss that made her realise she loved you. I don't understand."

He rolled his eyes and made a weird growling noise as if I was being dense. "She kissed another guy, Jen. That's what happened."

"I'm Allie."

He scrunched his face in annoyance. "What?"

"You called me Jen."

He waved his hand dismissively. "Oh, right. Whatever. She says I worked too much. I was never at home. She felt neglected. She felt I was more interested in spreadsheets and numbers rather than bedsheets and loving her."

Good grief; I felt like a bloody marriage guidance counsellor. "And were you?"

He paused for a while, contemplating his next words. "I worked long hours. Admittedly, we didn't spend much time as a couple. When I was home, I was easily distracted by financial programmes and articles. But I was doing it all for her. She wanted the big fancy house. I gave it to her. Well… she *said* she liked the little cottage we lived in but I knew what she wanted before she did. The big house was stunning. I knew it was what she really wanted."

I shrugged. "Maybe the cottage and her husband *was* what she really wanted."

He snorted derisively. "Yeah, and now she wants my bloody dog. She has the fucking house, for goodness sake."

"I think you maybe need to go and see her. Talk to her. Two adults conversing in a neutral place so you feel able to be honest. It sounds like you need it."

He nodded. "You always know what to do, Allie. What would I do without you?" He stood and walked over to where I sat and bent to kiss my forehead but caught the towel instead. "I'll call you later, gorgeous."

I was beginning to feel like a third wheel in our relationship. He had admitted he still had feelings for his wife and that should have forced me to ask him to leave but I was just as guilty. The way I had been missing Si told me that perhaps Evan wasn't the man for me. If he had been, I wouldn't have cared about what my drummer friend was up to. But he was all I could think about.

Although, I got the feeling things hadn't really sunk in with Evan. He was using me to keep his mind from what he really wanted. Not deliberately. He wasn't a cruel person. But it felt like he had yet to come to the conclusion that he missed his wife and the life they had shared. That the divorce was a mistake.

Only time would tell.

CHAPTER 27

Si

"Hi, Mum. How are you both doing?"

Mum huffed. "Hi, love. Oh, not too bad. Your dad has been suffering with a cold. Or should I say man-flu. I've been running around like a headless chicken after him. I'm exhausted. Honestly. You'd think he was at death's door."

I worried whenever I heard news like this on my calls home. "It's not serious though?"

She laughed. "About as serious as him scalding himself with his tea when he sneezed."

I grinned and shook my head at the mental image I conjured up of him leaping to his feet and shouting, "Aww, come on!"

"Poor Dad. So, what have you been up to apart from playing Florence Nightingale?"

She made a derisive scoffing noise. "Us? What do you

think? Not a lot of anything, as usual. But surely you must have some news?"

"I do, as it happens. Den is getting married."

There was a long pause on the line. "But... I thought he was gay?"

I laughed. "He's not marrying a woman, you daft thing. He's marrying his boyfriend, Roger."

"Oh, of course. Goodness me. I'm so scatter-brained sometimes. Well, that's something to look forward to then. When is it happening? Next year?"

"Next week more like. If they can organise it, they're getting married as soon as possible. Den is like a giddy bloody woman. He's carrying around wedding magazines like an accessory just now." I took a deep breath. "There's other news too."

"Really?" She didn't try to hide the intrigue in her voice.

"I kind of met someone."

She squealed like a teenager, forcing me to pull my handset away from my ear. "I knew it! I just knew you'd meet someone. So, what's she like? What's her name? Is she pretty? Are you in love? Ooh, I'm so excited for you, Simeon, darling."

"Bloody hell, Mum. Talk about bombarding me."

She made that scoffing noise again. "Come on, moaning Minnie. Just tell me."

"Okay, okay. Her name is Bobbie. She's my new drum tech and she's really good. She's... erm... quirky."

Another pause. "How do you mean?"

I took another deep breath, knowing full well that my mum wasn't judgemental but feeling like I needed to warn her for some reason. "She has her head shaved at one side, the rest gets dyed a variety of colours, and she has tattoos. Lots of tattoos. And a nose piercing." My words came out in a rush, and I was panting like I'd run a marathon at the end as I waited for her reaction.

A relieved huff travelled across the airwaves. "Good grief, I thought you were going to tell me she was the head of a bloody cult or something. Don't scare me like that, Simeon. So long as you like her and she treats you well, I couldn't care less if her hair is all the colours of the rainbow and she rides a bloody unicorn. Appearance is never something that's shocked me. I've lived with two teenage boys, remember."

I have no idea why I had been so worried about telling her. "Thanks, Mum. She's American and I love her accent. We have a lot in common too. She also lost her brother. And get this, he was a drummer, just like Joe. How spooky is that?"

"Oh, gosh, yes. That's uncanny. But so long as you're happy. You are happy, aren't you, Simeon?"

I paused for thought for a moment before answering. "I think I am. I mean, it's early days yet, but I enjoy spending time with her. And she makes me laugh."

Mum sighed. "You *think* you're happy? Just promise me something. Be sure you're not settling, eh? I mean it's not so long ago that you were in love with someone else. Someone the opposite of this girl in every way. I just don't want you to rush things and get hurt."

I loved how concerned she was, but sometimes I couldn't win. "Mum, Allie has moved on. That's what I need to do. And I haven't proposed marriage to Bobbie. I just like her. That's all."

"Oh dear. Now you're angry with me. I'm sorry for interfering, sweetie. I just worry."

I softened a little at her admission. "I know you do. Anyway, speaking of Allie, have you heard from her lately? I was surprised she didn't come to the festival we headlined in Scotland."

"Hmm, she mentioned that. She was going to come along with her young man, but... I think maybe it was too soon for such a step."

Intrigue needled me. "Too soon in what way?"

"Well, it would've meant sharing a tent, camping together. But I don't think she wants to rush things either."

For some reason, I was relieved to hear that maybe Allie and her bloke weren't having sex yet. But I swiftly reminded myself I was moving on. Leaving the past *and* Allie behind me. It shouldn't matter to me who Allie was sleeping with. It was time to get my own life together and look to the future. And if that future included Allie... I mean *Bobbie*. Shit. B. O. B. B. I. E. If my future included *Bobbie*, then so be it.

Yeah, who was I trying to kid?

The rest of the conversation with my mum was about neighbours building a home extension and the clock tower in town being vandalised—amongst other local news. I ended the call and made my way inside the hotel to the bar where the rest of the guys were. Except Nick. He'd been AWOL for a couple of days, attending to important business, apparently. We had all been informed that exciting things were afoot and I couldn't wait to hear his news.

When I arrived at the bar, Den and Roger were together in a huddle, talking about all things wedding, no doubt. Chris and Stig were having some debate about guitar manufacturers, and the crew were dotted around the place in their usual cliques.

I stood waiting to be served when hands covered my eyes.

"Guess who?"

I immediately recognised the fragrance of Bobbie's perfume. "Erm... pfft... not a Scooby Doo," I teased.

She whacked me playfully on the arm as I turned to face her. She was pouting. "Well, that's just charming."

I winked at her. "Just kidding. I knew it was you. What are you up to?"

She slipped her hands around my shoulders. "Nothing, but we could change that if you feel like it?" The sultry whisper to her voice wasn't lost on me. But I wasn't in the mood for getting amorous. Irritatingly, since my conversation with my mum, thoughts of Allie and her accountant plagued my mind.

"Aww, I was just going to get a drink and chill for a bit with the guys."

Bobbie stepped away. "Oh, okay. No worries. Let's go and sit with Den and Roger then, huh?"

The disappointment in her eyes caused a niggle of guilt inside of me. "Yeah, then maybe later we can grab a bite to eat if you fancy?"

A wide smile spread across her face and a cute dimple

appeared in her left cheek. I hadn't noticed it before. "Deal."

Bobbie and I pulled out chairs opposite the newly engaged couple. "Hi, you guys. How are the wedding plans coming along?" I asked.

Den's face lit up. "Super-duper. We have a venue that will do the wedding and the do afterwards."

Bobbie scrunched her face and glanced at me. "Do?"

I chuckled at her confused expression. "Party," I informed her, and she formed an 'o' with her mouth and nodded.

Den continued. "The best bit is they can fit us in in two weeks!" His voice went up an octave and I waited for the windows to smash. "By the time we return from playing London and Birmingham, we'll be good to go."

Wow. Two weeks. That shocked me as I thought they were being totally unrealistic expecting to get a venue at such short notice. But Den had so many contacts; I definitely underestimated him.

♫♫♫

I was excited to be playing London again. The night after we arrived, Nick asked for the band and Den to gather in the private meeting room at the venue after the soundcheck.

Nick was flushed and pacing the floor when we arrived. He was twisting his hands in front of himself and I was so worried about what he was going to announce. Was he leaving the band? After the year he'd had, I wouldn't have been surprised.

I was relieved when he finally began to talk. "Thanks for being patient with me these last couple of weeks, guys. I know this tour hasn't been the usual bang, bang, bang of dates we're used to but I needed to ease back into things after what happened."

I wanted him to just spit it out. "That's fine, mate. We're your family and we get it. But you're worrying me. There's been so much secretive shit going on lately, I don't know whether I'm coming or going."

Chris laughed out loud. "Hey, dude, if you don't know when you're coming, you're either doing it wrong or you need to see a doctor." He carried on guffawing and I punched his arm. He and Stig bumped fists like the immature tossers they were and I rolled my eyes, but I couldn't help laughing too.

Turning my attention back to our leader, I said, "So, back to adult conversation. What's going on, Nick?"

He cringed. "Well, the thing is... I've bought a property in Gairloch. It's in the Highlands. I want to convert part of it into studios and make the rest into a home. I figure eventually we'll get sick of touring and I want something else to focus on too. Plus, I think it would be a great place to record our next album. What do you think?"

Chris stood and grappled Nick into a bear hug. "Bloody hell, mate. You don't do things by halves, do you? I think it sounds fucking awesome. Good on you!"

I stood to join them. "Great news, Nick. I love Scotland. And I think it's a good plan. No one wants to see old rockers pootling around a stage, do they?"

Stig slapped Nick on the back and then turned to address me. "You have heard of The Stones and Aerosmith, right? Those guys may not be twenty-somethings, but they could give us a run for our money. There's nothing wrong with being an aging rock star in my book. Lasses love it."

Okay, so he had a point. But I was trying to be supportive. "So, anyway, Nick, what are you going to call this studio? Are you naming it after us?"

Nick shook his head. "Nah. 'Fraid not, Si. It's aptly placed on Rockhill. So, it'll be Rockhill Studios and Rockhill Records, mate."

I grinned. "Perfect."

CHAPTER 28

Si

London was awesome, just as expected. Packed to capacity and the guys were buzzing. Bobbie watched from the wings, and every time I glanced her way, she beamed at me. The pride on her face made me wonder if I should just jump in with her. But I shelved the thoughts and pounded the kit like my life depended on it. My heart thudded along with every beat, and every chance I got, I wiped the sweat from my eyes with my bare arm. Fucking awesome gig.

After the show, we all showered and changed in the dressing rooms and headed out to an exclusive club for a few celebratory beers. Bobbie looked amazing. She wore a short black leather skirt, thigh high boots, and a backless black top that showed her tattoos and advertised the fact that she didn't need a bra. Her hair was freshly dyed a vivid purple and it really suited her.

She dragged me to the dance floor and we stayed there until the early hours, grinding against each other, kissing and touching, and letting the sexual tension build between us. I regretted the fact that we were on the tour bus and not in a hotel as I was ready to take things up a notch with her. Alas, the tour bus was waiting in all its stinky, man-carrying glory.

Bobbie took my hand and tugged me to a dark corner of the club where other couples were making the most of the shadows. She launched herself into my arms and wrapped her legs around my waist as her lips met mine and her tongue slipped into my mouth. A mixture of alcohol, lust, and libido took over, and I kneaded at the flesh of her arse and pushed her against the wall as I ground my erection into her. Sensations of pleasure fogged my mind and I almost forgot we were in a public, albeit dark, place. She nibbled on my lip and slipped her hand down between our bodies to touch me through the denim of my jeans.

I was ready to explode until she whispered into my ear, "Si, I think I'm in love with you."

Fuck.

I stopped moving and held my breath. *What the hell?* I hardly knew her. Love had only crossed my mind as a distant hope for us, but I was nowhere near that yet.

A heavy hand landed on my shoulder and someone belched loudly in my ear. "Come on, little drummer boy. Den says you need your beauty sleep. And we both know he's right. It's nearly six a.m., dude."

Talk about saved by the bellend. I was so grateful to Chris right then, I could've kissed him.

As if he just realised what was going on, Chris continued, "Whoops. Sorry, mate. Hi, Bobster. Sorry, babe. Didn't see you there. Got to take this skin basher away, I'm afraid. Den's orders. You can bash Si's skin another time, eh?"

"Fuck's sake, Chris. Perv," I growled.

Although I couldn't see his face, I could sense feigned innocence in his, "What?" response, before he walked away.

Bobbie lowered her feet to the floor and she kissed my cheek. "To be continued, huh? Now, let's get you back to the tour bus so you can dream of me and all the things you want to do with me."

My stupid erection flinched at her words. What can I say? I'm a man.

♫♫♫

The bus journey from London to Birmingham the following day passed by in a blur. I slept for a big chunk of the journey, and when I was awake, the other guys were sleeping. I was relieved not to be bombarded with innuendos from Chris and took solace in the silence, concentrating on the whirring of the tyres against the road.

The one thing I was plagued by as we travelled was the memory of Bobbie and her confession of love. *Should I tell her how I feel? That I hope we're going somewhere but that I can't say I love her? Not yet, anyway. Would that hurt her?* I didn't know until I bit the bullet.

We arrived at the arena for the soundcheck and Bobbie was banging out a drum solo on my kit. When she realised I was watching, she stopped playing and her cheeks coloured pink.

"Hey, are you after my job?" I teased as she clambered awkwardly from the seat.

"God, no. I was just… the acoustics in this place are really rad."

I held up my hands. "I was only kidding around. It's fine. You're really good, Bobbie. How come you don't play in a band? Or set your own up?"

She stared at the floor. "Oh… well, I'd rather be here." She lifted her gaze. "With you." She cleared throat. "With Sonic Idols, I mean. You're just the icing on my cake of awesomeness." She smiled sweetly but it was brief. "And listen, about last night… I'm sorry if I freaked you out. I'd been drinking… you know… got carried away."

I stepped towards her and placed my hand on her shoulder, giving it a gentle squeeze. "You just took me by surprise, that's all."

She leaned her cheek onto my hand and closed her eyes for a moment. "Do you think you and I have a chance, Si?" Her wide-eyed expression was filled with hope. "I don't throw myself at guys and I'd rather know if we have… something, at least, before I sleep with you. Because I do want to sleep with you. But I don't want to misread the signals again."

I sighed. "Look, I'm new to the whole relationship thing. I have no clue what I'm doing. But I want to try. I do mean that, Bobbie. I'm just so used to the shag now, think later mentality. No strings, you know? But I'm very much aware that's not who you are. So, you might just have to bear with me. Although I totally understand if that's not enough. But if you *can* cope with my bumbling attempts at an us then I promise to keep things strictly PG. Until I know for certain how I feel."

She stared at me, the cogs in her mind almost audibly whirring as she processed what I had said.

Then she smiled and stepped closer. "Maybe not strictly PG, huh? We could throw in a little R rated action too? But just not... you know, go all the way. Not until you're sure."

"SOUNDCHECK IN FIVE!" came over the sound system.

I leaned to place a chaste kiss on Bobbie's forehead. "Sure. Now, buzz off, will you? Your arse is too distracting in those jeans and I've got to be all professional and shit."

She grinned and shook her head. "See you later, drummer boy." Then she turned and walked away, swaying her hips on purpose, and I watched unabashedly as she did so.

♫♫♫

We rocked Birmingham, obviously. And after the gig, we were all cajoled into a press conference and fan meet and greet—which all took place a little too late in the night for my liking. I was knackered and wanted to sleep.

We started by posing with fans for photos, signing autographs—some on body parts—and chatting to local newspapers. Then we were ushered through into another room which was filled with national press.

Questions were randomly fired at the guys, and luckily, I was getting a reprieve. Or so I thought.

"So, Si, rumour has it there's a new lady in your life. Are we to expect wedding bells in the not too distant future?" The place fell silent.

I laughed. "Yeah. You sure are." Before I could finish, a cheer erupted and a rumble of conversation traversed the room. Camera flashes temporarily blinded me and the rest of the guys stared open-mouthed in my direction. Once things had quietened down, I continued, "They won't be my wedding bells, I should point out. They'll be ringing very soon for Den, our manager, and his partner, Roger, as they tie the knot. You'll probably be better waiting for hell to freeze over than wait for my nuptials." The guys burst out laughing and slapped me on the back. No idea why they were so relieved.

The female reporter who had asked the question spoke again. "Mr Delaney, has anyone ever told you you're a big tease?"

I made direct eye contact with her and gave her a cheeky wink. "It been said before, yeah." Her cheeks turned crimson and she fanned herself as the rest of the crowd 'Oohed' in unison.

Bobbie was waiting for me after the press conference. She reached up to kiss me and said. "You were great in there." Luckily, the press had been escorted out of another exit at the back of the arena so no one saw the exchange between us. Well, no one apart from the guys who all whistled and cat-called like kids.

We were heading in the bus to a hotel for a decent night's sleep, ready for the long journey north to Dumfries for the wedding. We were setting off at crazy o'clock, so sleep was paramount.

Bobbie linked arms with me. "Can I escort you to the bus?"

"Sure. Are you guys following us up to Scotland tomorrow?"

Her smile disappeared and she shook her head. "No. Limited space, apparently. I guess I don't know Roger and Den that well to be classed as close friends."

I had a crazy lightbulb moment, and before I could stop myself, I blurted. "Be my plus one!"

Her eyes widened and she covered her mouth with her hand. "Seriously?"

Wishing I could somehow suck the words back in, I urged, "Look this won't change things between us, okay? We would be going together but that doesn't mean anything is different. I wouldn't want to get you there under false pretences. We can get separate rooms. I just thought… I know you'd like to be there."

She stopped walking and turned to face me. Placing her hands firmly on my arms, she smiled. "You're not going to get all caught up in the emotion of the day and propose. I get it. But we could use the time to get to know each other a little better maybe? Unless you're regretting asking me in which case—" We started walking again.

"No not at all," I lied. "So long as you're not expecting—"

"Si, I'm expecting to go to a wedding and have a nice

time with you. Period. Now stop worrying. I have to figure out where the hell I can shop for a dress."

We arrived at the bus. "Right, well you can come along with me on here tomorrow. So long as you don't mind a bunch of rude, obnoxious male companions."

She laughed. "How could I resist such an appealing offer?"

CHAPTER 29

Allie

The phone rang and I was in no rush to answer it. "Hello?"

"Hey, gorgeous. It's me, Evan. What are you up?"

I glanced at the clock. "It's eight o'clock in the evening. What do you think I'm up to?" I laughed. He clearly didn't know me well yet. I was sitting on the couch in my joggers, braless and in a baggy T-shirt with my hair scraped into a ponytail. I had no make-up on and was settling in for a night of crappy TV.

He chuckled. "Got your glad rags on, I bet. Ready to go paint the town red."

"Erm... more like paint this wine bottle and the contents of the fridge empty, I'm afraid. Not really dressed for going out."

He sighed. "That's a shame. I was going to suggest I

take you out for a nice meal and then we could come back to my place... have a little wine... see what happens next..."

The unspoken words were deafeningly loud down the line. He wanted us to take that next relationship step. But I wasn't sure. I had learned very recently that sex complicates things. With drastic consequences. And I had also learned that maybe his wife was still in the picture, even if he hadn't quite realised it yet.

"Look, I'm sorry, Evan, but I'm really not in the mood tonight. Maybe we can arrange another night? I've got some paintings to get framed. That little gallery on Horsemarket in Kelso have agreed to give my work a shot." It was kind of true. The gallery had agreed that but the paintings were all ready to go. It just seemed like a good excuse.

"That's great, sweetheart. I'm very proud of you." Ugh, why did those words sound so condescending coming from him? "You'll be a fully-fledged artist before you know it." *Yup. Condescending.*

I bit my tongue so as not to say something I may regret. "Yeah. You never know. Anyway. Better get on. See you soon. Goodnight." I hung up before he had a chance to reply, and I hoped he might realise how his words had affected me.

He had been spending so much time talking about his ex that I was getting to the point where I was going to have to say something. Our dates were becoming tedious and my decision to put up with the fact was making me question myself. I had been alone for so long that I wondered if it was just that I was stuck in my ways and having someone else in my life was an intrusion. He was nice enough, but there was still no obvious spark there. He didn't ignite my blood. Not like Joe had.

And not like Si had either.

And therein lay my real reason for sticking with Evan. I was trying to prove to myself that Si was just a temporary fling. That I didn't feel anything real. I couldn't allow myself to feel anything real. It wouldn't be right, after all. Would it? It was easier to take the path of least resistance and try to make something work with someone else. Someone who didn't remind me of what a shitty person I was every time I kissed him.

The TV announcer teased that there would be footage of Sonic Idols on the magazine show *Ceòl Oidhche,* or Music Tonight as I knew it, which was coming up next. I went to the kitchen and grabbed my bottle of wine and a big bag of crisps in readiness.

The band had played Birmingham the night before, and by all accounts, it had been another sell out show. A huge success, yet again. I was so proud of Si and wished I could pluck up the courage to ring and tell him so. But after hearing those words from Evan, I decided it would probably come over wrong. So, for now I would make do with watching him on the TV.

As the show started, my heart began to pound like one of Si's drum solos as I waited to see the band. I took a long gulp of my wine and stared at the screen. The presenter finally gave me what I was waiting for.

"Ladies and gentlemen, as you all know, I'm a huge fan of Sonic Idols." Cheers and whistles followed. *"They've been here on the couch with me, and I have to say, Nick Dacre is*

one of the nicest guys I've had the pleasure to interview. So, imagine my delight when I caught news of their recent shows in the UK. London and Birmingham were both sell out shows." More cheers. "*And the band took part in a post-gig press conference that turned out to be very interesting indeed. Before we get into that, here's a clip of them playing Birmingham. Enjoy.*"

The screen cut to the band and I watched with a grin on my face as Nick stomped around, singling out girls in the audience to sing to. Stig bounced around like Tigger on energy drinks, and Chris was in a world of his own, eyes closed as he played like the guitar in his hands was a sexy woman. I squinted at the screen, annoyed that, up to that point, they hadn't filmed Si. Then suddenly, there he was. Shirtless and wet through, beating the crap out of his kit with a sexy as hell look of concentration on his face. Every so often, he glanced to his left and smiled widely towards the wings. I wondered who he was smiling at. As the camera panned around, I caught a flash of purple hair and tattoos on a girl clapping along. She had an equally wide smile on her face. And a look of pure adoration.

My stomach lurched and my heart skipped. Who was she? And more to the point, why the hell did I care?

Once the clip had finished, the audience cheered yet again and the camera was focused, once more, on the show's presenter.

"*How about that, ladies and gentlemen? Good or what?*" The audience whooped. "*Now, I teased that the conference had been interesting. Here's why…*"

Another clip of the guys appeared on my screen. This time they were sitting behind a long desk, with towels around their shoulders, looking happy but exhausted, and with glasses of water before them. I heard a voice from the audience speak.

"So, Si, rumour has it there's a new lady in your life. Are we to expect wedding bells in the not too distant future?"

I held my breath as the press conference fell silent. I hadn't realised I was standing up until my feet carried me a step closer to the TV. The camera zoomed in on Si and he grinned, running his tongue along his full bottom lip. He leaned into the microphone.

"Yeah. You sure are."

My already pounding heart plummeted towards the floor, taking my stomach with it, and a sob erupted from somewhere deep inside me. How the hell can he be getting married? It wasn't so long ago I discovered he was in love with *me*. I didn't understand any of it, and when the presenter appeared on TV again, my ears were buzzing and my eyes were fogged with tears. I watched with blurred vision as the presenter clapped along with his audience.

"You heard it here first, ladies and gentlemen. We have a Sonic Idols wedding on the horizon."

I reached for the remote control and waved it angrily at the TV, pressing violently at every button until it was finally silenced. Then I shakily placed down my wine glass, dropped the remote control on the sofa, and slumped down onto the cushions to cry. And to figure out why the hell the news had affected me so badly.

CHAPTER 30

Si

The country house hotel in the little Dumfrieshire village was such an idyllic setting, and I could totally understand why Den and Roger had chosen it. Den had booked the whole place as a private event, and further rooms at a place close by.

It was going to be a very small affair with only the couple's closest friends and family in attendance. Den had made this sacrifice so that 'his boys' could be there without the worry of a fan frenzy. Roger was absolutely fine with this as he didn't have much family to speak of. I was really looking forward to being there when the two guys exchanged their vows over the anvil, in true Gretna Green tradition. It would no doubt be the only wedding I was likely to attend for a while.

My double bedroom was small but sweet, with everything I could possibly need. I was going to enjoy spreading out across the whole bed for the nights I was there. Bobbie had chosen to get her own room, and I was quite relieved about that. We had agreed that sharing a room wouldn't do the whole 'taking things slow' scenario any favours.

The night before the wedding, we all met in the bar for food and drinks. We got to officially meet the woman who had stolen Nick's heart in Scotland. Wow, she was bloody stunning. Funny, feisty, and so sweet too. Ugh… I was surrounded by people in love and it was making the green-eyed monster in me rear its ugly head. I wanted them all to be happy, don't get me wrong. But I wanted that too. I wanted a slice of the loved-up cake, but it appeared it had all gone.

A while later, after I'd had a few drinks, someone tapped me on the shoulder and I turned around to see Bobbie standing there. She grinned up at me. "Well, hello there, handsome. Do you come here often?"

I rolled my eyes. "To Scotland? No, thankfully. Bane of my bloody life, this place. It's sucked away most of my band and my bloody heart." Okay, that was the drink talking. Her brow creased in confusion and she opened and closed her mouth. I thought I should interject before she asked what the hell I was going on about. "Ugh, ignore me. Just love this place, that's all I meant. It's stolen my heart." I made a circular motion around my temple and rolled my eyes. Little did she know that I was talking about Allie.

"Oh… yeah, it's really beautiful. I'd love to live here someday. Anyway, what's a girl got to do to get liquored up around here?"

I laughed at her theatrical *Annie Get Your Gun* accent and called the bartender over.

At the end of the night, I walked Bobbie to her room and stood there awkwardly, wondering if I should kiss her or not.

She stuck her key in the door. "Are you coming in? I have some mean sachets of coffee. I stole extra from the bar. I could make us a drink."

I huffed, the alcohol in my brain confusing my thoughts. *I could go in for coffee, but we'd end up in bed. I just know it.* "Erm… to be honest, I think I should go get some sleep. Don't want puffy eyes to start the wedding day."

She pursed her lips and nodded. "Okay." She leaned closer and pulled me down so that her lips hovered close to mine. "Just so you know, there was going to be some of that R rated stuff on the table if you *did* come in." She placed a kiss on my lips and I had to fight with myself to pull back.

I allowed my mouth to widen in a grin. "Fuck me, you're hot as hell, you know that?"

She ran a finger down my chest and tilted her head to the left, looking at me from under flickering eyelashes. "That's what I hoped you'd think. Now. get lost before I try to convince you to change your mind. And we both know you'd take no convincing." Before I could answer, she had walked through her door and closed it behind her.

My resistance was waning, and I stood staring at the door, chewing on my lip, contemplating knocking. Instead, I called through the wood, "Wedding's at twelve so I'll pick you up at half eleven." She didn't reply so I walked away to make use of the shower and my imagination in my room.

♫♫♫

I stood admiring my suit in the full-length mirror on the back of my room door. I scrubbed up okay, really. I had managed to tame my hair too, which was a bonus. I attached the flower thing to my lapel exactly as Den had instructed the night before when I had been too drunk to really get what he was saying. But it looked okay.

Once I was ready, I made my way along the corridor to collect my date for the wedding. My date. Who'd have thought that I, Si Delaney, lover of all things Allie, would have a date with a girl who I could see potential for a future with? I was no Chris. I wanted to meet someone and fall in love. I wanted to have someone to share tour stories with and to snuggle up to when I wasn't travelling. Hell, I wanted someone to take on tour with me so I could snuggle up to them when I was travelling. I could squeeze someone petite like Bobbie in my bunk.

I shook my head and mentally patted myself on the back. *You're doing all right, Si. Take it steady and you and Bobbie could be it. She could be the one.*

I knocked on Bobbie's door. There was a hammering in my chest and my palms were clammy. I took these as very good signs. Signs that I was beginning to have feelings for my little drum tech and her cute arse.

The door opened and I gasped. Bobbie's hair was completely different. She had combed it down so that the shaved area was covered and it was blonde. Completely blonde. She was wearing this slinky pale blue dress—the colour of a spring sky—that clung to her curves and showed just the right amount of tattooed cleavage to be classy but sexy. I allowed my gaze to trail down her body and noticed the grey peep toe stiletto shoes she was wearing and the matching clutch in her hand. I was no fashion guru, but damn, she looked fucking hot.

"Ahem… is that drool, Si Delaney?" Her voice snapped me back from whatever sexual fantasy I had disappeared into and I wiped my chin. There was no drool. "Ahhh, got you good, Mr D. But I'm guessing from the fact that you haven't spoken yet, you either like very much or you think you've left the iron on."

I cleared my throat and tugged at my tie, suddenly very much aware of the rising temperature in the hallway. "Oh… I like. *Lots*."

She stepped towards me and nibbled on her lip seductively. "Wait, until you see what's underneath."

She swished past me, letting her door close. "Come along, Mr Delaney. We shouldn't be late."

I adjusted the front of my trousers and straightened myself up. After a deep, calming breath, I followed her, keeping my eyes on that delicious arse.

CHAPTER 31

Allie

I was still reeling from Evan's visit the night before. I hadn't expected him to turn up on my doorstep. And I certainly hadn't expected him to ask me to move in with him.

"I really think we have a future, gorgeous. I have money. I have a beautiful new place in Kelso. I know we haven't been intimate yet, but I think... I think that's been my fault. I've been going on about Jen and the divorce so much that I must have appeared as though I wasn't committed to you. But I am. When you know, you just know. And I think we could grow to love each other. Don't you?"

I gawped at him, completely blindsided.

"Say something, Allie. Please? Look, you can mess about with your arty stuff until you decide what you want to do full time or you can come and work for me. That would be great. That way we could spend time getting to know each other better. It's a win-win situation. I really think it would work. And I hate living alone. It's so tedious. We could keep each other company. You could cook and look after the house if you didn't want to work for me. And I would have you to come home to instead of a silent house."

Suddenly, it dawned on me. He wanted a housemate, not a girlfriend. You shouldn't move in with someone unless you already love them. And I didn't love him. Over the time I'd got to know him, I had realised he was opinionated, self-centred, self-absorbed, and patronising. The way he spoke about me and my 'arty stuff' and the way he called Sonic Idols' music 'that God awful noise' was so disrespectful. He left no room for my thoughts and didn't care about my feelings. I didn't need that in my life.

As if a lightbulb had flicked on in my mind, everything became clear. My reaction to Si when we spent that brief time in our affair. The way I had reacted when he had announced to the world he was getting married. The way I hadn't stopped thinking about him since he'd been gone.

I was in love.

With Si Delaney.

But shit, I had to move fast. If there was still a possibility that he was in love with me, I had to tell him how I felt. I would call his mum and glean some information from her. Surely this wedding was going to be ages away. I must have time to make sure it wasn't real. Surely it was a publicity stunt? That's it! It must be! There was no other possible explanation.

"Are you going to pack your things, Allie? You can move in tonight." Evan's voice pulled me from my revelation and I shook my head.

I stared him right in the face and took a deep breath. "Evan. You don't like my paintings. You hate the music I love. We don't like the same movies. You still love your wife even though you won't admit it. From what you've said, the split was all your fault and what you considered an affair was a blip. She didn't sleep with another man. She got chatting to someone who fancied her. Not the other way around. And she only did that because she felt unwanted and neglected. Your pride got in the way and instead of admitting you were wrong, you let it get to the point of divorce. Call her. Tell her you bloody love her. Get her to come and live with you. That's what you need. That's what you want. Not me. I'm *nothing* like your ex. We have so little in common that I can't see us having a future, Evan. I'm just a distraction. A companion. Someone to chat to after a busy day at work. Your dog is more of a companion than I could be. We have no spark. But from the stories you've told me - over and over - about you and Jen, all you *have* is spark. She's your bloody soulmate, for goodness sake. I think you're crazy if you don't get your arse up to the Highlands and tell her so right now."

His brow creased and he stared silently at me, his chest heaving as if he'd run a marathon. And then his eyes widened. "Bloody hell. You're right, Allie. You're absolutely right. I've been a blinding idiot." He ran his hands through his hair and then tugged at the strands like a man at the end of his tether. "Shit. Do you think she'll take me back?"

I sighed as my shoulders relaxed. I had been right all along. "You don't know if you don't try, do you?"

He leaned forward and kissed my cheek. "Thank you so much, Allie. I think you've finally knocked some sense into this stupid head of mine."

And with that, he was gone.

Left with only my thoughts I went to bed trying to conjure up a plan of how I could find out about Si without being direct. I had to protect myself.

♫♫♫

The following morning, as soon as it seemed to be a reasonable time, I picked up the phone and made the call to Yorkshire.

We chatted for a while, Si's mum and I. "Is Mr Delaney over the flu now?" I asked, skirting around the real reason for my call.

"Yes. Almost back to fine fettle, love. You wouldn't even think he'd been so poorly. Although, he's still having a grouch every so often. It was all drama if you ask me."

"And how are you?" Once again, I avoided asking the question I needed an answer to.

"I'm okay. I've been trying to sort the garden out but the weather down here has been rotten. What's it like there?"

"It's been really warm, actually. I've been gardening too."

"That's good. More chance of it being nice for the wedding today then."

My heart leapt. *Shit. It's today? How the hell has that happened so damn quickly?*

I cleared my throat. "Have… have you heard from Si?"

"Oh, yes. He's been very excited about the wedding. It's a shame we can't be there but with his Lordship and his ailments, we thought it best not to go spreading germs. It's going to be a very quiet ceremony though, apparently. I thought you might have had an invite."

Tears stung at my eyes as the realisation that I had ruined my chance of happiness finally began to sink in. "Oh, no. If it's a small ceremony… and anyway, I'm not sure I could've made it. I have some art exhibitions going on, so, you know… busy. I… really wish them well though." My voice wavered and I hoped she hadn't noticed.

Mrs Delaney huffed. "Me too, love. It's all a bit rushed if you ask me, but they're adults. I was surprised about them getting married at Gretna, but who am I to argue? It's obviously come back into fashion." She laughed and I held my breath so as not to let my pain become evident. "Ooh, sorry, love. Someone's at the door. I'll have to go. Speak soon, okay?"

I swallowed down the ball of emotion that had lodged in my throat. "Sure. No worries. Bye for now." I hung up the call and closed my eyes as tears over spilled.

If only I had let myself believe that what I was feeling for Si was real. If only I had realised before he met someone else. If only I hadn't been such a damn *coward* and I had just told him to bear with me. That I definitely had feelings for him but I was trying to deal with the guilt of falling for my dead fiancé's brother. He would have understood, surely?

All the if onlys in the world wouldn't change anything though. He was getting married to someone else. He was finally happy. And my timing couldn't have been worse. Just as he realised he was over me, I realised I loved him with all of my broken heart.

CHAPTER 32

Si

The wedding room was set up with rows of wooden chairs facing the front where the anvil stood. Candles were lit all around, giving a cosy and warm feel to the exposed stonework. Bobbie and I took our seats along with the other guests. Nick and Cat waved over when they arrived and they came to sit beside us, followed by Chris and Stig, who had come as each other's plus one.

We were surrounded by white roses, and the fragrance was reminiscent of a balmy summer day. In fact, when I closed my eyes, I could have been back at home in the garden of mum and dad's house with Joe and Allie, guitar music playing as Nick sang whatever new song he was writing, and a blissful look in Allie's eyes. A serenity brought about my brother and the love he had for her.

Something tapped at my leg, ripping me from my

memory, and I snapped my eyes open to chastise whoever it was.

Bobbie was staring wide-eyed at me. "Don't you dare fall asleep."

I shook my head. "No. No, I wasn't falling asleep. I was just thinking about Joe, sorry." I cringed.

Her features softened. "Oh, no. That's okay, sweetie. Times like this make me think of Dean. It makes me sad that I'll never get to see him walk down the aisle with his new bride. I miss him so much."

I reached to squeeze her hand and ignored the minor fact that Joe would have been marrying the woman *I* love if he were still here, and I would've been so happy for him, pushing my feelings aside because, not only was he my brother, but he was my best friend in the world. I bit down on the inside of my cheek in the hopes that the pain would shock me into remembering that my future was sitting beside me.

Bobbie was hopefully going to be my future. Okay, so it wasn't love... not yet. But I'd been thinking overnight about the fact that I should give things a serious go with her. And the only way I could do that would be to make love to her and show her that I was committed to making us work. But all would be revealed in time. There was no rush. Today was all about Den and Roger. Tonight, however...

Once all the guests were seated, I glanced at Bobbie and smiled. She ran her thumb gently over the back of my hand and leaned in to kiss my cheek. I swear there were tears in her eyes. No doubt she was still thinking about her brother and how much she hurt from losing him, and it struck me again how much we had in common. All part of our foundation. A foundation we could build upon if I just let it happen.

The celebrant gestured for us to stand and music began to play. Den and Roger had decided to walk down the aisle together and the whole congregation turned to see them holding hands and smiling lovingly at each other as the sounds of Herb Alpert's "This Guy's In Love With You" floated from the sound system and around the room. The love they had for each other was evident in their eyes, and for a moment, I felt that it was entirely possible for me to achieve what they had. Theirs had been a whirlwind romance by every definition, but who had the right to tell them they had rushed into it? Not me, that's for sure. Just the way they looked at each other whenever they were together was proof enough that they were destined to be married.

Once the men reached the front of the room and were standing before the anvil, the celebrant began to speak. He talked about love being unconditional and that marriage was something you shouldn't enter into without knowing it was right. I didn't see a single hint of hesitation in either man's eyes. I have to admit to being a little bit emotional myself. Who knew that a strapping, six-foot odd drummer like me would get weepy over true love? I was definitely going soft in my mid-twenties.

It came to the time for the exchange of vows and the celebrant announced that the couple had chosen to write their own.

Den was first. "Roger, some say there's no such thing as love at first sight, but I say, just like a certain, hunky, bearded TV character we both love, they know nothing." Laughter rumbled around the room at Den's impersonation. "The fact is, I've been on this Earth for over fifty years, and until you walked onto my tour, I had *never* had that glimpse of forever with one man. But on that first day, you looked up and smiled at me and it was like my future played out on a big screen. Okay, so there were a lot of clips of us running through fields of corn; you were bare-chested, obviously." Another rumble of laughter. "But from that moment, I knew I wanted to get to know you. To spend as much time with you as possible. And to be with you forever. Yes, it's happened fast, but what's the point in waiting? So, I stand before you today, Roger, with hope for a long and bright future filled with laughter and, hopefully, a pug puppy. I've always wanted a pug. And I think we should call him Hector. But, I digress. I want you to be my forever. I love you."

Applause erupted and everyone stood as Den placed a ring on Roger's finger and then curtseyed to the congregation. Then he dabbed at his eyes, trying his best to be discreet, bless him.

Once everyone was seated again, Roger took a deep breath. "Phew. How the heck do I follow that?" Everyone laughed again. "You know that feeling when you're on a rollercoaster and you're heading towards a downward part of the track and your stomach is all fluttery? You know it's going to be scary, but ultimately, you're going to have a blast. That's how I felt when I met you, Den. I'd heard about you before and knew from the stories that you were a tough guy to deal with. But the look on your face that first time we met... all that was missing was the cartoon love hearts floating above us. It was mutual, you see. That love at first sight thing. I was so tongue tied and nervous but… you were just so wonderful. You *are* wonderful. You make me laugh each and every day and I swear you've prolonged my life by a decade simply by doing that. You're kind. Thoughtful too. The way you look after your boys… wow. I'm in awe, Den. You're the most hilariously funny man I've ever had the pleasure to meet, and every day, I wake up excited. Like a giddy teenager with so much to look forward to. And I can't wait to be your husband. And for us to start our lives officially as a married couple." He patted at his waistcoat pocket and his eyes widened. Shit, he'd forgotten the ring. "Oh… erm… I seem to have…" He glanced down the aisle towards the exit and the door opened. He turned his face briefly back to Den and a grin widened across his bearded face. Then he crouched and shouted, "Come on. Come on, boy!"

Everyone in the room shared questioning glances until Den squealed and his hands covered his mouth. A jingling could be heard and then scampering feet. Roger stood again, and in his arms was a little sandy coloured pug puppy with a wedding band attached to his collar on a ribbon. I almost lost it at that point. My throat constricted as I watched tears streaming down Den's face.

Clearly trying to remain composed, Roger inhaled deeply and said, "Den, my love, I thought Hector, our new pug puppy, could bring you your ring." He handed the pug to Den and removed the ring from the dog's collar. The dog licked the tears from Den's face and it's stubby little tail wagged like crazy.

He was a sobbing wreck as Roger placed the ring on

his finger. Once the ring was safely in place, he grappled his new husband into his arms. "Oh, thank you, Roger. He's beautiful and I love him to bits. I love you too. Thank you so much."

With tears in his eyes, the celebrant, announced, "Dennis and Roger… I now pronounce that you are married."

Another loud applause erupted and I looked on as Roger and Den shared a sweet, romantic kiss.

CHAPTER 33

Si

I had never really been a fan of wedding receptions. All the ones I had been to as a kid had been dull as shit, but this one was shaping up to be great fun. First off, we sat down for a really tasty steak, and it was so juicy, I thought I'd died and gone to heaven.

I caught Bobbie laughing at me, and with a mouth full of food, I asked, "What's up with you?"

"Every mouthful you take is like a mini orgasm. I swear I'm getting jealous of a slab of damn meat."

I waggled my eyebrows suggestively. "Ah, well. I will have to make it up to you later then."

Her smile disappeared and she leaned towards me. "What do you mean?"

I swallowed as her warm breath sent shivers down my

back. "I mean that you promised to show me what's under your dress and I intend to take you up on that offer."

Her breathing rate increased and her pupils dilated. "Really? But we said we wouldn't do anything until you were sure. Does that mean...?"

I leaned forward and took her bottom lip between my teeth. Gazing straight into her eyes, I nibbled gently before releasing the reddened flesh, and I kissed her. "I think you know what it means, Bobbie."

She slipped her hand into mine and pulled me down to take my mouth in a hot, searing kiss. "You wanna know what's under my dress?"

I kissed a path from her mouth towards her neck and whispered, "Mmhm. Why don't you tell me?"

She clamped her teeth briefly on my earlobe, sending a shockwave of pleasure straight to my groin. "Nothing."

Oh. My. God.

I wanted the rest of the people in the room to disappear so I could swipe everything from the table and take her right then and there. But no sooner had she teased me almost to the point of no return than she pulled away and gave me a sweet smile.

She smoothed a finger around my cheek. "Hold that thought, Mr Delaney."

There was a clinking of glasses and everyone turned to focus their attention on Den, who was now standing to give a speech.

"Ladies and gents, as you know, this has all been a very fast turn around and I can't thank you enough for rearranging your schedules to make sure you could be here."

Chris piped up, "Yeah, well it's a wonder we got the

time off. Our boss is a total douche. A real task master."
Everyone laughed and Den rolled his eyes.

"I'll have you know I've heard very good things about
your boss. Roger here adores him, don't you, Rog?"

Roger held up his hands in surrender. "What can I
say? I'm a sucker for a cute smile and a fake tan." More
laughter followed and Den bent to kiss his new husband
on the forehead.

"Anyway, as I was saying, it means the world to Rog
and me that you could all be here. And I want you to
know I've footed the bill for the bar, so fill your boots,
folks. Cheers!" He held up his glass and everyone shouted
their response in unison.

Roger stood next and everyone quietened down. He
handed the wiggly bundle of fur he was holding to Den
and smoothed his tie down.

He cleared his throat and then began to speak. "Don't
worry, we're not going to bombard you with long
speeches. I just wanted to say thank you to you all, but
mainly to Sonic Idols. You've taken me into your team and
made me feel like part of your family. It's a position I will
cherish." He reached down and held his hand out to Den,
who grasped it. "This man beside me has come into my
life at a time when I never thought I would love again. I
lost my first partner to a heart attack five years ago and I
hadn't looked at another man since. But meeting Den has
made realise that maybe there isn't just one soulmate out
there for us all. Maybe we get another shot at true love,
even if we didn't think it was possible. So, thanks, Denny.
I love with you all my heart." He leaned to kiss Den as the
guests applauded. "Now, if you'd all like to go through to

the adjacent room, there's a dance floor and another bar! Cheers!"

Bobbie squeezed my hand. "Do you think he's right? That there's more than one true love out there for everyone?"

I gazed down at my petite blonde companion and smiled. "Do you know, I really think he could be."

Once we were all ensconced in the room next door, the dance music started. People sat in their groups, laughing and chatting, and the atmosphere in the room was so good. So positive.

The DJ's voice came over the speakers and announced, "Ladies and gents, could I have your attention, please? It's time for our newlyweds to take to the floor for their first dance as a married couple. Let's give them a round of applause."

The opening bars of "Can't Take my Eyes Off You" began, and Den and Roger walked onto the dance floor. A spotlight shone down on them and they began to sway to the music. They sang along to the lyrics which seemed to fit their situation so well, and everyone looked on with warm hearts and smiling faces.

When it came to the famous chorus, the room erupted as every single voice joined in. Bobbie grabbed my hand and pulled me towards the dance floor where everyone else had now congregated. Once it was time for the instrumental part, the singing voices suddenly became terribly bad trumpet sound effects, and of course, Bobbie and I joined in. This was followed by more loud renditions of the chorus and whoops and cheers that almost lifted the roof off the place.

The song ended in one massive group hug, consisting of everyone in attendance. Den and Roger were in the centre of the circle and each word was belted out until I felt sure the neighbours to the venue would complain. But oh. My. Word. It was such a bloody laugh.

I couldn't remember the last time I had laughed so much and I began to wonder if it was all down to the company I was with. Especially Bobbie.

The night wore on and Bobbie and I danced for most of it. At some point, people started to slope off to their rooms. Lightweights. I was in for the long haul. I didn't want the night to end. But the DJ announced that there would be two more songs and so it was clear it would be ending all too soon.

"Love Bites" by Def Leppard was the next song to be played, and I slipped my arms around Bobbie's waist and pulled her close. I tried not to think about the lyrics too much. The DJ certainly hadn't made the best choice; playing this particular song at a wedding may have been a bad decision but it was one of my all-time favourite songs so I closed my eyes and swayed Bobbie in time with the music.

I bent to kiss her and slipped my tongue into her mouth. She tasted of wine and wedding cake, and I decided at that precise moment that I had to take the leap. It was a leap of hope and faith, but I had to believe that what Roger had said was true. Allie wasn't mine and never would be. But here before me was a beautiful, sweet girl who wanted to be with me. To give herself to me. And I had to be man enough to admit that I wanted her too. Lust was playing a big part in it, as was alcohol, but deep down, I knew she was perfect for me. There were so many reasons why we should be together. Our shared grief. Our love of music. The fact that we got along so well and that there was a definite sexual attraction. I was at the top of that rollercoaster Roger had mentioned in his wedding speech, and I had to just hold on and enjoy the ride.

A part of my heart would always belong to the auburn-haired girl from Scotland, but she didn't love me.

Bobbie did.

"Hey, shall we take a bottle of champers upstairs and find out what your non-existent underwear looks like?" Ugh. It wasn't the most romantic proposal I could have presented her with. But it didn't seem to matter.

"Absolutely. Just let me grab my bag." She disappeared briefly before returning to my side and taking my hand. "Let's go." She pulled me towards the exit and I willingly followed.

CHAPTER 34

Allie

With eyes sore and swollen from crying, I stared at the clock. It was one in the morning which meant that Si would officially have been a married man for hours. I had been watching the news off and on all night and was surprised there had been no leaked footage of the wedding. I guessed Den had ramped up security in light of recent incidents involving the band. And having experienced first-hand the frightening side of the band's fame, I could totally understand why there had been no press in attendance.

But it didn't help me and my need to see him. To see his face. To know that he was okay and happy. But that was crazy, because he must have been ecstatic. He was married, for goodness sake.

Married.

It made me sad how final that was. I wondered what her dress had been like. Did she look stunning and had she had that bridal glow about her? Had he looked adoringly at her as they said their vows? And were they in bed right now, making love?

Probably.

A fresh batch of tears sprang from my eyes and I bent double as the anguish I felt manifested as physical pain in my stomach. How could I have been so damned stupid? Okay, so falling for Si hadn't been intentional. And it was damned weird considering *who* he was. But when it comes down to it, you can't help who you fall in love with. You can choose to do nothing about it. You can choose to ignore it, but that doesn't make it go away. I think subconsciously I had known from the first time we made love. There had been this connection between us. An invisible thread that joined us. Partly, it was the grief we shared, but there was more to it than that. But I ignored it and dismissed it. I pretended I had imagined the feelings and pushed them down. Only now that I knew it was love, I knew the feelings weren't imagined. They were real. But thanks to my own unwillingness to see what was right under my nose, I had lost him.

Just like I had lost his brother.

I picked up my mobile and flicked through my photos until I landed on the one I had secretly taken of the song lyrics Si had written for me. At the time, I had taken the photo without realising why the song meant so much. But now I realised why the poetry had tugged at my heart and why I couldn't stop reading the words and wishing he still felt that way...

Your heart beats next to mine but I wait for you to leave,
I've wanted for so long to wear my heart upon my sleeve.
I want to see you laugh, to see the light upon your face.
The one he used to put there, that no one could erase.
I've loved you for so long now and you don't even know,
how much my heart will break when it's time for me to go.
I want to see you laugh, see the light upon your face
and I wish that I could put it there, but
I can't be in his place.

CHAPTER 35

Si

We reached my room and I checked my watch. It was past one in the morning and here I was, ready to take that oh-so-important step with Bobbie. The step that would show her I was willing to make a go of a serious relationship with her. I opened my room door and stepped inside. As soon as the door closed behind us, she leapt into my arms, just as she had that night at the club. Our mouths collided and our breaths rasped. I wanted her. To be inside of her. To feel her around me.

She wanted me too, that much was clear as she ground herself into me and I slipped my hand underneath her to discover that she was, in fact, naked under her dress. A voice in the back of mind told me I would regret this. That I wasn't on the same page as Bobbie and that I would only hurt her in the long run. But I pushed my conscience back and did my best to ignore it. Fear of moving forward had never got me anywhere, after all.

Bobbie stopped kissing me and rested her forehead on mine. "Is it okay if I just go back to my room and freshen up? We've been dancing and I want to make sure I'm as sexy as I can be."

I tried to calm my lust-filled, ragged breaths. "But I want you now. Don't go."

The responding smile told me I had almost convinced her. But she dropped her feet to the floor and shook her head. "Let me put it another way. I need to go back to my room to get into something a lot less comfortable."

"Ohhhh!" It dawned on me that she must have brought sexy underwear. "Well, in that case…" I kissed her again and smoothed my hand down to her breast, tweaking her nipple through the tight fabric. "I had better let you go."

She licked her lips and stepped back. She reached into her clutch bag and grabbed her room key. Jingling it a little, she stepped towards the door. "Yeah, you'd better. But don't start without me, okay?"

I shook my head as I watched her leave. "Oh, no. I'm saving myself for your return."

She slinked out of my room and closed the door behind her.

I stared at the door briefly, wondering what I should do now. Should I get naked and wait in the bed, or would that be too presumptuous? Should I open the bottle of champagne we had taken from the bar and pour us a drink? It would have to be in teacups though, as we forgot to get glasses.

The whole thing was starting to feel a little bit like a hook up, whereas I had thought this was going to be me showing her I was willing to make some kind of commitment. Didn't sexy undies come later in a relationship? Although, I hadn't done the relationship thing in a while... or ever... so I decided I should just go with the flow.

As I stood there trying to straighten my mind about it all, I heard a ringing coming from her bag. I ignored it and let it ring. It stopped and I presumed it had gone to voicemail so I went back to my pondering.

I decided to at least take off my jacket and tie. Once I had done that, I began to roll up my sleeves, but her phone started to ring again. *Maybe it's important. Maybe I should take it to her so she can answer it? Ahh, but no, that would ruin her surprise.* I imagined she would want to return in a robe to cover up whatever she was wearing and make a big entrance. The phone stopped again.

I kicked off my shoes and pulled off my socks and sat in the chair by the window. The phone started ringing again. It was getting on my nerves and I was thinking it must definitely be important, or whoever it was would just leave a message and be done. I reached over the bed to her clutch bag and slipped my hand inside to retrieve the phone.

I glanced at the illuminated screen in utter confusion. *Dean? That's odd. She must have a friend called Dean as well as a deceased brother.*

Figuring I should explain that she wasn't available, I hit the green handset symbol and lifted the phone to my ear. "Hello, Bobbie's phone?"

There was a silent pause at the other end, so I repeated, "Hello? Bobbie's phone? Who's calling?" I felt like a bloody secretary.

"Um… hi. I'm sorry, is Roberta there please?" The caller was male and had an American accent.

Who? "Oh, I'm sorry you must have the wrong number. This is—"

"Bobbie's phone. Yeah, you said. Is Roberta *there*, please?"

I was getting a little pissed off now. "I'm sorry, *mate*, I don't know anyone of that name. Did you not hear what I said?"

"Jesus, *fuck*. How dumb are you, man? Roberta *is* Bobbie. I should fucking know. She's my goddam sister."

What the fuck kind of sick joke is this? I pulled the handset away from my ear and checked the screen again. The name on the display was definitely Dean. I scrambled around my alcohol addled brain trying to get my thoughts straight. There had to be an explanation. Maybe she had another brother and he used their dead brother's phone and she hadn't been able to face changing the name on the… but wait… she said there were only two of them. Dean and Bobbie…

My heart leapt in my chest. Something was very fucking wrong. "Who…who is this, please?"

Obnoxious bastard sighed heavily. "Seriously? My name is Dean. D. E. A. N. Dean. Roberta is my kid sister and I've been trying to get to talk to her for God knows how long now. Our parents are worried sick about her. If you have her, you'd better put her on the goddam phone, or I swear I'll fucking—"

"I don't *have* her. And I don't know what you're suggesting by that, but... Wait, are you Dean the drummer? Her older brother who drums in a band?"

The surly prick at the other end of the line snorted. "*Drummer*? Dude, I work construction. The only things I hit are nails. What the fuck are you talking about and where's my sister?"

I rubbed my fingers over my eyes and tried to digest what he was saying. "Like I said, I don't *have* your sister. She's here, yes, but of her own free will. Well... not here as in right here, but she's in the building..."

"You're rambling. That makes me more worried. Spit it out."

"Bobbie... erm... Roberta is absolutely fine but she's out at the minute. I'm sorry... I'm just a bit... erm... I don't... Look, c-can I get her to call you back?"

"Shit. Look, dude, from the confusion in your voice, I'd say she's done a number on you. She does this. She goes off the rails. She disappears for months at a time. She said she was going to Europe to follow some band. We thought she was kidding around. But she hasn't called home in weeks and now we're getting worried that she hopped a plane and went there after all. She's a liar, man. But she's still my kid sister. I just want to check she's okay."

I sighed as the world I had begun to imagine crumbled around me. "She's... she's here in Scotland just now. And she *did* follow a band."

"Aww, crap. Scotland? I knew it. Shit, it must be so late there. It's like seven in the evening here. Is she... is she okay, though? I mean, she hasn't done anything crazy, has she? She's not in any trouble?"

"She's… she's okay. But… can I ask you something?"

"Sure, man. Look, I'm sorry I jumped on you at the start of the call. I'm just freaking out here. Go ahead and ask me anything."

I took a deep breath, unsure if I wanted to hear the truth. My chest ached and I rubbed the spot above my heart. "Has she ever lost a brother to a serious illness?"

"Lost as in *dead*? Nah. I'm her only brother and I'm still here. Why? What'd she say this time?"

I ignored his question and continued, "And were you and she named after Dean Martin and Bobby Vinton?"

"Bobby who?" *Okay, that answers that question.*

"And have you *ever* drummed in a band?"

"I'm sorry… what's your name, man?"

I sighed. "Si. My name's Si."

"Okay, listen, Si, I hate to be the bearer of shitty news but I can almost guarantee that whatever she's told you, chances are, she was fantasising. It's what she does. She creates these imaginary worlds in her head and decides to become a different person. She's like a fucking female Walter Mitty or something. Don't get me wrong, she's not crazy or anything. Just imaginative and damned selfish. She does it to get what she wants and it usually works. Says it makes life sweeter. But no, I've never picked up a drumstick in my life, never mind joined a band. Roberta played a little in school but stopped before college. Although, bizarrely, she's kind of gifted at it." He sighed as if exhausted from worrying. "Look, can you just get her to call me? I know she probably won't but you could at least try to convince her. My mom and dad worry so much. If you ask me, they should waste there energy elsewhere but... well, she's still their little girl. I call every so often to just make sure she's okay. See if she needs money. I don't want her resorting to stupid ways of getting cash, if you catch my drift. What my folks really want is for her to come home and stay here. But she won't settle down. I doubt she ever will. But could you just ask her to call me? So I can put my mom and dad's minds at ease. Selfish little bitch doesn't think about them while she's off on her wild adventures." The venom was evident in his voice at his disdain for his sibling. "Just a quick call. That's all I ask. Can you do that for me, Si?"

The ache inside got worse and I wasn't sure if it was from the betrayal or from anger. Or both. "Yeah, I'll do my best. Bye, Dean."

I hit the end call button and stared at the handset as the door to my room opened.

CHAPTER 36

Si

Bobbie curled her leg around the door and rotated her foot. "Well, hello there. Did someone order room service?" It felt completely contrived. Especially in light of my recent conversation.

She was still wearing those sexy stiletto shoes from the wedding. I didn't respond. How could I?

When she didn't get the desired reaction from me, she poked her head around the door and frowned at me. "Oh, I thought you'd fallen asleep. I'm sorry I took so long, but I wanted to look good for you."

She pouted and did that fluttery fucking eyelash thing. My nostrils flared and I fought to keep my cool. "Hey, no worries, *Roberta*. Why don't you come on in?"

She stepped into the room and did a little sashay with her back to me as she untied the rope around her robe.

She flung the tie backwards onto the bed and dropped the robe off one shoulder but then froze.

"What did you just call me?"

I clenched my jaw. "You heard me right."

She swung around to face me, her cheeks pale and her eyes wide. "But… but how…?"

"I've just had a lovely chat on the phone. Long distance, of course. *Very* long distance, in fact. All the way from the great beyond." I widened my eyes and waved my fingers in a mocking fashion.

She pulled the robe closed and wrapped her arms protectively around herself. "Oh, no. You're mistaken. That will have been Dean my *friend*." She shook her head. "He calls to see how I am… you know, since his namesake died."

"Cut the fucking crap, *Bobbie*. You're a liar. You've been lying all along." I stood and pointed my finger at her. "It was all utter bullshit. Wasn't it? Admit it."

She fidgeted and stuck her tongue into one side of her mouth as her jaw jutted out. "No. No, I haven't lied. How could you *think* that? You could've thought of a better way to dump me than to make up shit about my dead brother calling you. Thanks, Si. Thanks a lot." Her voice wavered as she turned on the pathetic water works.

I scoffed. "So, you're sticking to your stupid, crazy arse story?" I shook my head in utter incredulity. "My God. You've got tenacity, I'll give you that much."

"My brother is *dead*!" She bellowed at me. "He died in a terrible accident. But, of course, you're the only one allowed to grieve, huh? It's allll about Si Delaney. Well, I've got news, buster, other people have lost someone they love too. I thought we had that in common. I thought we could help each other to heal."

I laughed out loud without the slightest hint of humour. "So, he died in a 'terrible accident' now?" I punctuated my response with air quotes. "Don't you think you should've got your lies straight in your own head before you went on to try and manipulate me?"

Her brow creased and she reacted as if she had a bad smell under her nose. "Duh. He died in an accident *because* of his illness, dumbass."

Oh, she was hilarious. But in the worst possible way. "Let's start telling the truth here, okay? Your name is Roberta. Your brother works in construction and it would be fairly tricky to do that if he was dead. Oh, and you're a fucking lying, manipulating bitch. Now, I suggest you get your shit together, get out of this hotel, and go find another fucking job because you are *so* done here. Finished."

She burst into fake tears and screamed at me. "He is dead! Why are you saying this?"

"Because I've just spoken to him on the fucking phone! His name came up as Dean. I asked him outright. Just stop lying."

She stamped her foot. "Well, why does it even matter? Okay, so Dean is alive. But I love you. I won't do it again. Just stop yelling at me. It's not like I killed your brother!"

I shook my head slowly and clenched my fists into balls at my side. I wanted to shake her, but I fought my urges and tried to calm my voice. "I don't ever want to see your lying fucking face again, do you hear me? You took the one thing you knew about me. The thing that hurts more than *anything* and you used it to get what you wanted. Who the fuck *does* that? What kind of sick fuck do you have to be to lie about the death of a loved one just so we had something in common? What the fuck is wrong with you?"

My eyes stung and my jaw ached from clenching so hard, but I spat my words out with as much venom as I could muster because she deserved it. "I thought you were special. I thought for the first time in my fucking life I had met someone who got me. Got what I'd been through. I told you stories about my brother. I shared my innermost grief with you. And all that was based on a fucking lie. Have you any idea what you've done? How much you've hurt me? Do you even fucking care? Yes, I might be a man, and yes, I might look tough on the outside, but my brother was my best friend. My hero." My jaw quivered and I inwardly berated myself for showing any emotion, but I couldn't stop it. "And the pain I carry over losing him makes me so fucking weak on the inside that I never let anyone in. *Never.* But I let *you* in, Bobbie. I trusted you. And for what?"

She stared open-mouthed at me, her eyes blank. "But I *can* play the drums. I didn't lie about that. And I know how to set up a kit."

What the fuck? I gripped the strands of my hair and shook my head. I was exasperated. Dumbfounded. "Are you even listening to me? Can you even comprehend the damage you've caused? Eh? I don't give a shit if you're fucking Neil Peart. You've betrayed me in the worst possible way. Now get out. Please just get out." I pointed at the door. My chest heaved and my head throbbed. It was two in the morning and I was exhausted.

She stood there. Like a statue. The blank stare on her face made me wonder if she was actually crazy. I stared back, giving no quarter. She wouldn't manipulate me again.

Eventually, she shrugged. "Well, you have to admit, it was fun while it lasted. Shame we didn't have sex. I'm really good at that too."

I was determined not to let her get the last word. "Goodbye, Roberta. Go call your brother and tell him everything. He'll be so proud of you, I'm sure." I could've done with a bucket for the sarcasm dripping from my words.

She grabbed the rope for her robe from the bed, turned, and left the room, slamming the door behind her in one last defiant move.

Once she was gone, I collapsed onto the bed with my head in my hands, wondering if—and hoping that—what had just happened was by some chance a twisted fucking dream. And furthermore, realising the irony of the lyrics to the song we had danced to at the end of the night.

Love didn't just bite, it pulverised.

CHAPTER 37

Si

Standing in Den and Roger's room, I felt like utter shit interrupting their honeymoon. Okay, so it wasn't really a honeymoon as such. It was the morning after the wedding and they weren't going anywhere apart from on to the next gig of our UK tour. But I still felt bad.

Once I had finished explaining what Bobbie had done, Den gave a horrified gasp. "That little bitch! I can't believe she played you like that, Si. Are you going to be okay? I know you liked her a lot."

Roger interjected, "But don't worry about finding a new tech. I know people. We'll get it sorted for you ASAP."

I held up my hands, filled with guilt. "Look, guys, don't worry about it all now. I don't want to spoil things for you. This is your special time. I just thought you should know, that's all."

Den placed his hands on my shoulders. "Hey, when have I ever turned you away? And of course we need to know. But you're spoiling nothing. We have plenty of time for romance, don't we, Rog?"

"Hell yes, we do."

"And I know I'm your manager, Si, but we're family too. Maybe not by blood, but I chose you boys as my family and Roger gets that. Don't you, Rog?"

His husband grinned. "Oh, boy, do I? I feel like I've adopted Sonic Idols as part of the package deal!"

Relief flooded my veins, and for the first time in twelve hours, I began to relax.

"Seriously though, Si, are you okay? That was a low thing she did, that Bobbie, Bertrand, or bobblehead. Whatever the hell her real name was."

I chuckled at his bizarre choice of names but nodded. "I'll be fine. I've just learned the hard way not to trust new people though. I still can't believe the lies. And the fact that she preyed on my grief over Joe."

And I really couldn't. How could someone be so fucking cruel and manipulative?

Den squeezed my shoulders. "Hey, not every girl you meet will be like that. She was a one off. Believe me."

I wished I could believe him but I knew it would be a while before I would make myself so vulnerable again. I could already feel the walls building up around me.

I shrugged. "Yeah, let's hope so. Anyway, you guys enjoy the last couple of honeymoon hours you've got left. I'm going to take a walk. Clear my head."

"Good plan, lad. We're setting off for Newcastle just after lunch. Roger will get you a drum tech sorted."

Roger, who was clutching his phone, waved and nodded. "On it like a car bonnet, chuck."

I thanked them both again and left them to it. I passed by my room to grab my shades and hat and then I set off to explore the cute village we were staying in.

I'd heard lots about Gretna Green and the fact that couples would elope to the village to marry without their parents' consent. As I stood outside the Blacksmiths Shop, I wondered just how many love stories had culminated in this quaint little white building. I stepped inside to the part that was now used as museum to display memorabilia from the weddings that had taken place over the years and imagined what it must be like to be so desperate to be with someone that you would travel hundreds of miles from home to make it official, regardless of what others thought. Instead of dread at such musings, my heart warmed. To love so fiercely and be loved back in equal measure must be the most amazing feeling a human being can experience. I immediately thought of Allie and the lengths I would've gone to just to be with her, regardless of what others had to say. Moot point, but it didn't stop me thinking.

As I read the letters on display from those who had crossed the border to take advantage of Scotland's marriage laws back then, I wondered if marriage was an outdated institution now. As far back as 1754, couples had run away to commit themselves to each other on this very spot, and yet here I was in the twenty-first century, with all its modern-day trappings, unable to find a sane woman to love me unconditionally. But there really were still people who felt that marriage cemented their relationship and believed wholeheartedly in it. As I explored my feelings, I realised that, in spite of the shit Bobbie had put me through, and in spite of the fact I couldn't be with the one I truly loved, I was one of those people.

♫♫♫

Once we were back on the road, I breathed a sigh of relief. Performing was my safe haven. I knew where I was on a stage surrounded by my guys. No fear, no tension, just fun and the rhythm.

I stared out of the window and watched as we crossed the border into England, and the landscape changed from hills and fields to houses and industry.

The seat dipped beside me. "Hey, Si. How you doing, mate?" I turned to see Nick's concerned, crumpled stare fixed on me.

I shrugged. "I'm okay, I think. Still a bit pissed off, but I'll survive."

He sighed and shook his head. "I still can't believe she turned out to be such an evil witch. You really didn't deserve that. It's a bloody good thing Den fired her or I certainly would have."

"It's okay. I'm just glad she's gone."

Nick fell silent for a while and we both stared at the morphing landscape passing by us.

He eventually spoke again. "So... have you heard from Allie lately?"

I heaved a defeated sigh at being reminded of the one woman that, without a doubt, I could trust. "Nah. She's got a new man in her life."

"Ah. Sorry about that. I wish things could've been different for you two."

I was surprised by his comment and turned to face him fully. "You do? I mean... you don't think it would've been weird? Me and her being together with Joe being her... and me being his...?"

Nick shook his head and frowned. "Si, you can't help who you fall in love with. Simple as that. I just wish she had felt the same."

And once again, I was reminded that, although I loved Allie with all my heart, hers now belonged to someone else.

♫♫♫

"Good evening, Newcastle! Are you ready to roooock?" Loud screams and cheers ensued in response to Nick's question. "Yeah? Yeah? Well, are you ready to get... HOT AND HEAVY?"

I laughed as I strained to hear my kit above the thousands of piercing voices and my heart hammered at my chest, fuelled purely by adrenaline. Nick turned to grin at me and I pointed one stick at him as I beat the snare with the other and pounded my foot on the base pedal.

The night was going so well, and as always, for a few short hours, I was Si the rock star, drummer heartthrob, not Si the loser, recently betrayed by a psycho bitch.

Nick stomped the stage like the pro he was and began to announce the eighth song on our playlist. "This next song goes out to everyone who's been lied to and cheated on. To everyone who trusted and got betrayed. But it also goes out to everyone who fought back and rose above." He turned to face me again. "This one's for you, Si!"

Oh, fuck. Nick had just announced to the world... well, Newcastle... that I had been crapped on from a great height by someone. I know he meant well, but I made a mental note to slap him after the show.

I hit out the heartbeat rhythm of "No Going Back" and Nick began to sing the scathing lyrics as if Bobbie could hear him. For the first time ever, I could relate to the song that Chris had penned after being cheated on by a famous fashion model.

Your beauty may have knocked me from my feet
But you broke my heart with lies and deceit
You wanted fame and fortune to make you whole
Just a silly little girl with beauty but no soul

Now you say you're sorry for what you lack
Well, it's too late honey
'Cause there's no going back

No going back
No, you won't break me
No going back
It took your cruel lies to wake me
No going back

So who's the loser now?
No going back
And I'll make it through
Yeah, I know how

CHAPTER 38

Allie

The arena was packed and everyone was jumping to each and every beat Si hit out. I was surrounded by so many smiling face, all singing the Sonic Idols' words back to them. I almost burst with the pride I felt for the guys I had once known so well.

It had been too long since I had seen them play live, and I had been so excited that I managed to get a ticket for their Newcastle arena show just before they sold out. I had been there all those years ago when they penned "Hot 'n' Heavy" and I loved the fact it was still a fan favourite after all this time.

I had a great view of the stage from my position on the second tier to the side and watched Si as his muscles worked hard and a sheen of sweat covered his toned body. He wasn't glancing into the wings like he was when I watched on TV, and I wondered where his new wife was. Maybe she wasn't here tonight. Maybe she had tired of the performances already. Although, I sincerely doubted that. Regardless of the songs being the same, every show was different. Or at least, that's how I remembered them. *No. She must be here somewhere.*

When I had arrived at the arena, I had toyed with the idea of making my presence known to the band, but the thought of coming face to face with Si's blushing new bride would've been too painful. So I resolved to watch from a safe distance. Then, after the show, I would return home to Kelso and get on with my life. I had to put the whole Si business behind me. My realisations had come too late so what choice did I have?

Towards the end of the concert, I was wrung out emotionally as almost every lyric of every song had spoken to me on a personal level. Then Nick addressed his adoring fans.

"This next song goes out to everyone who's been lied to and cheated on. To everyone who trusted and got betrayed. But it also goes out to everyone who fought back and rose above." He turned to face Si on the drum podium. "This one's for you, Si!"

My heart and stomach plummeted towards the floor in unison. What did Nick just say? I glanced around me as if the rest of the fans would be able to shed light on the matter. But of course, they were completely oblivious to me and the reasons I was staring open-mouthed and wide-eyed at the stage.

Was Nick joking? Or had Si just had his heart broken? Was it his new wife who had been the heartbreaker or was he—and I hoped not—talking about me and the way I had seemingly toyed with Si's affections?

Confusion clouded my mind and my breathing accelerated until I was almost hyperventilating. Panic gripped me and I had to get out. I had to find out what the hell was going on but didn't know how to get to the truth. There could be two *very* different meanings to Nick's cryptic comments but I had to know for certain which it was.

Panting and with blurred vision, I shoved my way through the crowd towards the exit, where a security guard stopped me. "Are you all right, pet?"

I glanced up at his worried expression and nodded. "Oh... yes, I'm fine. I just need to leave."

"Can I get you some water? You look awfully pale considering how hot it is in there."

I waved my hand dismissively and shook my head but smiled. "No. No, really. I'm fine. Or I will be once I get to my car."

"Aye, all right, pet. I'll get the door for you." He pushed the exit open and I stepped out into the chilled evening air.

"Thank you." I peered around the car park and realised I had come out of the wrong exit. I set off running around the outskirts of the building until I located the correct parking area. By the time I reached my car, I collapsed against the door, thankful for the coldness of the metal against my heated skin. I was breathless and my face was damp with sweat. I opened my car door and climbed inside to sit for a moment and catch my breath. Once I felt human again, I stuck the key in the ignition with shaking hands and turned the engine on before heading out of the car park and following the signs for Leeds.

♫♫♫

At half past eleven that night, I pulled the car to a halt outside the Delaney's home. I suppose I could've just called, but whatever was going on, it felt necessary to hear it direct. I turned off the engine and tried to calm my rising nerves again.

I rested my head on the steering wheel. "Ugh, what the hell are you doing, Allie? Are you totally bloody insane? Well, you *are* talking to yourself so there's a very good chance of that. Come on. It's now or never."

On weak, shaking legs, I climbed out of the car and walked up to the front door. I tapped lightly so as not to wake the whole neighbourhood and then waited.

A light came on inside the house and Si's dad opened the door, greeting me with a worry-filled expression. "Allie? Is everything okay, love?"

"Y-yes... erm... no. I just..."

He held out his hand. "Come on in. You look terrible."

"Who is it, love?" Si's mum called from the top of the stairs. When she saw me, she dashed down. "Allie, sweetheart, what on earth are you doing here at this time of night? Are you okay? What's happened?"

Mr Delaney patted his wife's arm. "Take her through to the lounge. I'll make some tea."

I followed Mrs Delaney into the familiar, friendly room, and we both sat.

"I'm so sorry to turn up unannounced like this. I don't know why I didn't just call. I suppose I was part of the way here anyway. Newcastle isn't far," I rambled.

"No, it's fine, love. You're welcome here any time, you know that. But you're worrying me. Why were you in Newcastle? What's going on?" I sat silently staring at her, trying to figure out what to say so I didn't sound completely crazy. "Allie?"

I rubbed my hands over my face. "I... erm... oh, God. You're going to think I'm a lunatic."

Mr Delaney reappeared with three steaming mugs clutched awkwardly in his fingers and he placed one down for each of us.

I took a deep breath and began. "I was at Si's concert in Newcastle. At the arena. He was brilliant. But..."

"But what, sweetheart?"

I flitted my glance between the two worried-looking people across from me. "Can I ask you something and can you be completely honest with me?"

Mr Delaney nodded. "Always, love. Always."

I closed my eyes, squeezing them shut as if it would ease what was to come, and I blurted. "Has Si's wife left him?"

Silence.

I opened my eyes again to find his parents gaping at me.

His dad spoke first. "S-Si got *married*?"

Mrs Delaney burst into tears. "And he didn't even bother to tell us? I can't believe he would do such a thing. We've always been so close. We're his parents."

If I wasn't utterly confused before, I certainly was now. "But… I thought you knew?"

Mr Delaney's face was bright red and I couldn't tell if it was bubbling rage or heartbreak causing it. "We knew nothing about it, Allie. He's not known the girl that long. That's probably why he didn't mention it. Knew we'd say he was mad jumping in to a wedding. Bloody hell. I wonder if she's pregnant." He shook his head.

Good grief, is everyone losing their marbles? "But, last time I called you said he was excited about the wedding."

Mr Delaney nodded as his wife continued to sob. "Yes, that's right. He was."

Overcome with equal measures of exhaustion and exasperation I lifted my arms and let them drop again. "Well then you *did* know!"

Mr Delaney frowned and leaned towards me. "We knew about Den and *his* wedding but it doesn't mean Si had to jump into having one too. And to not even bloody tell us!" His voice became louder as anger began to win over his emotions.

Then the penny dropped.

I held up my hands. "H-hang on. It was *Den* getting married? You were talking about Den when I called? Not Si?"

Mrs Delaney sniffed and wiped at her eyes. "Yes, love. What has Si said about his own wedding? Is it that drum technician girl with the tattoos?"

Relief flooded my veins and I heaved a huge sigh through puffed cheeks. "Okay, I think I owe you a massive apology. It looks like I've got the wrong end of the stick. I saw Si on TV talking about wedding bells when a reporter asked if he was getting married and I—"

Mr Delaney's face was returning to its normal colour. "Put two and two together and got five?"

I cringed. "It appears so, yes."

He nodded. "I see. So, you didn't see the next part of the clip where he said it was his manager getting wed?"

I covered my face as my cheeks heated and peeped out through the gaps in my fingers. "No."

"So, Simeon isn't married?" Mrs Delaney's wide eyes showed her relief.

Mr Delaney squeezed her knee. "No, love. He's not."

She shook her head. "Oh, thank goodness! Thank goodness!" She hugged her husband but then turned her attention back to me. "But, hang on. You said he had been dumped."

I went on to explain Nick's cryptic song announcement and dedication to Si at the concert.

"Oh, no. My poor boy. That drum tech girl must not have been right for him after all." There was a distinct appearance of disappointment in her eyes. She only wanted her son's happiness, after all. She assessed me with her gaze again and her eyes narrowed. "Allie, can I just ask, why were you so bothered by all of this anyway? You came all the way here at almost midnight to find out the truth. Why on earth would you do that?"

A lump of sadness restricted my throat and I tried to swallow it down, but my eyes had already welled up and betrayed me. "Because... because I'm in love with him. I'm in love with Si."

CHAPTER 39

Allie

The drive home from Leeds was filled with mixed emotions. My conversation with the Delaneys following my admission had been wonderful, yet heart-breaking. As I drove, I replayed it over and over in my mind.

Mrs Delaney had cried and said that she had suspected I had feelings for Simeon but couldn't interfere seeing as I had loved Joe. She just hadn't felt right saying anything. "But *you* need to speak to him, Allie. You should tell him how you feel. That way you'll get your answers. More answers than we can give, love. We can't speak for him."

I nodded and lowered my gaze, realising I was speaking to the wrong people. "I know. I know, but... please don't tell him I was here, okay? Don't tell him anything about this. From what Nick said at the concert, he's just had his heart stamped on. I don't think me admitting my feelings will help. I think the timing is completely wrong."

Mr Delaney shook his head. "Strike whilst the iron's hot, Allie. You can't leave things like this to chance. You should say something. Or at least find out if he still feels the same about you."

My eyes began to sting. "I can't. I'm too scared. I rejected him before. I was too afraid to acknowledge my feelings and I pushed him away. How could he trust me now?"

Mrs Delaney smiled warmly. "People change, love. People make mistakes. You're human. I know my son and I know he'll understand."

"No. I have to be certain. I don't want either of us to get hurt. Please just leave it for now. Let me try and figure out a way to find out if he still feels the same. If he does, great. If not... I'll move on... or at least I'll try to."

Mr Delaney sighed. "I understand what you mean. But just so you know, you have our blessing. I know you said that you didn't pursue a relationship with Simeon because of your past with Joe and you were worried about what we would think. But honestly, Allie, we loved you when we thought you were going to be married to Joe and we still love you now. You'll always be family to us, no matter what. And if Si is who your heart wants then who are we to deny you and he that happiness?"

Tears over-spilled my eyes and I released a pent-up sob that had been desperate to escape. I stood and the Delaney's stood too to engulf me in a hug that showed me just how wonderful they really were. Why had I been so worried? I'd really had no need to be. If I'd known how accepting they would be, I wouldn't have been feeling so lost and heartbroken. Instead, I would be curled up in bed with Si after a brilliant show in Newcastle.

But that was then. Before I discovered his feelings and rejected him. The now was what concerned me. Had he given up on the prospect of love? Had he given up on me?

CHAPTER 40

Si

Manchester was the next stop on the UK leg of our tour. A place we had played many times as our fan base there was huge. After Manchester, we were apparently heading to Scotland again, to Nick's new studios to do a bit of recording. It wasn't the main recording of our new album but a bit of a dummy run to see how the studio setup was working and to iron out any issues. The studios weren't quite finished but Nick was happy with the work his Scottish crew of engineers and builders were doing, and if things went according to plan, we would record the whole new album there. It was a bittersweet pill for me. I was over the moon for Nick but not so happy to be in that part of the UK again as it held only bad memories for me. Getting your heart pummelled twice has that effect.

Seeing Nick's face light up whenever he talked about

his new venture and his future there with Cat was enough to make even the likes of Chris think about settling down. Although, he would need to find someone daft enough or strong enough to deal with him. But it appeared I wasn't the only one who wanted something real.

I was at the table at the front of the bus with my e-reader. Nick came and sat opposite and placed a mug of coffee on the table for me. "I hear you've been doing some song writing."

I placed my reader down and frowned. "Oh yeah? Who told you that useless snippet?"

He shrugged. "Doesn't matter who told me. Is it true?"

I chuckled as my cheeks heated. "I've been messing about but I'm not sure I'd call it song writing."

"Hey, don't sell yourself short, mate. You should let me check out what you've got. I think it'd be a great idea for you to write something for the new album."

I sighed as I remembered Allie reading my lyrics and her reaction. "I'm not sure anyone would like what I've written, to be honest. Allie definitely wasn't impressed."

"Was it something you had written about her?" I nodded. He scrubbed at his beard with his hand. "It can be quite a cathartic way to get your feelings out. I think you should stick with it."

"Yeah, well I'll think about."

"Have you tried talking to Allie since she found out how you feel?"

I shook my head and took a sip of my drink. "No point, Nick. She's moved on. I need to do the same. Although, I think I'll give relationships a wide berth for a while. I reckon I just need to sew my wild oats for a bit."

He pursed his lips and shook his head. "A year ago, I would've been inclined to agree with you. I would've said go for it. Get your rocks off with whoever, whenever you can. But now—"

"But now you're all loved up, Nick. You've found the one. That elusive thing called true love. I envy you. I really do. But maybe it's not meant for everybody. Maybe it's not meant for me."

He stood, stepped towards me, and patted my shoulder. "I know you don't feel that way deep down, Si. You've been lied to and it fucking hurts like a bitch. I get that. But in reality, love is something we all crave. And someday, you'll find it. I know you will." And with those wise words, he walked towards the back of the bus where the other guys were jamming.

♫♫♫

With the soundcheck completed earlier in the day, we had eaten lunch and had a chance to rest. At the venue, I was sitting with the rest of the band in the dressing room, waiting to go on.

Stig sat beside me. "What do you reckon to your new drum tech then, Si?"

I shrugged. "Seems okay. He's done a good job from what I could tell. Kit seems set up right which is all that matters."

He nudged me. "Not quite as nice to look at as that psycho though, eh?"

I chuckled. "Yeah, well I don't really care about that. So long as he does a good job, he'll do for me."

Stig's expression changed to one of concern. "Do you miss her?"

"Bobbie? I miss the idea of who I thought she was. I miss the idea that she projected. Someone who understood about Joe and understood my passion for playing. But I don't miss her as a person."

"What about Allie? Do you miss her?"

I scrunched my face. "What's up with you Jeremy bloody Kyle? Are you trying to make me cry or something?" I joked.

He grinned. "If I wanted to make you cry I could do it, believe me. Nah… I just know how you felt about her. And I gather from chit chat that she pretty much turned you down."

I shook my head in exasperation. "Chit chat? You mean Chris, more like. Yeah, well, Allie and I were never destined to be anything other than friends. It's shit but I have to learn to deal with that. Anyway, if Joe had still been alive, we wouldn't be having this conversation because I would never have done anything to jeopardise their relationship. Joe meant too much to me."

Stig's expression turned serious again. "You don't have to do that, you know?"

"Do what?"

"Justify yourself. We all know you and Joe were close. And we all know that you would never have tried to steal his girl. You don't have to worry that that's what we're thinking. We're brothers. All of us. We just want you to be happy, and if it had turned out that Allie loved you back then we would have supported you wholeheartedly. You do know that, don't you?"

Did I? No, I don't think I did. I hated finding out that everyone knew I had feelings for my brother's woman. Hated how that made me look. And I didn't want people thinking I was glad Joe was gone so I had a shot. I didn't see things that way. At all. Not that she would've even looked at me twice if Joe was still around. Although, why everyone felt the need to confess their innermost thoughts about the whole Allie situation was beyond me. How many times did I have to repeat myself and say that none of it mattered because she had moved on?

Stig stared at me expectantly. "I'm sorry it didn't work out, mate. And I mean that."

"Yeah. Cheers, Stig."

CHAPTER 41

Allie

Two days without sleep. Two days trying to figure out how the hell to find out if Si had totally given up on me. Two days of feeling lost and defeated.

I finally gave in and picked up my phone to call the one person who could give me an honest answer, and who I could trust to not talk to Si and tell him I was fishing around.

"Allie? Hey, how are you doing, girl? Not spoken to you for bloody ages." Nick's warm, friendly voice made my heart squeeze. It made me realise just how much I missed being in the inner circle of the band.

I cleared my throat, conscious of the fact that I was already experiencing that tightening of emotion. "Hi, Nick. I'm… I'm good. You?"

"I'm great, thanks. But you don't sound sure. What's up?"

"I'm calling for a specific reason and I honestly don't know how to begin to ask you the things I want to ask. But I can't stand feeling like this any longer. So, I'm just going to ask, if that's okay?" My words came out in an almost incoherent rush.

"Allie, you can ask me anything. What's up?" There was the distinct tone of worry edging his voice.

"Is Si with anyone right now?"

"Si? Erm… I don't know He was going home for a couple of days to his folks. But I don't know where he is right at this second. Why? Is everything okay?"

"No, no. I mean with anyone as in… romantically?"

"Ahhh." Nick sighed. "Poor lad. No, he just had his heart trampled on by this drum tech. He really liked her. But you know Si. He's not really one for diving in head first… so to speak." He chuckled. "Anyway, she told a load of lies about her brother dying and him being a drummer. Made out they had all this stuff in common. And Si was ready to take the leap. Then—get this—her fucking brother called up and Si spoke to him."

Oh my word! What kind of psycho was she? "No way!"

"Yup. Poor Si was heartbroken. Not because he loved her; at least I don't think he did. It was the betrayal that got him. The way she used Joe's death to get to him. Pretty low blow if you ask me."

Anger knotted my insides, and for the first time in my life, I wanted to punch another woman square in the face. "How dare she? The bitch!"

"We all said exactly the same. Anyway, Den fired her

before I could. So, he has a new guy. Some older bloke who used to tour with Whitesnake back in the eighties. Nice guy."

Images of punching some woman I had never even met began to swirl around my head. How dare she treat Si that way? What the hell had she gained apart from a lot of enemies?

"Are you still there, Allie?"

I shook myself from my violent fantasy. "S-sorry. Yes, I'm here. Is he okay? I wondered what the hell you were talking about at the concert the other night."

He gasped. "Newcastle? You were in Newcastle? Why didn't you come backstage? We would've loved to see you."

"Erm… I couldn't. Because I… I had to leave early. Stuff to do, you know?"

There was a pause. "Allie? What's your real reason for calling? I suspect there's something deeper than just checking in, considering the way you babbled at me at the start of the call."

I took a deep breath. "Yes. Yes, you're right. Do you know if Si… has he… did he say anything…" I wasn't brave enough to form the words in my head which was making it difficult for them to come out of my mouth.

"Hang on. You want to know if Si still has feelings for you, don't you?"

What the…? "H-how do you know *that*?"

"Let's just say I have a sixth sense about these things. Look, Allie, I'm going to be completely straight with you. Si's been through a shit time lately. I know what happened between you two when he came to see you. *And* what happened again when you were in Yorkshire. He took your rejection pretty fucking hard. And then all this stuff with that witch just about finished him off. I know he still cares for you. So, please... *please* don't mess with his head, okay? And definitely don't mess with his heart. He's like my kid brother and I know him well. He wants and deserves someone to love him totally. He's got a heart of gold, Allie. I think you know that. And I won't stand by and watch him get pummelled again. Not even for you. I love you, but I can't let that happen to him. So maybe you should keep your distance, eh?"

Ah. "Oh... oh, yes, of course. Yes, you're right. No, I'll stay away. I just... I just wanted to check he was okay, that's all," I lied, and tears trickled down my cheeks. This was not how I hoped this call would go.

"I don't want to fall out with you, love. I know you mean well. Of course I do. And I promise I'll keep an eye on him. Look, I'd better go. I'm on my way up to the new studios in Gairloch and my girl's waiting for me. I'll introduce you to Cat someday. She's fucking amazing. And feisty like you. I think you two would get on like a house on fire. Gotta go. Take care, love."

I swallowed and forced a smile even though he couldn't see me. "Yes. You too. Have fun." I ended the call and crumpled to the floor. My heart shattered into a million tiny pieces. I had my answers. So now I would need to move on.

CHAPTER 42

Si

Back in my old room again temporarily. Only this time, the memories were of more than just me and Joe as kids. I stared across at his bed and remembered Allie smiling at me from there as we talked about all sorts of crap. She was one of those women who look even more beautiful when they've just woken up; all make-up free and rosy-cheeked from sleep. Those brief times we shared had made a serious impact on my heart and being here again without her filled me with a deep melancholy. I wondered what she was doing. And I wondered if her accountant was making her happy.

I suppose I was relieved really that the thing with Bobbie hadn't gone anywhere. I didn't love her. My heart still belonged to Allie. And I had finally realised that there was absolutely no point in trying to be with someone else until I was over her. So, if anything good could've come from that shit... I didn't like it, but at least it meant I could focus on playing and song writing.

Yeah, song writing... *me*. After my chat with Nick, I'd decided to give it another go. I wasn't sure anything I wrote would ever end up on a Sonic Idols album, but at least I had an outlet for the emotions I usually kept locked up inside me. I'd penned a song about Joe and I had finished the one about Allie so I was on a bloody emotional rollercoaster on its downward spiral. But oddly enough, I felt better for it.

My parents had been weird ever since I arrived home for my visit. Every time I mentioned Allie, they clammed up and changed the subject. I presumed they had found my balled-up sheets of paper, filled with puke worthy lyrics, in my bin when I had gone on tour, and they put two and two together. Their reluctance to talk about her was probably their way of protecting me. Bless them.

I was only staying for a couple of days before we headed up to Gairloch to check out Nick's studios, so at least they wouldn't need to walk on eggshells for much longer. I was needled with guilt that they felt they had to be like that. And on so many occasions I almost confronted them about it. But there was never really a good time. I resorted to spending a lot of time in my room just so they could relax. And I even considered leaving early. But I missed them when I was on tour so I was stuck between a rock and hard place.

We had just eaten lunch and the topics of conversation had revolved around Nick and the new studios. Den and his wedding had also cropped up but I think my mum and dad remembered that Bobbie was connected to that particular event so they again changed the subject. We were then back on Nick and his studios and they talked about how brave he was to be taking such a risk. Although, I knew different. It wasn't a risk. I knew deep down that his studio venture would be a success. And with Cat by his side, he was bound to be a winner. She seemed so perfect for him. She was beautiful, feisty, and had a wicked sense of humour. And good grief, how she bloody adored Nick. Then again, he went all starry-eyed when he talked about her too. So that was another situation where horrific circumstances turned out great and I was so happy for him.

I was, however, getting worried about Chris, and I voiced my concerns to my folks. Something was going on with him but I didn't know what. I hoped that a few days up in Gairloch might help him too. They agreed and advised that I should just be there for him as he had been for me.

After lunch, I retreated to my room once again and I stood in front of the notice board in my room, smiling at the photos of me and Joe and the postcards from trips we had each taken with school. There were also postcards that our folks had just posted locally to us because they knew we liked to receive mail. There were cards with pictures of cute animals. Cards with beautiful scenery and even cards with just one word as the picture, like *Family*. I was blessed to have had such a wonderful childhood. And the two amazing people downstairs were the ones to thank for that. If only they wouldn't worry about me so much. But then again, if only I didn't give them *reasons* to worry.

I ran my hands through my hair and huffed the air through my puffed cheeks. "Sheesh, bro, I've really done it this time. If you're up there looking down on me, I want to say I'm sorry. I love you *so* much. I hope you still know that. And I would *never* have admitted to anything about Allie if you were still here. Even though you apparently knew. I was your brother first and foremost." I shook my head as my eyes began to sting. "I'm carrying such guilt around. Guilt because I didn't come to your show that night. Guilt because I fell in love with your woman. And guilt because I *still* love her even though I've tried so hard not to. Please don't hate me, Joe. If I thought for a second you hated me, I..." My voice cracked and I rubbed at the dampness around my eyes. "I'm *so* sorry. Okay? For everything. I wish I could talk to you. Through a medium or a psychic or something, you know? Just to find out if you still love me. Or if I've ruined everything we ever shared because of how I feel and what I've done. But to be honest, I don't think I believe in all that shit anyway." I laughed. "I know you were a great believer in all things mystical, but me? Nah. I think I'm more of a realist. I've been a shit brother and I acknowledge that. 'Nuff said. Hearing someone I don't know pretend to be passing on messages from you to confirm it would just hurt. In fact, why the hell am I talking to your photo?" I chuckled and shook my head. "I'm obviously going crazy. But anyway, bro, the band still talk about you. Still joke about your daft antics. They still miss you. And *I* miss you. Oh, God, I miss you like you wouldn't believe. I just... I wish I knew you still loved me back. That you can forgive me."

I leaned towards the noticeboard, and as I did, one of

the photos slipped on its pin. I stared, open-mouthed at the photograph and froze. For a split second, I couldn't believe what I was seeing and a shiver travelled the length of my spine. On the notice board was a postcard with only the word *Love* printed on it in brightly coloured letters. And the photo that had slipped was one of Joe, Allie... and me. But the way it had slipped meant that Joe had disappeared behind the word Love, leaving just a photo of me staring up at Allie with that love-filled gaze.

And then I knew.

I sniffed and wiped my eyes again. "Thank you, Joe. Thank you."

CHAPTER 43

Allie

It's funny how colours seem a little duller when your heart is broken. The fact that it was stupidly self-inflicted heartbreak seemed to make matters worse. I stood at my easel, staring blankly through puffy eyes at the canvas I had started a week before. I had no inspiration. None. All that filled my head was what ifs. What if I had taken the chance back when Si admitted he loved me? What if I had really thought through my feelings and decided that I would own them no matter what? What if I wasn't such a bloody coward? What if I didn't worry so much about what people thought? What if, what if, what bloody if.

All a bit late now, but it seemed that beating myself up was at the top of my agenda every day. I had tried running, but yet again, the music on my playlist tortured me, and unfortunately, running in silence gave me too much thinking time.

I had tried to keep busy. I went out with the local art group to try some outdoor painting but it chucked down with rain and I felt guilty. Like the weather was reflecting my mood. I even apologised to them all as I packed my things up and left and they looked at me like I had fallen out of a tree. So, regardless of the fact I was my own worst enemy I seemed to be better in my own company.

The Delaneys had called on several occasions and left lots of concerned messages, but I couldn't bring myself to answer or return their calls. What would I say? "Oh, yeah. I spoke to Nick and he pretty much told me to sod off out of Si's life"? Yeah, that would make me look like a real fighter. The truth was, I didn't feel I had the right to fight for him. He had been nothing but honest with me and I hadn't returned the favour.

And now it was much too late.

For goodness sake, Allie. Pull yourself together. No point in sitting around wallowing in self-pity. Get your head on straight. You've a lot to look forward to in life. You don't need a man.

I didn't need *a* man. I needed a *particular* man. And so, the war inside me continued. My head tried to rationalise my heart, and my heart just kept saying, "I told you so".

Having walked away from my canvas for the third or fourth time that same week, I sat in the garden with a cup of tea on my little table and my eyes closed, listening to the birdsong. I became aware of a ringing sound and I fumbled around to find my phone which had fallen under my chair.

"Hello?"

"Allie? Hi, it's Nick. I think we need to talk."

"We do? What about?"

"Look, I've had a very long chat with Mr and Mrs Delaney."

Uh-oh. "You have?"

He sighed. "Yeah. I feel bloody awful, Allie. Why didn't you tell me? Why didn't you tell me you're in love with him too?"

I fell silent, unable to conjure up the right words. And wondering what the hell difference it would've made anyway.

"Allie? You there?"

Say something, you muppet. "S-sorry. Yes, I'm here."

Another sigh. "Thank goodness. I thought you'd hung up. I wouldn't blame you after our last conversation. I'm so sorry. I honestly had no clue that you felt that way about Si. No clue at all. Things would have ended very differently if I'd known. It really does change everything. I'm such an interfering idiot. But... I don't understand why you couldn't tell me."

I rubbed my fingers over my stinging eyes. I was so tired of crying. "I couldn't say anything, Nick, because you were right. He'd been through too much already and I would've just made things worse. I don't want him to be hurt anymore. So, I figured I would just try to move on." My voice wobbled and I feigned a cough to try and cover it up.

Nick chuckled. "Oh yeah? I can tell you're *really* succeeding with that plan."

"Sarcastic pig."

He laughed louder. "Yup. You know me so well. Look. I'm truly sorry. I want to make it up to you. I want to sort this whole thing out. But I need you to trust me. Do you trust me, Allie?"

Daft question. I would trust Nick with my life. He had always been like a brother to Joe and only had Si's best interests at heart. "Absolutely. Why?"

"Okay. I have a plan."

CHAPTER 44

Si

I have to admit to being a bit like a kid waiting to go to the sweet shop for the whole journey up to Nick's studios. We were taking the tour bus simply because it was easier than trying to sort individual forms of transport for us and our gear. But the bus wasn't exactly fast. Nick was already up there as he couldn't wait to get home to Cat, and I was looking forward to seeing her again. Last time had been too brief and I was too busy with Bobbie to talk properly and get to know her.

Chris was very subdued and I contemplated trying to find out why on more than one occasion, but every time I made to do so, he either disappeared into his bunk or stuck his earbuds in.

I finally managed to catch him off guard around three hours into the journey. "Hey, what have I done to piss you off, Chris?" Okay, so it wasn't subtle, but then again, subtlety wasn't exactly his style.

He scrunched his brow and stared up at me. "What are you on about, dude?"

I sat down opposite him at the table. "Every time I see you you're giving me the fucking stink eye. I know something is up and I want to know what it is. Did I say something wrong? Are you angry because of the stuff I told you about Allie?"

He shook his head. "It's not all about you, you know. I know you've had a shitty time of it lately, mate, but stop thinking the fucking world revolves around you."

Ouch. "Hey, that's bullshit. You know it is. Come on. Spill it."

He dropped his gaze to his phone which sat before him on the table. "Maybe another time. Look, I'm sorry for getting pissy, all right? You haven't done anything. Nothing at all. I'm just on a downer. I promise I'll talk to you at some point but just not right now. Can you leave it for now?"

Worried about pushing things too far, I sighed. "Look, you were there for me when Joe died. You were there for me when things went wrong with Allie. You've always been there for me. And I want to return the favour. So, when you're ready, come and find me, okay? No judgement, no awkward questions. Just two good friends putting the world to rights. Deal?" I held my hand out towards him and he grasped it.

"Deal, buddy. Now… seeing as you're here, I have a joke for you."

I rolled my eyes but couldn't help grinning as the

Chris I knew and loved reared his ugly head again. "Oh, yeah. Go on then."

He sat up straight, and with a cheesy grin, he spoke. "So… how is a drum solo like a fucking huge sneeze?"

I smiled and shook my head. "Oh, God. Go on…"

He started laughing before he got the words out. "You know the bastard's coming but there's fuck all you can do to stop it." He threw his head back and guffawed like a bloody idiot.

His stupid laugh was infectious and it was so good to see him happy that I joined in. "Yeah. Haha! Good one, Chris. Good one."

♫♫♫

We pulled up to Rockhill House and my jaw fell open. I had seen it in photos on Nick's phone, but nothing had prepared me for how beautiful it was in real life. Absolutely huge but with understated elegance, if that even makes sense. Okay, so it was a mansion, but it wasn't gregarious or tasteless. It was absolutely stunning. Double stone stairways arched up to the front door and the door itself was a huge, carved oak slab.

Nick and Cat were waiting at the top of the steps like the Laird and Lady of the manner, and I couldn't wait to get up there and hug them both. I jogged up to greet them and was enveloped in a group embrace.

"Aww, it's so good to see you both," I told them in a muffled voice, thanks to being engulfed by tons of long hair.

"It's good to see you too, Si. I bet you're exhausted," Cat said as she smiled up at me.

I shook my head. "Nah. Too excited for that."

Chris and Stig joined us, and Den and Roger followed on as we were invited inside. The entrance hall. The tiled floor and high ceilings were like something off a movie set and I gawped around like a little kid.

Nick started the house tour and we all walked around with huge grins plastered on our faces. The living areas were already starting to resemble a family home and I could picture Nick, Cat, and a couple of toddlers running around the place. He was one lucky SOB, that's for sure. The kitchen was quite modern. Not finished yet, but there was going to be every mod con and a huge island counter top in the centre. There was a cinema room, and an office big enough for several staff, and a reception area for the business side.

"I'm not taking you to the studios yet. I'm saving the best until last." He winked and gestured for us to follow him up a flight of stairs.

He showed us to the bedrooms next. I stopped counting at six. The bedrooms were pretty much decorated as they were left when he bought the place, although they looked clean and comfortable.

"This area is getting a complete overhaul when Cat decides on a design scheme." He whispered dramatically behind his hand, loud enough for her to hear, "But she's far too bloody picky if you ask me."

She whacked him and laughed as her cheeks coloured pink. "Hey, I just want it to look good, you rotter. They'll all be thinking I'm a diva."

Nick pulled her into his side. "You? A diva? Not at all, my precious girl." He kissed the side of her head and she rolled her eyes, still smiling.

"Si, this is you," Cat told me as she opened a large door. "You should have everything you need, but if not, just shout. Or ring the servant bell. It still works. Although there's no servants now." She giggled.

"Cheers, guys. This looks lovely." I wasn't kidding. It looked like one of the better hotels we had stayed in as a band. High ceilings, floor to ceiling arched window, and a dressing room off to the side.

Cat pointed to the opposite side of the room. "You have your own bathroom. It's a little dated but it's all working."

"Great. I'll just drop my bag in here." I stepped into the room and dropped my bag by the bed.

Once all the guests had been shown their rooms, it was time to go see the studios. We walked down two staircases into the basement area and my excitement rose exponentially with every step we took.

"So, there are going to be four recording studios to begin with. And two big soundproofed practise rooms. Each studio will have a fully kitted out control booth and state of the art sound equipment. Studio one, the biggest, is just about ready, but I might need to enlist you guys to help bring some gear down in the lift."

My eyes widened. "There's a bloody lift?"

Nick laughed. "Yeah. It was necessary partly because of access for bands who want to bring their own gear, and also because I want this place to be accessible to everyone. Wheelchair users will be able to use the studios too, thanks to the doors being widened and control stations being on hydraulic lifts to put them at the comfortable height for whichever engineer is in charge of production for the session."

He had thought of everything and I was so impressed. Studio one was massive and equipped for a full band to do either simultaneous recording or individual by sectioning off areas with moveable walls. It was incredible. Like nothing I had ever seen before.

"Bloody hell, mate. This is fucking awesome. What's the sound quality like so far? Have you tested it out?"

Nick glanced at Cat who blushed again. He pulled her into his side. "Cat and I recorded a song together. The sound's pretty fantastic, actually."

Stig piped up, "Bloody hell. She's gorgeous *and* she sings?"

Cat waved her hand dismissively. "Ugh, no. I play guitar mainly. I'm not a singer."

Nick kissed the side of her head. "Hey, don't sell yourself short. Guys, she has a bloody amazing voice. In fact, I was thinking if we needed female backing vocals—"

"Nick, don't say that. They won't want me for backing vocals." Cat's face was bright red now and she looked horrified.

Nick held up a finger. "One sec."

Cat followed him. "No, don't play it. Please don't play it, Nick."

"Too late," he called from the booth.

Cat stood with her hands over her face as the sound of guitars came over the sound system. Nick's vocals kicked in first. It was definitely a song he had written. I could tell by the style. Then Cat's voice came in. We all stood open-mouthed. She was amazing. Talk about a multi-talented woman.

Den stepped forward and put his arm around Cat's shoulders. "Cat, seriously, love. You can sing on our albums any time. With a voice like that we may just kick Nick out. How are you fixed for a stint on the road with a crew of smelly men?" We all laughed and Nick folded his arms over his chest in a mock sulk.

Cat gazed back at Nick. "Only if I can bring Nick along."

"Bloody hell. Someone pass me a bucket, will you?" Den winked and laughed.

Once the track had finished, we all applauded and Den talked about how we should at least get her up on stage at some shows to perform that particular track. Cat tried to put him off but she didn't realise how Den worked. He would make it happen.

Afterwards, we all chatted about how the sound quality was on a par with—if not better than—some of the studios we had worked in. The whole band agreed that we should record the next album at Rockhill.

Nick clapped his hands together. "Right, guys, I think you should all bugger off and leave me to have some time with Cat. No doubt you're all knackered, anyway. Oh, but Si, can you give me a hand taking some stuff up in the lift, mate? There's a leather chair that Cat's decided needs to go upstairs. If you can take that up while I close up down here that'd be great.

Chris nudged me. "Is that because he's the muscle of the band rather than the brains?"

I jibed back, "Well, you're definitely not the brains of the outfit, Malham." Everyone pointed and laughed at Chris as he turned beet red. I looked back to Nick and nodded, happy to help. "Sure, no problem. Which chair is it?"

The other guys wandered back towards the staircase and Nick pointed me to the chair he wanted me to take. I managed to manoeuvre it into my arms and he pressed the call button on the lift. The door opened right away and I backed inside.

"See you up there, mate. Cheers for your help." Nick closed the door.

The lift started to move and I placed the chair down.

When I glanced up again, my heart almost stopped. "Jeez, fuck!"

I wasn't alone.

"Hello, Si."

With wide eyes and a racing heart, I asked, "What the hell are you doing here, Allie?"

CHAPTER 45

Si

The lift juddered to a halt and I waited for the door to open but it didn't. I turned to glance at the panel and the lights were flicking between two floor numbers.

"What the fuck?" I didn't know what to deal with first. The fact that Allie was in the lift with me or the fact that the lift was bloody stuck.

Allie stepped towards me. "I... I thought we should talk. Want to sit down?" She gestured to the chair I was supposed to be moving upstairs.

I crumpled my brow and rested my hands on my hips. "Hang on. Is this a set up?"

Allie shook her head. "Me being here? Yes, a little bit. The lift being stuck? Not that I know of, but you know what the guys are like for pranking."

I ran my hands back through my hair. "I'll call some-one." I grabbed the handset that was fixed to the wall.

Before I could speak, Nick's voice was heard. "Hello? Si? Sorry, mate. We're on the case. Not sure what's going on but we'll get you out as soon as we can. Sit tight and don't worry."

I clenched my other fist. "Nick, I swear to God, I'll—" The line went dead. He had hung up on me. *Shit head.*

I looked back to Allie and she was trying hard not to laugh. That got me rattled. "What's so funny?"

She shrugged. "There's nothing like a captive audience, eh?"

I huffed, pissed off that a) I was stuck in a confined space with Allie with no escape and b) I was going to have to talk to her about shit I no doubt wanted to avoid.

Clenching my jaw, I told her, "If you wanted to talk, you could've just phoned me."

"I felt that what I needed to talk to you about was better said face to face."

I leaned against the wall and slid down it until my arse hit the floor. "We've been over it all, Allie. We're both on different pages. I get it. Can't we just leave it at that?" I rested my head in my hands and my elbows on my knees.

She came and sat beside me on the floor of the lift. "I heard someone stomped on your heart again."

I rolled my eyes. "Oh, great. Who told you about Bobbie?"

"I spoke to Nick. I can't believe she did something like that to you. I'm so sorry."

I shrugged. "Yeah, well it appears I have 'emotional punch bag' on my head and it's only visible to women."

She sighed. "I guess I deserve that."

Guilt twisted my stomach. "Look, I'm sorry, okay? I'm tired after a long day of travelling and I'm not really in the mood to rehash my errors in judgement."

Sadness clouded her eyes. "Is that how you see me? An error in judgement?"

I tilted my head and stared at the ceiling. "Ugh. No, I just... I don't want to do this, Allie. Not now and certainly not when we're stuck in a fucking lift."

She was sodding persistent. "Si, I have stuff I need to say to you. Can you just give me a chance?"

I fixed her with a stern glare. "I think you said everything you needed to say to me last time I saw you, don't you? I got it. Believe me. And I understand. It's like I said before, I'm not Joe and I can't take his place in your heart. I heard you loud and clear. Can't we just leave it at that?"

She pleaded at me with her beautiful, emotion-filled eyes. "Just hear me out, okay?" I shrugged like a petulant teenager and wished the lift would just move so I could go hide in my bedroom. But alas, it didn't, and she continued talking. "That first time we had sex, that's all it was. It was all I wanted. To feel desired again. To be close to someone again. But in the cold light of day, I realised I had made a mistake. I had tried to substitute you for Joe and I had taken advantage of your grief. We were both struggling and I should have comforted you, not seduced you. My guilt over that was immense, Si."

"Well, it takes two and all that. I don't remember you forcing yourself on me."

"Let me finish, please?" I gestured for her to carry on but could no longer look her in the eye. "Seeing your tattoo just brought me to Earth with a thud. You loved your brother so, *so* much. And I felt like I had sullied that out of pure selfishness. That was why I was so upset. It wasn't anything you had done wrong. It was all on me. Do you understand what I mean?"

"I get you, but like I said, we were both there, Allie. It wasn't just you. I took the guilt about my feelings for you around with me for years before that. I had no clue Joe knew how I felt. Once I knew that, I felt like such a bastard. He loved me regardless of the fact that I loved you. And then I went and broke the promise I'd made to myself. I swore I would never do anything about my feelings for you because you were Joe's. Not mine. And what the hell would people think of me if they knew what we had done?"

"I had that same worry. That's why I couldn't deal with it. And then when I found out that you loved me, that back then you didn't just have a crush on me, I felt so much worse. Like I had not only betrayed Joe, but that I'd somehow betrayed you too."

A heavy silence fell between us for a few moments until I broke it. "You know, Den and Roger got married at Gretna Green, and when we were there, I went to look at the old blacksmiths shop museum. Did you know that people would travel for miles just to get married there? They would run away to marry their true love, regardless of what anyone thought. Regardless of people's objections and the trouble it might cause. It amazed me that people could love each other so deeply that they would fight to be together no matter what. And it struck me then that I want that. I don't want to be worried what people think of me. If I love someone, I want to be able to shout it from the rooftops, not stay behind closed doors out of sight. I want to be as determined and reckless as those people who elope just so they can be with the one they love. Because at the end of the day, that's all that matters. Being together. Being with that one person you know can make you happy. Don't you think?"

I glanced at Allie and she had tears trickling a path down her pink cheeks. "I totally agree."

I swallowed hard, trying to keep my own emotions at bay. "So, no more apologies, okay? No more going over old ground. We were just never meant to be."

Her lip trembled. "Is that how you really feel? That we were not meant to be?"

I reached up and wiped the tears from her cheek. "I don't have to like it, but I guess I do have to accept it."

She grabbed my hand. "But... does that mean you're over me?"

I smiled as sadness weighed me down and my throat tightened. "I didn't say that. But I will *try* to get over you. I promise."

"What if I don't want you to?"

I frowned and my heart flipped. "What if you don't want me to what?"

"Get over me."

I shook my head. "But that's why you're here, isn't it? To draw a line under it all so we can put it behind us."

She shook her head as more tears came. "Si, I do want to draw a line under my mistakes. But... but you're not one of them. I want our fresh start to begin now."

I scrambled up to my knees, my heart racing and my

head buzzing. "Allie, what are you saying? I don't know what you're saying. What are you saying?"

As I rambled like an idiot, she laughed through her tears. "I'm saying I fell in love with you back in Yorkshire. The day you rescued me from the paparazzi. You were so selfless, and I didn't want to admit my feelings because I was terrified about what people would think. You're my dead fiancé's brother and I'm not supposed to feel that way. But then I spoke to your mum and dad and they were so lovely. They made me realise that love is love, and so long as we hurt no one, we should just be together. So, I want to be like those people you read about at the museum. I want to take risks and be out in the open. With you. And you're not in *his* place Si. You're in your own. And that place is in my heart and my head. I love you. I'm in love with you, Si. So, if you still want me... I'm yours."

I opened and closed my mouth but words wouldn't come. Was this all a dream? Had I imagined it all? I stared at her, realising all over again just how beautiful she was. Just how much of my heart she occupied, but I couldn't move. If it was a dream, I wanted to hold on for just a little while longer.

She raised herself up to her knees until her face was level with mine and cupped my damp cheek. "Say something. Please, Si."

I shook my head. "I'm sorry. I just... I thought for a bizarre moment you just told me you love me and I'm trying to get my head around—"

Before I could finish my sentence, she crushed her mouth to mine in a soul searing kiss, and I swear the ground moved. A loud cheer erupted from somewhere over my shoulder and Allie and I turned to see the band, Den, and Cat standing outside the open doors, clapping. There wasn't a dry eye amongst them.

I looked back to Allie and smoothed my thumb across her cheek, gazing into her eyes and knowing deep down that I would be kissing those lips as often as possible from that moment.

Nick stepped towards us and hugged us both. "Guys, there's a little surprise for you both in Si's room."

I puffed the air from my lungs. "Another one?"

He laughed. "Yeah, maybe not such a big one this time, but... you deserve some alone time."

I grabbed Allie by the hand and took off at speed towards my room with her giggling behind me. It was the best sound I had ever heard.

I opened the door and we stepped inside. Allie gasped. "They did all this for us?"

My face ached from all the smiling but I didn't care. Fresh flowers had appeared on every surface and candles were dotted around the room. The thick drapes were drawn, closing out the daylight and creating the most romantic atmosphere. It was better than any hotel I had ever stayed in.

I turned to Allie and slipped my hands into her hair. "Is this real?"

She smiled and smoothed her hands up my chest. "I hope so. Because if it's a dream, I'm never waking up."

I glanced over to the nightstand and spotted a mini speaker attached to my iPod. Nick really had thought of everything. I walked over and flicked through the track lists I had created over the years until I found the one simply titled "Allie". It was a track list I had never expected to play again. It was the track list of every single song that reminded me of her. Songs I never dared listen to again after the first time I heard them. Yet there I was, about to hit play.

Allie walked over to join me and encircled me in her arms, resting her cheek against my back. "We've waited for this for so long, haven't we?"

We... *we've* waited. Those simple words sent my heart soaring. This was what we *both* wanted.

Bon Jovi's "Always" began to play and I turned around to face her once again. "We have. So, let's make the most of it."

I leaned in to kiss her. Her lips were soft and her kiss filled with a restrained passion, so I slipped my tongue along the line of her lips and she parted them for me. The feel of her mouth on mine sent shivers darting like sparks throughout my body as Jon Bon Jovi sang about forever. And that was what I wanted with Allie.

Forever.

She pulled me back to the bed and began to undress. I watched, mesmerised by her slow and sensual movements, her eyes fixed constantly on me. Once she was naked before me, I dragged the clothes from my body and joined her on the bed where I took her in my arms again, caressing every inch and kissing every place I touched. I rolled her beneath me and sank myself deep inside my love and her back arched as she sighed and trailed her fingertips down my back. I watched as she moved with me, her hooded gaze taking everything in too. She was finally mine and I was where I had wanted to be for so long. Bending to take her sensitive flesh in my mouth, I revelled in the erotic noises she made and knew she was close to her release. Reconnecting with her gaze once more, I watched again as she breathed deeper, grasping for me in desperation, and I took her mouth one last time as she cried out, her ecstasy triggering my own.

Everything was different now. Everything felt right. Making love to her that time really was making love. And I wanted to stay there in that bed for as long as possible, never breaking that spell.

As we lay in each other's arms later that night, Allie smiled up at me and said those words I would never tire of hearing, "I love you, Si Delaney."

I shook my head, unable to believe what was happening between us, but with a heart bursting because it *was* happening. "And I love you, Allie Kendry. Always have... always will."

EPILOGUE

Si

I have no bloody clue what all this secrecy is about. I'm sitting here in the car with a blindfold on and it's a sweltering June day. Allie left me here and went back into the cottage. She's been gone a while and I'm hoping she doesn't take too much longer or I might expire from the heat. She was very firm about the fact that I can't take the blindfold off until we arrive at wherever the hell we're going. She's given me my iPod and told me I must not, under any circumstances, remove the ear buds until she indicates that I can. She hasn't told me how long I'll be sitting like this and I've learned not to bother asking as she just gives me that sexy, pissed off look.

She squeezes my leg and then I feel the car engine start and we take off. I'm listening to the track list she's created just for me and I'm sure I look like a blindfolded idiot, sitting here with a huge, excited grin on my face as "You and Me" by Alice Cooper filters into my brain. God, she's such a bloody romantic. But that's absolutely why I love her. It's my birthday today and I know she's got something special planned, otherwise I would be driving. The next song to grace my ears is a Bon Jovi classic. "Always" was the first song we made love to on the day she told me she loved me in the stuck lift at Nick's place. Only I had discovered it wasn't actually stuck. Nick had planned the whole damn thing. Sneaky sod. I'm so glad he did though. This last year has been the best of my life. I moved all my stuff into the little cottage in Kelso and we've been playing house ever since. Waking up to her beautiful, make-up free face every single morning is the best feeling.

The locals are great too. It's strange how they've just accepted they have a famous rock star living close by. It was a little busy just after I moved in. Lots of kids calling by to offer to do odd jobs and such, but things settled down eventually and now it just feels like home. Like Allie and I have always been together. I'm living the bloody Scottish dream. What is it about this place and Sonic Idols? It's like we have some kind of spiritual connection to the place. And yes, I did say spiritual. After the incident with the photo back in my old room, I'm not discounting anything. I'm very open-minded these days.

I shake my head and rest it back as I remember making love to her to the Bon Jovi track on that wonderful day at Nick's, like it was the first time again. Her naked curves laid before me, but all mine. The love in her eyes was real and the connection was more than just physical. Our bodies moved in perfect synchronisation and I worshipped her. Because she's the love of my life. And I now know I'm the love of her present and future. And that's all I need.

I must have dozed off, because the next thing I know, my face is being stroked and I open my eyes to find the earbuds gone but the blindfold still in place.

"Si, keep the blindfold on, okay? But we're here. I'll come around to help you out of the car."

As she helps me out of the car, I warn her with a grin still on my face, "This had better be good, Kendry, or you'll pay later."

"Oh, I think you'll like it."

I know we're outside as the air smells fresh and clean, but it's still warm which is good. At least it hasn't rained. Maybe Joe is smiling down on us.

She takes my hand and leads me forwards. "Watch your step here," she tells me, and I obey as I can't see a bloody thing.

I hear whispers but can't quite make out what anyone's saying, and then a door closes and everything is silent. A familiar scent fills my nose but I can't quite place my finger on it.

"Si, I'm going to take your blindfold off now. And then we need to have quick chat before we go any further."

Okay, the plot thickens. Shit. I hope she hasn't booked me a bungee jump or something daft like that. I'm shaking now. The nerves have kicked in. What will I do if I'm not happy with my surprise? How will I tell her? The last thing I want to do is upset her.

I feel her reach behind my head and unfasten the

blindfold, and as the light begins to filter through my eyelids, I blink to let my pupils adjust. When I'm able to focus again, I see Allie standing before me. God, she looks stunning. I don't even take note of my surroundings. She's all I have eyes for.

I trail my gaze over her and shake my head. "You're bloody gorgeous, you know that?" Her eyes start to well with tears and I panic. "Shit. What did I say?" I step forwards and wrap her in my arms, kissing her tears as they escape down her flushed cheeks.

"I need to talk to you about something. Have you seen where we are?"

I glance around the little space that appears to be an entrance hall. The walls are white and there's a wooden door closed behind us and another closed one before us. "It looks familiar but…" I rack my brains, trying to figure out where I am. But once again, I'm drawn to her and how utterly beautiful she is. "It doesn't matter where we are. You're here with me and that's all I care about."

Suddenly she lowers to the floor and I follow her with my gaze. *What's she doing?* I smile down at her and shake my head. "I'm sure we can find you a chair, you'll dirty your dress sitting on the…" It's then that I realise she's wearing white. Well, yes. That *will* get dirty on a stone floor…

"Si, I wanted to make your birthday extra special this year. But now I'm terrified. We've been together for a year and it feels like a good time to have a special day. Now, I know how fascinated you were with this place when you came here that first time but I need to ask you a question."

I once again assess my surroundings and realise where

we are. We're in the Blacksmiths Shop at Gretna Green. My eyes widen and I look back to Allie still kneeling on the floor before me.

My heart tries to escape through the buttons of my black shirt. Now it dawns on me why she told me exactly what to wear. Black shirt, waistcoat, black jeans, trim my fuzzy over-grown beard...

She clears her throat. "I know this is a little unorthodox but... Si Delaney, I love you with my whole heart and I'd like to know if you'll marry me?"

I can't quite believe this is happening. I stare at her for a few moments as I try to get my head around everything. But then I see the panic in her eyes and realise I need to answer.

"Are you... are you serious? You want to do this here? Today? And *you're* asking *me*?" *Okay, that was a stupid set of bloody questions, Delaney. Get a fucking grip.*

She nods as she wipes at more escaped tears. "It's all set in motion. All you have to do is say the right word."

I swallow and try to speak but my voice breaks. I clear my throat and try again, realising I too have damp trails down my face. "Allie, my answer... my answer is two words... HELL YES!" I bend and scoop her up into my arms, swinging her around. She squeals with what I hope is delight and then I crush my lips to hers.

I've waited and dreamed of this moment since I was sixteen years old and I still can't believe *she* asked *me*. It's like I've won every lottery in the world simultaneously.

The door before us opens and suddenly I'm greeted by a raucous cheer and I'm overwhelmed with what I see. The room before me is filled with my closest friends and my family. Mum and Dad, the band, the crew; they're all here. Allie has arranged all of this for me. For *us*. The band is standing near the anvil, armed with instruments; Chris and Nick with acoustic guitars and Stig has maracas. My face widens in a grin and I shake my head.

They start to play and I immediately recognise the intro to "Alison's Starting to Happen" by The Lemonheads.

Allie takes my hand, and in true Den and Roger style, we begin to walk down the aisle together, towards the celebrant, as the lyrics float through the air towards us and the whole congregation claps and sings along like they've heard the song a million times before. I'm guessing Nick has had something to do with that.

We reach the anvil and I turn to face my stunning bride-to-be. She leans to kiss me and I know without a shadow of a doubt that there is no better way for me to start my married life with Allie than right here, right now.

ACKNOWLEDGMENTS

As always there are so many people I want to thank and acknowledge but as always I will probably forget someone. Please know this is not deliberate! Those who know me well will know how scatter-brained I can be!

I would like to first say thank you to my Mum and Dad for being a huge support to me. It's been a tough few years for so many reasons yet you never fail with your unending support and love. Know that you mean the world to me.

Rich, you will always be my very own bearded heart throb. And even though you can't sing, drum or play guitar I would honestly choose you over Eddie Vedder any day. To my gorgeous Emo chick. I know you love me more than Fall Out Boy really. And I love you more than any of the Emo Quartet possibly could.

Friends. Whether we met conventionally or via the book

world, please know that your encouragement, support and friendship keeps me uplifted. Thank you.

JC, Karen, Caroline, Louby and Christine. Thank you for helping me to make Si the best he could be. And thank you for wanting more of Sonic Idols.

To the amazing bloggers who continue to share and spread the love for us Indie Authors—you are one heck of a fantastic breed! Keep that stuff up!

To all my author friends, especially the Indie Girls Club, squishy hugs to you all!

And finally, to my own musical idols—Pearl Jam, Soundgarden, Alanis Morisette, Bon Jovi, to name a small few. Thank you for your wonderful music. It continues to inspire me to write and lifts me when I'm down—a gift I'm so grateful for.

ABOUT THE AUTHOR

Lisa was born in Yorkshire, England. Her passion for writing began at a young age when she started to pen stories and poetry whilst at school. Nowadays she can be found tapping away at her laptop almost full time. When she takes a break from writing she spends time looking after her daughter and husband or walking her two canine companions.

After relocating with her family to Southern Scotland in 2012 she began to write her Scotland based debut novel, Bridge Over the Atlantic (published 2013). In 2014 the novel was shortlisted in the Contemporary Romance category of the Romantic Novelists Association RoNAs. This meant a trip to London for an awards ceremony where she had the opportunity to meet her favourite authors—some of whom were also shortlisted in the same category.

Three years after beginning her writing career in earnest Lisa now has a total of ten contemporary romance novels published—several of which have become best-sellers on Amazon, iTunes and Barnes & Noble—and three erotic romances under the pen name Lissa Jay. Her erotic debut, Bad Company also hit the bestselling eBook charts in the USA and the UK on Amazon and iTunes.

Being a crafty and creative person, Lisa spends any spare time singing in a trio with a guitarist and drummer or making book related items to give away to her readers via her Facebook page.

www.ingramcontent.com/pod-product-compliance
Lightning Source LLC
Chambersburg PA
CBHW031214120726
47905CB00002B/327